Come the Hour

Come the Hour

Peggy Savage

ROBERT HALE · LONDON

© Peggy Savage 2011
First published in Great Britain 2011

ISBN 978-0-7090-9319-0

Robert Hale Limited
Clerkenwell House
Clerkenwell Green
London EC1R 0HT

www.halebooks.com

2 4 6 8 10 9 7 5 3 1

Typeset in 10/14½pt Palatino
Printed in Great Britain by the MPG Books Group,
Bodmin and King's Lynn

Chapter One

August, 1938

Amy sipped her tea, looking out of the kitchen window on to the garden. The sun was shining – a beautiful summer's morning. The borders were bright, sparkling with flowers, roses and geraniums and marigolds, all tumbled together. All flowers were welcome, apart, perhaps, from red poppies – she did not want those memories. Mr Hodge was already out there on his knees, attacking the weeds. A long branch of the old cherry tree was propped up on a crutch like some sprightly old man, full of life, but shaky in the limb. It reminded her, fondly, of her father. The garden and the sunshine and the rainbow of colours should have calmed her, soothed her, but she couldn't blot out the prowling beasts of worry that roamed and threatened at the edges of her mind.

The children's swing was still there, even though they were more or less grown up now. She hadn't the heart to take it down. Sometimes she sat on it herself, lazily swinging, just being. It was part of the tranquil years that had gone by, a tranquillity that she had imagined would always last.

Mrs Parks, duster in hand, looked in around the door. 'Do you want anything, Doctor, or shall I get on with the rooms?'

Amy straightened up and smiled. 'No thanks, Edith. I'm fine. Just having a cup of tea.'

Mrs Parks disappeared and the comfortable sound of the Hoover came from the sitting room.

Amy turned back to the window. How long had they been here? It must be nearly twenty years now. Holland Park had been a good choice, a large, pleasant house with a garden where the children could play, and an easy journey to central London so that Dan could get to work. A haven. It had almost blotted out those years of horror and despair. She smiled, a wry, humourless smile. What idiot had thought of calling it the 'Great War'? Wrong word. It wasn't great – it was hideous, foul, inhuman. There were many words to describe it, but not 'great'. She assumed that description had been coined by some politician who had never seen any part of it for himself.

They didn't talk much about the war, she and Dan. Nothing that anyone could say could take those horrors away. But through the years Dan had always been there, always known when the memories were thrusting up like the rotting, twisted, blasted trees of wartime France, or when the dreams were bad. He would hold her close, soothing and calming. The quiet house, the soft streetlights, the occasional passing car, were all that the night held now. Those fears and dreams had retreated, almost gone, until now. Now her defences were crumbling, the dreams returning. Surely, surely to God, no one would be mad enough or bad enough to do it again. The twins' birthday was next week. They would be eighteen.

Dan breezed into the kitchen, straightening his tie. 'Every day,' he said, 'I have to practically force my daughter out of the bathroom. What does she do in there?'

'I don't know,' Amy smiled. 'Girlie things. Shampoos and face creams and goodness knows what.'

'We'll have to put another one in,' he said, 'sacrifice one of the bedrooms.'

'It's only for a few weeks now,' she said, 'and they'll both be gone for a while. It's going to be very odd without them, isn't it?'

He kissed her lightly. 'It might be nice, just us two again.'

She poured him his tea and he sat down at the table and filled a bowl with cornflakes. She handed him the milk. 'What are we going to do about their birthday?'

'Can't think about that now, my love,' he said. 'I've got to go early. I've got a long list this morning, starting with a possible appendix.' He took a hurried spoonful. 'But I know the orthopods get a stream of accidents with boys on motorbikes, so if Charlie wants a motorbike, the answer's no.'

She laughed. 'I think he'd rather have money. I think they both would. A bit more to spend.'

'Well, they can't go mad,' he said. 'Paying for their education at the same time is going to stretch things a bit. One of the pleasures of having twins.'

She smiled. A warm smile this time. She knew how he felt about his children.

He crunched more cornflakes. 'What are you doing today?'

'Surgery in Notting Hill this morning, and then shopping with Tessa this afternoon. She needs some books – a *Gray's Anatomy* for a start – mine's too tattered to use. We'll go to Lewis's. She wants to read up as much as she can before she starts.'

'Fancy our little girl doing medicine,' he said. 'She's so like you, Amy.'

'And you. I suppose it's not surprising if both your parents are doctors.'

'That doesn't seem to have influenced our Charlie,' he said. 'He doesn't seem to have any idea what he wants to do.'

'I know,' she said. 'But he'll find out.' She suspected that Dan was a little disappointed that Charlie didn't want to follow him into the profession, though he denied it. 'He'll know by the time he's got his degree.'

He took a swallow of tea and got up. 'Got to go. I'll see you tonight.' He stood close to her and took her chin in his hand. She could see the grey that was starting at his temples and the little lines around his eyes 'You've got to stop worrying,' he said. 'Nothing has happened. They'll sort it out. Neville Chamberlain's a good man – well intentioned.'

'Charlie ...' she said, her voice wavering.

'I know. It'll be all right.' He kissed her mouth and left.

She sat down at the table, nursing her cup, though it was cold now. She put her elbows on the table and rubbed her brow. Would it be all right? Dan didn't voice any fears, but he couldn't hide anything from her. She knew that he was worried, and that worried her even more. The Prime Minister might be well intentioned, but the whole world seemed to be in a mess and there was Winston Churchill, warning and warning. They were already planning to give gas-masks out to the children and forming an air-raid precaution service. What was that for, if everything was all right?

The twins. Tessa, starting medicine. She had been so thrilled to get in. She is like me, Amy thought, always keen on science, always known what she wanted since she was a small child; Charlie, reading history, both of them going up to Cambridge. They were twins, but they were so different. Tessa seemed so tough, so confident, so sure of herself. Charlie was a bit of a dreamer, quiet and thoughtful. He didn't say much about his thoughts or his feelings. But there was something there in Charlie, a strength that she recognized and respected. You could only push Charlie so far.

Tessa came into the kitchen, yawning. She was wearing slacks and a blue blouse, her fair hair tied back with what looked to Amy like an elastic band. She saw her mother looking. 'I think I'll get it cut short,' she said. 'It might dangle into things in the labs.'

Amy smiled. 'Good idea.'

Tessa sat at the table. 'Is there any tea?'

'I'll put the kettle on,' Amy said, 'and make some fresh.' She filled the kettle and put it on the gas. 'Where's Charlie?'

Tessa yawned again. 'Still asleep, I expect. We got back rather late.'

Amy was well aware of when they had got back, though she would never let them know. Even at their age she still couldn't sleep properly until they were safely back at home. 'Good party?' she asked.

'Not bad.'

Amy put some tea in the pot and waited for the water, leaning against the kitchen cabinet.

'There were a lot of army types,' Tessa said, 'going on about a war. They carry on as if it were something good, as if they were looking forward to it.'

Amy began to feel as if she couldn't breathe. 'It isn't something good,' she said, 'for the winner or the loser.' She poured the water on the tea, gave it a stir and poured a cup for Tessa. She watched her as she sipped her tea. She was proud of her. It still wasn't easy for a girl to get into medical school – not as difficult as it had been in her day, but still not easy. There was a lot of competition, and still a lot of prejudice. Amazing, that, considering what women doctors had done in the last war.

8

'Can you come this afternoon for the books?' Tessa asked.

Amy nodded. 'I'll meet you at Lewis's bookshop at two.' She paused. 'What were they saying – the army types?'

'Oh – you know, "We can't let the Nazis get away with it; Germans at it again; we licked them once and we'll do it again." They sounded as if they couldn't wait.'

Amy turned away so that Tessa couldn't see her face. Does it never change, she thought? One generation after another. All those boys in the last war marching cheerily off to France, not realizing, not knowing. 'It won't happen again,' she said. 'No one would be mad enough to do that again.'

'You never talk about it,' Tessa said. 'I don't know what it was like for you and Dad. Was it absolutely horrible?'

'It's best forgotten.' Amy looked away, fiddling with the teapot lid. It could never be forgotten, but she had been able, for the most part, to bury it. Until now.

Charlie appeared, tousle-headed and sleepy, wearing flannels and a white shirt rolled up at the sleeves. He sat down at the table. Amy poured more tea.

'You look a bit hung over,' Amy said.

'No I'm not,' he said. 'I didn't drink that much.'

'He got in an argument,' Tessa said, 'about the morality of war.' She gave him a smiling, exasperated glance. 'He just does it to argue. He doesn't believe half the things he says.'

'It's the fun of the debate,' he said. 'It's an intellectual exercise.'

'Well, there's no point in having that particular argument with the army,' Tessa said, 'is there?' She looked at Amy. 'It got quite heated. They seemed to think he was a conscientious objector or something. He was lucky not to get his block knocked off.'

Charlie grinned. 'Remind me not to join the army. The drunker they get the more they're looking for a fight.'

'I suppose if you train for a war,' Tessa said, 'you naturally want one. Otherwise it's all for nothing.'

'It won't happen,' Amy said sharply. 'Not again.'

Charlie said nothing – just looked at her over the rim of his cup, a look that she couldn't interpret. Was it questioning, cynical, resigned?

She didn't know. For a moment she could only see the little boy, romping in the garden. Sometimes he looked so much like Dan that her heart turned over: tall, dark hair curling a little, his father's sensitive mouth. 'I've got to go,' she said. 'Get your brother something to eat, Tessa. He looks as if he needs it.'

'I'm not that hung over,' he said.

Tessa got up and kissed her mother's cheek. 'I'll see you at Lewis's, then. Isn't it all thrilling?'

Amy laughed. 'I hope you'll still think so when you're doing dissection.'

'Of course I will,' Tessa sad happily. 'I got used to it with all those frogs and rats at school. Body parts don't frighten me.'

Body parts. The words set another beast roaming and threatening. For a few horrified seconds Amy was back in one of the operating theatres in France, among the shattered limbs and appalling injuries, among the body parts thrown away for disposal into the bins. She thrust the thoughts away. She picked up her bag and opened the door. 'Oh, Tessa – ask Mrs Parks to get some strawberries, will you? We'll have them for pudding tonight.'

'And cream,' Charlie said.

Amy put her bag into her little Austin Ten. She sat in the car for a few moments, trying to forget her worries. There were worries enough where she was going, down to the poorer streets at the end of Ladbroke Grove and the Harrow Road, to a mixture of hard pressed but respectable working-class families and downright slums.

They had hoped and expected, she and Dan, at the end of the war, that those men in the trenches would come home to a better life, better housing and food, better jobs. The slump had put paid to that. 'A country fit for heroes', the government had promised. Now the men, even those with jobs, said that you'd have to be a hero to live in it. Times here in London were bad enough, but some industries were still going. What must it be like in other places? She had seen those men from Jarrow, with their shabby clothes and cracked, worn shoes, strained and exhausted as they walked into London, asking only for justice. What was going to happen now? Something worse?

She started the car and drove into Holland Park Avenue, then turned left into Ladbroke Grove. She drove past the large Victorian terraced houses, many of which were tenements now. She was in and out of these houses all the time, visiting her patients. Families lived here in two or three rooms, many with no bathrooms and shared toilets. And there were now so many ageing women, living out their lives alone in one dingy room, their husbands and sons lost and thrown away in unknown graves in the ravaged fields of France.

The surgery waiting room was filling up with women and small children and babies. She knew the heart-breaking battle that many of these women were fighting, to feed and clothe their children, to keep their pride and respectability. Cleanliness wasn't cheap, or easy, in some of these tenements. Many of the children were wearing worn out plimsolls or shoes that were too big for them, and obvious hand-me-downs. As she walked through the waiting room she noticed that several of the children had impetigo, nasty-looking sores on their faces around their mouths. There must be another outbreak going round.

Nurse Jones was already there, laying out the consulting room, patients' notes, prescription pad, turning on the sterilizer.

'Morning, Jean,' Amy said. 'We've got impetigo again, I see.'

Jean nodded. 'And nits. You can see some of them from the door.'

Amy sighed. 'We've got some nit combs, haven't we? And Derbac soap? And Gentian Violet?'

Nora nodded. 'Yes. I'll make up some small bottles.'

The purple paint was all that Amy could offer for the infected sores – that and advice about cross infection. Not that that would help much – many of the children slept three or four to a single bed, two at the top and two at the bottom.

She went into her consulting room and laid out her equipment, stethoscope and auriscope and ophthalmoscope. Then she put out the contraceptive jellies and creams and diaphragms. Many of these women were desperate for contraceptive advice, and that still wasn't easy to come by. Most of them couldn't afford what they called French letters, or their husbands wouldn't use them. They had one child after another, year after year, or they risked their lives and went to a back-street abortionist, risking death from haemorrhage or infection.

She plodded through the children with impetigo and summer colds and gastroenteritis. She weighed the children. If the babies and infants were undernourished enough she gave the mother a note to get 'doctor's milk' at school – free milk, but they only got it until the child gained a normal weight. Then it was stopped again.

Her last patient was trimly dressed in a neat cotton blouse and skirt. Mrs Nora Lewis. Her address, Amy saw, was in one of the rows of terraced houses off the Harrow Road.

'Mrs Lewis,' Amy said. 'Please sit down.'

Mrs Lewis sat down carefully on the upright chair. She looked nervous, Amy thought. Many of her patients looked nervous, especially if they were going to ask for contraceptive advice. They seemed to be expecting rejection or shocked opposition. Even after Marie Stopes opened her clinics many women still didn't quite believe that they could get help with planning their families, and there was still opposition in certain quarters.

'I would like some of those jellies,' Mrs Lewis said, in a soft, Northern accent. 'My husband uses something but I'm always afraid they might break.'

Amy smiled. 'How many children have you got now, Mrs Lewis?'

She blushed faintly. 'Only one. I'd have loved to have more but I can't. I had something called toxaemia last time and the doctor said I shouldn't have any more. He said it would be dangerous. I don't want to leave Sara, my little girl, with no mother.'

Amy nodded. 'I understand.' She reached for a packet. 'Here you are. The directions are inside.'

Mrs Lewis sighed with relief – relief, Amy expected, at not being treated as if she were immoral. 'Is there anything to pay?'

'Only if you can afford it,' Amy said. 'Is your husband in work?'

Mrs Lewis nodded. 'At the moment. He's a carpenter, a real good one. He's got a job in a furniture factory. There wasn't anything in Manchester. He had to take whatever he could get and there wasn't much. He had some terrible jobs. So we came here.'

'I'm glad he got something,' Amy said.

Mrs Lewis picked up her handbag, preparing to leave. 'Do you think there's going to be a war, Doctor? Do you think they'd bomb London?

I could go back to Manchester, to Trafford Park, but there are factories there. They might bomb those too. I wouldn't know what to do for the best.'

'We'll just have to hope not.' Amy's worries surged again.

'But they're already giving out gas-masks for the children. They must think it's going to happen.'

'I'm sure it's just a precaution,' Amy said.

Mrs Lewis got up. 'Have you got children, Doctor?'

'Yes,' Amy said. 'Twins, a boy and a girl. They're nearly eighteen.'

'Oh.' Mrs Lewis's face mirrored her own worries. 'My little girl is nearly twelve. Sara, she's called. She's just got a scholarship to the grammar school.'

'That's wonderful,' Amy said. 'She must be very clever.'

Mrs Lewis smiled – a thin, humourless smile – and walked to the door. 'She is, for what that's worth. She says she wants to be a doctor when she grows up but I can't see much chance of that. You'd have to be well off for that, wouldn't you?' She went out, closing the door behind her.

Amy sighed. Mrs Lewis was right, she supposed. There wasn't much chance of that, the way things were, for a child like Sara.

Amy had a home visit to do after the surgery, to one of the tenement houses off Ladbroke Grove. Room four, she was told, on the first floor.

The front door was open and she walked inside and up the dingy stairs. These houses were all much the same. This one had dark-brown shiny paint below the dado and a dull green above. She knew what she would find – a cramped room with a single bed, a chest of drawers, a battered easy chair, a wireless. In the winter these rooms were often freezing cold, scarcely heated by a guttering gas fire. Her patient, almost always a woman, would be swathed in layers of tattered cardigans, often with woollen mittens on their chapped hands. At least it was warm today.

She knocked at the door and went in. 'It's the doctor, Mrs Kelly,' she said.

Mrs Kelly was in bed, wearing a worn but clean nighty, her hair in a net. 'I've got a bad cough, doctor,' she said.

Amy helped her off with her nighty. She was thin and scrawny. Most of these old ladies were undernourished. She listened to her chest and looked at her throat.

'Your chest is quite clear, Mrs Kelly,' she said, 'and your throat's a bit sore. I think you just have a cold. I'll leave you a prescription for some cough medicine.'

Mrs Kelly put her nighty on again. 'Thank you Doctor,' she said. 'The landlady will get it. Your two-and-six is on the chest of drawers.'

Amy took the sixpence, leaving behind the two shillings. Some of the ladies got annoyed if she took nothing. They had their pride. Sometimes they paid her off at sixpence a week. Sometimes she didn't charge them at all.

She gave a little shrug, feeling uncomfortable, a goose walking over her grave. Ever since she had come into this room she had the odd feeling that she was being watched. There was a large photograph of a young man in uniform on the chest of drawers, and beside it a single flower in a little vase He was almost certainly a son, killed in the war, but it wasn't him watching her. She raised her eyes and gave a sharp intake of breath. All around the picture rail there were perched grey, sooty-looking pigeons. They were sitting quite still, looking down at her with beady, malevolent eyes. 'We are watching you,' they seemed to be saying. 'What are you doing with Mrs Kelly?'

Mrs Kelly saw her surprise. 'They're my friends,' she said. 'I feed them and they know me.'

'You really shouldn't …' Amy began, but Mrs Kelly waved her words away.

'I know,' she said. 'I know all about the diseases they're supposed to have but they've never done me any harm. They're my friends. They keep me company.'

Amy left and got into her car to drive home. She sighed. How sad, how shameful, that in this huge city her only friends were a bunch of scrawny London pigeons. War, and the aftermath of war. How shameful.

She drove home for a quick lunch. Charlie wasn't home – out with his friends, probably.

Mrs Parks was busy in the kitchen. 'Do you want lunch, Doctor?' she asked.

'Just a sandwich please.' Amy ate her lunch at the dining-room table and drank a cup of coffee. Mrs Lewis had stayed in her mind, and her little girl – Sara, was it? She sounded so bright and ambitious. Why couldn't these children be helped? Why did so few working-class children ever make it to university? Half the country's brains were going to waste.

She finished her brief lunch, drove to Gower Street and waited for Tessa inside Lewis's bookshop. She glanced through a selection of second-hand books for medical students, some of them thumbed and grubby, some of them almost new. She smiled. You could tell who had worked hard.

Tessa arrived. Amy watched her as she came through the door, bright, happy, confident. Tessa could do what she wanted; achieve what she wanted, not like little Sara Lewis. They were so lucky; they had so much. Sara Lewis's chances of doing medicine, as her mother said, were just about nil. Even if the fees were somehow paid, the expenses were enormous – books, lab coats, instruments, and keeping alive for six years. And then, if you wanted to be a general practitioner, you'd have to buy into a practice. It all took money.

'Hello, Mum.' Tessa kissed her cheek. 'I need the *Gray's* and a book on embryology. Come and help.'

Amy followed her. 'I expect things have changed since I was a student.'

Tessa laughed. 'I don't think anatomy has changed much. We haven't evolved at all, have we? We're just the same.'

Yes, Amy thought, her mood dark, humanity was much the same – just as mad, apparently.

'Bacteriology,' Tessa said. 'I'd better have that. I shall need to know about the little blighters.'

Amy pictured her in the pathology lab, inspecting the colonies of bacteria growing in Petri dishes, learning which was which, looking down a microscope at the little dots and dashes on the slides – at those tiny, tiny things that were so deadly.

'What's up, Mum?' Tessa said. 'You look rather serious.'

'Oh – nothing.' Amy smiled. 'I was thinking about bacteria. At least we have sulphonamides now. We had nothing before.'

Tessa looked at her for a moment. She knows what I'm thinking, Amy thought. Why do we even have to think about war?

'Let's go and have tea,' Tessa said. 'Can we go back to Derry and Toms? I want to see the roof garden again.'

Amy drove to Kensington High Street. They went into the store and up in the onyx and black-marble lift to the Rainbow restaurant on the top floor.

'I love these lifts,' Tessa said. 'Very Art Deco.'

'Tea first,' Amy said, 'then we'll go up to the roof garden.'

The waiter brought tea and cakes.

'Mum,' Tessa said, 'why did you change to general practice after the war? You did surgery then, didn't you?'

Amy nodded. 'You and Charlie came along and I didn't want to be out all day and never see you. And I wanted to do more for the families. Some of them lead wretched lives, Tessa, even now.'

'Do you think there'll be another war?' Tessa said. She spoke quietly, without emotion, without fear or excitement.

'I don't know,' Amy said.

Tessa pressed her lips together. 'It's Charlie ...'

Amy forced herself not to react, not to show her terrors to her daughter. But she was a woman now, about to embark upon a career that would bring her face to face with distress and disaster. She couldn't give her childish assurances. She looked down at her hands, clasped in her lap. 'I don't know,' she said again.

'Charlie says he won't just kill people. He says they can't make him.' She paused. 'They shot people who wouldn't fight in the last war, didn't they?'

Amy turned her head away, looking out across the restaurant at the well-dressed women taking tea, the quiet hum of conversation, the waitresses in their neat uniforms. For a moment she couldn't speak. 'They shot some men who ran away,' she said. 'It was utterly disgraceful. What those men went through ... They didn't shoot conscientious objectors.'

'I don't think he's a conchie, exactly,' Tessa said, 'But he says he won't just kill people indiscriminately; certainly not civilians, women and children.'

Oh Charlie, Amy thought. She couldn't see him hurting a fly.

'It's all right for me,' Tessa said. 'I'd defend my country against anybody if I had to, but I'll never have to make the choice, will I? I'll be doing the other thing, patching people up.'

She doesn't know, Amy thought. She can't imagine what it was like, the mud and the blood and the rats and the disease and the screaming hell of it all. 'Let's go up to the roof garden,' she said.

They went up to the garden and strolled among the trees and flowers.

'Amazing, isn't it?' Tessa said. 'All this and the pool and the pink flamingos, on top of the world.'

Amy nodded, but didn't speak. In the last war, German bombers had been seen from Kensington High Street, dropping their bombs, destroying and killing.

'Cheer up, Mum,' Tessa said. 'It may never happen.'

When his mother left Charlie got out his bike and rode to Kensington Gardens. He sat in the sunshine by the Round Pond, watching the children sailing their little boats. It was as tranquil as ever, since he and Tessa sailed their boats here with their parents, or with the nanny they'd had then. On the surface nothing had changed. Now, he couldn't be sure. No one could be sure. All those men last night, not much older than he was, going on and on about what was going to happen. Was it? Those army types behaved as if they were glad about it: excited, anyway. Was there going to be a war, and what would he, Charlie, have to do about it? What would he be made to do? What would all of them be made to do?

He felt a kind of tension, his insides contracting. It wasn't fear, exactly; he knew that. He even understood their excitement, those army chaps. He felt a sort of excitement himself. It would be a chance to overcome, to prove himself as a man. He had read enough history to hear that call. But that last war – it was not a battle, but from what he had read, or gathered from his parents' occasional remarks, it was a spirit-numbing weary war of attrition, a bare-knuckled mindless slogging until both opponents were on their knees, battered and barely conscious. He didn't even really know what it was about. Did anyone?

What he felt, he realized, was revulsion. He tried to imagine himself pointing a gun at some man, looking him in the eye, deliberately pulling the trigger and killing him. He tried to imagine himself hating someone he didn't even know. None of it seemed real or possible.

In front of him a young boy was trying to catch his little boat, that had floated out of his reach, and he looked to be in danger of falling in. Charlie got up and fished it out for him. The child's mother smiled and thanked him. He remembered, with a shock, that the Government was already arranging to give out gas-masks for children.

Chapter Two

1938

Dan scrubbed up at the sink in the small room beside the operating theatre. The first patient was probably an appendicectomy, then two inguinal hernias, then an exploratory laparotomy that might take some time. He scrubbed the soap up his arms, around his nails and between his fingers.

He did this several times almost every working day. The routine of it had calmed his memories, but now and again they would edge back in, subtle and undermining, knowing they were unwelcome. Sometimes a faint whiff of infection as he opened an abdomen, or sometimes the brutal wounds of a road accident would revive it all, and for a few seconds he would be back in the sickening horror of the war in 1914, in the overwhelmed and spirit-numbing hospitals in France.

It happened less frequently now, but Amy's distress this morning had brought it back. He remembered holding her in his arms at the war's end, the day she said she would marry him. He remembered what she said: 'At least we know that our children will never have to go through that hell.' Now that happy assurance was thinning and fading. He would not admit to her that he was worried too, that the prospect of another war filled him with dread: dread on Charlie's account, and for everyone, women and children included. It would not be confined to the military any more – the advances in aircraft design, the newest bombers, would see to that. German bombers had bombed the defenceless town of Guernica in Spain and killed a thousand helpless civilians. The Germans seemed to regard that as some kind of successful experiment. If killing and intimidation and submission were what you were after, he supposed that it was.

Bob Reed, his registrar, appeared beside him and began to scrub up. 'Morning, Dan,' he said.

Dan nodded in reply, 'Morning.'

'The appendix needs doing,' Bob said. 'He's pyrexial and has definite rebound tenderness this morning, so I put him first on the list.'

'Fine,' Dan said.

There was a silence as they scrubbed, then Bob said, 'what do you think's happening, Dan? They brought round gas-masks for my kids yesterday. My wife's in a bit of a state. Gas-masks! For children! Good God!'

'They say it's just a precaution.' Dan glanced at Bob, who was concentrating on his hands, frowning. 'I don't believe they would use gas on civilians. The repercussions would be terrible for them too.'

'You could say that about everything, couldn't you? The prospect of them winning would be bad enough. God knows what they might do if they were losing.'

'I don't think even they would use gas,' Dan said. He almost believed it.

'You were in the last lot, weren't you?'

'Yes,' Dan said shortly. 'I was in a hospital at Etaples.'

There was another silence. 'Bad?' Bob said.

There was no use in playing it down, especially to Bob, who was young enough to be conscripted. 'Yes,' Dan said. 'It was bad enough.'

'You know what the Ministry is saying?' Bob went on. 'If there's another war they're expecting at least a million civilians dead in air raids. They're stockpiling thousands of cardboard coffins, planning to dig lime-pits. I'm wondering whether to move my wife and kids out of London, but where could they go to be safe?'

Dan shook the water from his hands and reached for a sterile towel. 'No good anticipating the worst,' he said. 'We must hope for the best.'

They moved into the operating theatre, slid their arms into the sterile gowns held out by the nurses and snapped on rubber gloves. The patient was already on the table, the anaesthetist at his head. They spread the sterile towels. Dan incised into the abdomen and the peritoneum. There was no putrid smell of infection; they had got it in time. 'I think it's retrocaecal,' he said. He carefully moved aside the bowel.

The appendix was lying behind the bowel, the red, infected tip almost glowing. 'I've got it,' he said. 'It's definitely inflamed.' He removed it, careful not to release any pus into the abdomen, and closed up. Infection was the killer. It had taken so many lives in the war. 'I wish we had something,' he said, 'something to kill the damn bugs. The sulphonamides don't stop everything.'

They worked through the morning, and then changed into their suits and white coats and drank a cup of coffee.

Dan sensed that Bob was going to ask him more about the war. He was reluctant to talk about it, to drag it out of the protective covering he had managed to spread over it. The thought of a million civilian casualties, woman and children, appalled him. They could never cope. The hospitals would be overwhelmed in Britain, let alone the care needed for the troops. He knew too much. He knew what a million casualties looked like.

'How old are your kids?' Bob said.

'They're twins. They're eighteen next week.'

'Oh.' Bob's silence was expressive. Then he said, 'You've got a boy, haven't you?'

'Yes,' Dan said shortly. 'He's going up to Cambridge this year.'

'Perhaps he'd get an exemption,' Bob said, 'until he's got his degree. They did that in the last war, didn't they?'

'I believe so,' Dan said. 'At first, anyway.' Bob was speaking as if war were inevitable. He didn't want to talk about it any more and changed the subject. 'Good thing we did the laparotomy and caught that peptic ulcer. It wasn't far from perforating.'

The family assembled for dinner in the dining room. The french doors were open on to the garden and the faint summer scents filled the room. Mrs Parks brought in the roast chicken and the dishes of vegetables, and Dan carved.

'Get your books all right?' he asked.

Tessa nodded. 'Yes, some of them, but there are rows and rows of enormous tomes. How on earth do you get it all into your head?'

Dan smiled. 'I don't know, but it seems to happen. Hard work probably has something to do with it.' He handed round the plates.

'I had a letter from Kurt today,' Charlie said. 'He's invited me to stay with his family in Berlin for a week or so.'

There was a silence. Amy and Dan glanced at each other, Amy startled and worried. 'I don't think so,' she said. 'I don't think that's a very good idea.'

'Why?' Charlie said. 'Nothing much is happening, just talk, and it's not as if you don't know Kurt.'

'It isn't Kurt,' Amy said. 'He seemed to be a very nice boy, but you know as well as I do that things are very dangerous just now. We don't know what's going to happen.' She turned to Dan. 'Don't you think so?'

Dan nodded. 'It's not the best time to be travelling in Europe. What else does Kurt say?'

'Only that his parents would like to repay us for having him for those half-term holidays. You can read the letter if you like. People are still going to Germany on holiday, aren't they? Nobody seems to be that worried.'

'Can I come?' Tessa said.

Her father shook his head. 'Absolutely not.'

'Why?' she said, grinning. 'Is Kurt a Nazi, Charlie? Does he wear a swastika and stick his arm up and say *Heil Hitler*? Did he come here to spy on us?'

'He came to school for a year to improve his English,' Charlie said. 'We didn't talk about politics.'

Tessa put her finger under her nose and put her hand in the air.

'It isn't funny, Tessa,' Amy said. 'They've just taken over Austria without a by-your-leave.'

'Weren't they Germans really?' Charlie said. 'They wanted to be taken over, didn't they?' There was a silence. 'I'm only asking.'

'They are doing terrible things to the Jews,' Amy said. 'There is no excuse for that.'

'Why do you want to go, Charlie?' Dan said quietly.

Charlie met his father's eyes directly. 'Can you really believe everything that the papers say? I want to see for myself.'

Dan saw something in Charlie's face – a message that the boy, knowingly or unknowingly, was giving him. Perhaps, he thought, some kind of resolve. For the first time, fleetingly, he had the impression that the boy was no longer there, and he was looking at a man.

Charlie tucked into his chicken. 'I'd like to go' he said.

Amy frowned. 'We'll have to think about it.' She glanced at Dan. 'Dad and I will think about it.'

After dinner Charlie joined his father in the garden. Dan lit his pipe and they sat together in the warm, pearly evening, the light soft and the air still.

'Why must you go to Germany?' Dan said. 'If you want to travel a bit go somewhere else – France, perhaps. You could get home more easily from France.'

'I just want to see Germany for myself,' Charlie said. 'And I've never been there. I want to see what's going on.'

'You can't ignore what your mother said,' Dan went on, 'about Austria and the Jews. Any country that gets rid of men like Albert Einstein and Sigmund Freud must have something seriously wrong with it.'

'I don't ignore it,' Charlie said, 'but I want to make up my own mind.' After a few moments he said, 'The Duke of Windsor went there.'

Dan drew on his pipe. 'That's hardly a recommendation, and anyway, that was a year ago and things have changed. The sabres are rattling. You know your mother wouldn't get a wink of sleep until you were home again.'

'A week,' Charlie said. 'That's all. You don't think anything's going to happen in the next week or two?'

Dan shook his head. 'No. I don't think so. I very much hope not.'

They sat in silence for a few moments.

'You never talk about the war,' Charlie said suddenly. 'You and Mum. You never say what it was like.'

Dan looked out across the garden. 'We were doctors,' he said. 'We weren't in the trenches.'

'But you saw what it was like. I've only read the books and seen the pictures. I don't know how people felt.'

Dan took his pipe out of his mouth and looked at his son. Charlie drew in his breath. His father's look of dark, raw pain and distress was unexpected.

'Don't look like that, Dad,' he said. 'It won't happen to me.'

23

Dan looked away. 'You realize that if it ever did come to war with Germany you and Kurt would be on opposite sides – enemies?'

'I'm not stupid, Dad.'

'I just mean that it might be best not to get too friendly with him – under the circumstances.'

'And that's what I mean. Surely if more of us ordinary people talk to each other…? We're not that different, are we?'

Dan puffed on his pipe. The evening began to fade, the colours blurring and losing their brilliance. Strange, he thought, how colour is only light. He knocked out his pipe on the arm of the bench. 'I don't know any more. We'd best go in.'

Later Amy lay in bed, restless, unable to sleep or read. 'What shall we do?' she said. 'Shall we let him go? The whole thing might blow up at any moment.'

'I don't think it will,' Dan said. 'Not yet anyway. We're certainly not ready for another war.'

'Oh God,' she said. 'What's happening, Dan? The Germans have taken Austria, the Spanish are killing each other, the Japanese are bombing China. The world's gone mad again. And it's as if some hideous evil force has arranged it, timed it perfectly. It's just twenty years – just exactly time for the children to grow up. It's evil. It's unbearable.'

He put his arm around her. 'It probably won't happen,' he said. 'Maybe we should let him go, just for a week. He's only kicking his heels around here. He says he wants to see for himself.'

'What difference would that make?' she said. 'If the balloon goes up he'd have to do what he was told like everybody else.'

'It might make a difference to his personal conviction, and for Charlie I think that would be important.'

She sighed. 'You'd have to tell him how careful he must be. You know that an American tourist was badly jostled by a crowd because he wouldn't give Hitler the Nazi salute?'

'I'll tell him,' he said. 'He's very sensible.'

'He's just a boy,' she said, turning over.

Dan lay back against the pillows. Would it do any good, Charlie going there? Did he need that immediacy, that face-to-face experience, before he decided how to manage his life, the possibilities of the coming world? Things took place in other countries; reports came filtering through: misunderstandings, pride, hate, nationalism and patriotism. Statesmen were just men, after all, as wise and as foolish as anyone else. But Charlie's life was his own. Perhaps he did need to see for himself.

Charlie got out of the train at the Anhalter Bahnhof and picked up his suitcase. He didn't need a porter, he decided; his case wasn't heavy. At his mother's insistence he was only staying for a week.

The platform was crowded. The station smelt of hot oil and burning coal. Clouds of steam rose to the roof and disappeared. There were pigeons up there, he saw, just like at home. He looked about him. He was struck by the number of uniforms. The officers were very smartly dressed, their caps rising at the front in aggressive peaks, badges gleaming. The swastika was everywhere.

He had been through customs – a very thorough search – when he entered Germany. His passport had been inspected again on the train by a silent, suspicious frontier guard, and handed back to him curtly. He followed the crowd to the exit.

Kurt was waiting, smiling and waving. 'I'm glad you are here,' he said. 'We'll get a taxi.'

They left the station and walked to the taxi rank 'What is that building?' Charlie asked. It was close to the station, huge, rectangular, solid, ugly.

'Oh that – it is an air-raid shelter,' Kurt said. 'It would take many people.'

Charlie thought of the air-raid shelters apparently being designed at home – Anderson shelters, he thought they were called – what looked like a couple of pieces of corrugated iron for a roof over a hole dug into the garden – flimsy looking things compared with this. 'Are you expecting air raids?' he said.

'I don't think so,' Kurt said, 'but you never know, do you? But I do not know if anyone would attack Germany. It would be foolish, I think.'

Charlie glanced at him, but Kurt's face was expressionless.

They drove through Berlin on the way to the Brauns' apartment. Charlie stared out of the window. Berlin looked prosperous, he thought. Some of the buildings were obviously new, massive and impressive, with great sculptures at their façades – eagles, soldiers, Teutonic knights, and everywhere the swastika. The whole atmosphere was military, and military on a grand scale. The very buildings seemed aggressive. It was not a bit like London. He wondered how two great European cities could be so different. To him, London had an air of grace, of dignity, wrought by centuries of culture, and by stability, achieved and retained. Here the buildings were new, huge, gleaming blocks. We are stronger than you, they seemed to say, more modern, more powerful. Ignore us at your peril.

'Great buildings,' he said, and Kurt seemed proud.

'I will show them to you properly,' he said. 'They are worth seeing.'

'Do your parents speak English?' Charlie asked.

'My father does, quite well, my mother hardly at all.'

Charlie was greeted by Kurt's parents with the utmost politeness. 'Welcome to Berlin,' his father said.

Kurt took him to his bedroom. 'I expect you would like a cup of tea,' Kurt said. Charlie nodded.

Kurt smiled. 'Very English,' he said. 'I will send it. Dinner will be ready very soon.'

Charlie unpacked and put his clothes away. The furniture was dark and heavy, very German, he thought, and then smiled at himself. What did he know about Germany? Almost nothing. That was what he was here for. A maid brought him a pot of tea and sugar and milk on a tray and he drank it, looking out of the window. Across the street was a park with trees and flower-beds and straight paths, meeting at neat right angles. He washed his hands and face, put on a clean shirt and tie and a jacket and joined the family for dinner.

Kurt's father was quite short and plump, a heavy gold watch chain across his waistcoat. His mother and his little sister were both blond and blue-eyed.

'I hope you will like our German food,' Herr Braun said. 'It will make you strong.'

Charlie smiled at Frau Braun. 'I'm sure I will.'

'It was kind of you to entertain Kurt in the half-term holidays,' Herr Braun said, 'and show him around London. He will show you our Berlin.'

After dinner the boys went for a walk in the park.

'I'm looking forward to seeing the city,' Charlie said. 'The buildings look magnificent.'

'And many of them are new,' Kurt said. 'London is very interesting, but you do live in the past, don't you?'

'We have a lot of past,' Charlie said. 'A lot of history.'

'That is where we are encouraged to be different then,' Kurt said. 'We are supposed to look to the future now, to the new Germany.' He paused. 'Whatever that may be.'

They walked on. 'How are your parents?' Kurt asked.

'Very well.'

'And how is Tessa?'

Charlie glanced at him. Kurt's voice had changed. It had a warmth in it, and a wariness. It hadn't occurred to him before that Kurt might have been attracted to Tessa. He had never said anything. He wouldn't, of course. Charlie could see that now. The atmosphere in this country was unmistakable – military and aggressive. Kurt would not, could not, approach an English girl under the circumstances: the hovering of an uncertain and possibly dangerous future.

'Is she still going to be a doctor?' Kurt said.

'Yes,' Charlie said. 'She's very keen. What are you going to do?'

'Go to university,' Kurt said. 'I shall read modern languages. That might be useful in the future.'

Charlie wondered what kind of future Kurt had in mind, whether he envisaged a situation where the knowledge of languages might go beyond the simple advantages of everyday use. He had certainly been keen to learn English. He didn't ask. 'I'm going up to Cambridge,' he said, 'to read history.'

Kurt gave a little laugh. 'You are a dreamer, Charlie.'

Charlie felt a sudden rush of feeling. What was it? Pride, patriotism, love of family, of home, some kind of belief? 'Someone has to be,' he said.

Charlie went to bed early, tired from the journey. There was an atmosphere here, he thought, an urgency, a kind of aggression. They were on their way somewhere. Where?

The next day they did a tour of the city. Troops were marching at the Brandenburg Gate. Charlie watched them, impressed. Their faces, implacable under the heavy helmets, looked as if they were carved from stone. 'They look very fit,' he said.

'They are,' Kurt said. 'Our Chancellor says that he doesn't want the army to be intelligent. He wants them brutal.'

Charlie didn't reply. Kurt's voice held a faint touch of deeper meaning. He couldn't decide whether it was amusement or cynicism.

They moved on. They looked at one great new building after another, the burnt and damaged Reichstag, now, seemingly, under reconstruction; then the huge, modern complex of the Air Ministry building. Charlie didn't know where the British Air Ministry was, but he was sure it didn't look like this. The Germans obviously attached a good deal of importance to their air force. They found and admired the *Eagle and Swastika* sculpture by Walter Lemke.

'They are magnificent, these buildings,' Charlie said. 'They must have cost a fortune.'

'It was probably worth it,' Kurt said. 'They send a certain message to the citizens, about our great strength.' Charlie glanced at him, not sure what he meant, but Kurt's face again seemed to be carefully expressionless.

They passed a small group of men, many of them well dressed in suits and overcoats and carrying a small suitcase. They were being moved on by uniformed guards.

Charlie watched them go by. 'Who are they?'

'Just some Jews,' Kurt said, his voice low. 'Perhaps they have volunteered to do some work for Germany.' He paused. 'Or perhaps they are leaving the country.' He turned away abruptly. 'Let's go to the Potsdamer Platz and have coffee. You will like it there.'

The platz was crammed with cafés and restaurants and plastered with posters advertising reviews and cabarets.

'It is like a Christmas tree at night,' Kurt said. 'We will come.'

They sat at a table outside in the sunshine, watching the crowds, pretty girls, good-looking young men, many uniforms.

'It's all very impressive,' Charlie said. 'Germany is very modern.'

Karl said nothing, sipping his coffee. 'What's all this trouble with the Jews?' Charlie went on. 'What are they supposed to have done?'

Kurt lowered his voice. 'I don't think we will talk about the Jews.'

He didn't move, didn't look round, but Charlie could see the tension in his body, the wariness in his face. Kurt got up. 'I think we will go now.'

They dined at home again that evening.

'So, what do you think of our Berlin?' Herr Braun smiled a broad, complacent smile.

'The new buildings are magnificent,' Charlie said.

'They are the Führer's doing,' Herr Braun said. 'He has saved us from inflation, the communists, the Jews.' He took a mouthful of wine. 'We were cheated after the last war,' he went on, 'and look at us now – the most powerful country in Europe, if not the world.'

Charlie didn't know what to say. He just smiled. Herr Braun did not smile back. He seemed to regard Charlie's smile as some kind of challenge. 'We did not cause the last war,' he said angrily, 'and we were humiliated afterwards. Our land was given away, to the Czechs and the Poles. Our colonies were given away. Millions of Germans are forced to live outside our borders. What do you think of that?'

Charlie was deeply embarrassed. He could feel himself flushing. Kurt spoke to his father in rapid German and Herr Braun said no more, stabbing at his food in silence.

The boys went to the little park again.

'I am sorry about that,' Kurt said. 'My father gets very emotional about it. He was in the last war. He was wounded in the leg.'

Charlie kicked at a little stone. 'What did you say to him?'

'I said that you were not born then and it was nothing to do with you.' They walked on. 'It has left its mark, though.'

'It would,' Charlie said. 'I'm afraid I don't know much about it.'

'Never mind,' Kurt said. 'We will go to a lake tomorrow, the Wannsee, and take a picnic.'

Next day they took the subway train to the Lanke station and walked to the lake. They walked past prosperous houses and through a pleasant wood. The shores of the lake were crowded with families, walkers, and children running everywhere. The people looked prosperous, Charlie thought, the women in flowery summer dresses and shady hats.

'We'll take a boat out on the lake,' Kurt said. 'I need some exercise.'

They hired a rowing boat and Kurt rowed out on to the lake.

'You must forgive my father,' Kurt said. 'He is a great admirer of Herr Hitler.'

'I don't blame him,' Charlie said. 'The man has pulled the country together. I just don't understand why he has this hatred of the Jews, and I don't understand why he's risking another war.'

Kurt looked around him. 'We are on the lake,' he said quietly, 'so that no one will hear us. Please, Charlie, do not speak about the Jews or criticize the Führer while you are here. It could make a great deal of trouble for my family.'

Charlie looked at Kurt's troubled face and the darkness in his eyes. He felt a sense of sudden and profound shock. I'm a fool, he thought, an idiot. I know nothing. It simply hadn't occurred to him that he might be in a country where just his words or his expressed opinion could lead to such danger. The moment was a watershed. He felt as if a door had closed behind him, as if he had stepped into another world where he was naked and unprepared. He wondered what Kurt really thought about what was happening in Germany. He, Charlie, lived in a country that he had never questioned, that had never presented him with any real political conflict. He had never had to make such decisions. In fact, he thought, he had never been presented with any kind of conflict. His life had been smooth and untroubled. Perhaps that time was coming. He watched his childhood skitter away across the water.

He looked at Kurt with new eyes, a new understanding, at a Kurt who seemed so much older, so much more experienced, than himself.

'Remember, Charlie,' Kurt said. 'You are not in England now.'

'I – I understand,' Charlie said. 'I'm sorry.'

Kurt smiled. 'We'll go back now and have our picnic. My mother has packed *käsebrotchen* and smoked ham and salami and cheese and fruit.'

'A feast,' Charlie said.

On Charlie's last night they went to a nightclub. Most of the clientele were officers in their glamorous uniforms with their pretty, well-dressed girls. On each table was a telephone.

'You can ring up the other tables,' Kurt said, 'and ask a girl to dance or have a drink with you.'

'I wouldn't have the nerve,' Charlie said.

They drank a few beers before the phone rang.

Kurt answered it and smiled. 'It is for you. That young lady would like to dance with you.'

Charlie stood up and smiled and the girl walked to him across the dance floor. He wished his German was better. She didn't seem to understand him, except when he said he was English. At the end of the dance she left him and went back to her table. She said something to her companions, the officers and their girls, and they roared with laughter, holding up their glasses to him in some kind of sarcastic salute. Later, when he and Kurt left, they raised their glasses again. 'Good luck, Englishman,' one of them called, and they roared with laughter again. He imagined that the words hung in the air: *You'll need it.*

Kurt took him to the station the next day. 'I hope you and I will meet again one day,' Kurt said. 'As friends.'

Charlie knew immediately what he meant. It was the first time that either of them had hinted at the thoughts they would not express.

'It won't happen,' Charlie said. 'It can't.'

A group of soldiers marched on to the platform. They looked so confident, Charlie thought, as if the world belonged to them.

The guard blew his whistle. 'Do you remember the story of Croesus and the Delphic Oracle?' Kurt said.

Charlie shook his head. 'Not really. Why?'

'Look it up,' Kurt said. 'It is as true as ever.'

Charlie settled in the train. Kurt waved to him, and then was swallowed up in a crowd of uniforms. It was a strange relief when the train started, as if he feared that they would never let him leave. The atmosphere seemed to him to be oppressive, strangling. The people, he thought, had no freedom. Even if they disagreed with the regime they were not able to say so. Even to express such a thought invited retribution, a visit from the police. He had no idea what Kurt really thought. He found that he couldn't wait to get out of Germany. Crossing the border was a positive relief. There was no more beautiful sight than the English coastline, no better feeling than to find himself back in England.

His mother threw her arms around his neck as he came through the door, laughing with relief. 'Thank God you're home,' she said. 'I was worried all the time.'

Tessa kissed his cheek. 'Did you get up to no good? They say Berlin is a bit racy.'

'Good as gold.' Charlie grinned. 'I return unscathed.'

Later he sat with his father in the garden.

'Well,' Dan said. 'Did you see for yourself?'

'Yes,' Charlie said shortly.

'And...?'

Charlie looked around the garden, at the tranquil evening, at the old swing. 'I think we're for it, Dad. They're preparing for war, that's for sure. I'm not saying they want one, but they're getting ready. I've never seen so many uniforms, such an atmosphere. Their Ministry of Aviation building is as big as a small town.'

'Don't say that to your mother,' Dan said.

'I won't, but it isn't just that.'

Dan sucked on his pipe. 'What then?'

'It's hard to describe,' Charlie frowned, 'but there's something dark there, Dad, something very unpleasant. It's not like it is here.'

Dan was quiet, drawing on his pipe. 'How was Kurt?'

'Very well, physically. He didn't say anything but I get the feeling he isn't happy about it. His father is very pro Hitler.'

'He won't have a choice if war comes,' Dan said. 'I don't suppose they would show much mercy to conscientious objectors.'

'Dad,' Charlie said, 'do you remember anything about Croesus and the oracle at Delphi?'

His father was obviously surprised at the change of subject. 'Why?'

'Kurt said something about it just as I was leaving.'

'I believe Croesus asked the Oracle if he should go to war against the Persians and the Oracle said that if he did a great nation would be destroyed. So Croesus went to war and was heavily defeated. The great nation destroyed was his own.'

'Oh,' Charlie said, 'I see.' He didn't see. He wondered which nation Kurt had in mind. Perhaps, he thought, it was both.

Chapter Three

1938

Sara sat at the table in her little bedroom. She could come back here after tea and stay up a bit later tonight – it was school holidays. Her mum made her go to bed at half past eight on school days, even if the other children were still playing outside. She said sleep fed your brain. Outside in the street she could hear the other children playing, running and shouting. She preferred to stay here and read. She didn't want to join them. Sometimes she did go out, playing pig-in-the-middle or tag or skipping, but she seemed to have grown out of that kind of play, running about to no purpose.

She had another purpose, one that she could never talk of to the children in the street. They would look at her with bafflement and poke fun at her and call her names. It was going to be bad enough going out in her new school uniform and carrying the leather satchel that was a kind of grammar-school badge. That was if she got there. Her heart seemed to swell in her chest. The longing was desperate. She squeezed her eyes tight. Perhaps if she just wished hard enough it would all happen. She wanted to be a doctor more than anything in the whole world. Meanwhile, there were her books, years of study at her new school. But it wouldn't be hard – she loved it, loved the endless revelations of endless, thrilling science. There was so much to know and so much to learn. She couldn't wait. She couldn't remember when she had first wanted to be a doctor – years ago. Her mum's doctor was a lady, so it could happen – girls could do it.

Downstairs Nora was cooking what she called 'tea' – dinner really – that's what they called it down here. Fish and chips tonight, it being Friday. She wasn't Catholic but she had got into the habit back home in

Manchester. Everybody seemed to have fish on Friday: fish, chips and peas. She peeled the potatoes carefully, so as not to waste anything. What is happening, she thought – all this talk of war? She couldn't bear it. She'd been a child last time. It had never occurred to anybody that it could happen again. The threat had become for her a solely personal thing. A war would be directed right here, to her home, to her Sara. She couldn't expand the fear, spread it out, include the rest of the world, even the rest of her own country. It seemed to her that the whole purpose of a war would be to threaten Sara.

She stared out of the window, where Sara's bicycle was propped up against the yard wall. She had never realized what motherhood would be like, never anticipated this degree of loving and caring. Sometimes she wondered whether, if she had known, she would have wanted motherhood at all. This kind of love brought with it a low but constant anxiety – would Sara be all right? Would she escape the dreadful diseases that could kill a child: diphtheria, scarlet fever, TB? Now it was growing into a new fear – fear of a war, and even if there was no war, fear that she might not be able to give Sara what she wanted. A doctor! Her daughter a doctor! It would make up for everything that she herself had missed. Somehow, somehow, they would make it happen. She slipped the chips into the hot fat in the chip pan and the fat bubbled up, crackling and spitting.

Jim came in and kissed her cheek. He took off his jacket and hung it up on a chair-back.

'Any news?' she said.

Jim sat down at the table and she gave him a cup of tea. He knew what she meant. She wasn't talking about a war. Some dangers were closer than a war. 'No,' he said. 'The bosses seem to think the factory'll be all right. People still need furniture.'

Nora said nothing. Every day she was frightened that Jim would come home and tell her that the factory was closing and he was out of work again. She didn't know how she would cope if they had to go back on the dole again, back on fifteen shillings a week. Keeping body and soul together would be bad enough, but there was Sara and grammar school – so much to pay for. Thanks to the scholarship there would be no fees, but there was uniform and books and gym clothes and goodness knows what else. The uniform alone would cost a fortune; the wool dresses for winter and the cotton ones for summer, the blue gabardine mac and the blazer for summer, and the hat with a yellow hatband, the gym tunic, navy-blue knickers, indoor shoes. And then the books. The list of books alone was bad enough.

She pressed her lips together, and turned the fish over in the frying pan. She'd saved enough, she thought, bit by bit, shilling by shilling. The pound notes were slowly growing in the shoebox in the wardrobe. Sara was getting out of this, out of privation and scrimping and saving and getting nowhere. Sara was going to the grammar school if she, Nora, had to starve to death to get her there.

'Where's Sara?' Jim said

'Upstairs. Reading, I expect.' She went to the foot of the stairs. 'Sara,' she called. 'Tea's ready. Your dad's here.'

'She's always reading,' Jim said. 'I don't know why you're so insistent on that school. She'd be perfectly all right at the ordinary school with the other kids.'

'No she wouldn't,' Nora snapped. 'We've been through all this. She's clever. She's going to get on. She isn't going to be stuck in some dead-end job.'

'We can't afford it,' he said.

Nora put his tea before him with a little thump. 'Yes we can. I could get a job.'

He opened his mouth to reply but Sara came into the kitchen. She kissed her father on the cheek. 'Hello Dad.'

Jim smiled at her with affection, and some puzzlement. Where had she come from, this brainy child, and what were they going to do with her? No one in either family had ever been to a university, let alone want to be a doctor. What an idea! There seemed to be no way out of the mess the country was in. She'd be lucky to get a job at all. It was pie in the sky, especially for a girl.

Sara sat down at the table. 'Mum,' she said, 'why did you go to the doctor's? Is there something wrong?'

Nora glanced quickly at Jim, a faint colour rising in her cheeks. 'No love,' she said. 'Just a check-up. I'm fine.'

Sara took up her knife and fork and carefully dissected her fish away from the bone, admiring the little vertebrae in the spine, the way they so cleverly locked together. 'It's a lady doctor, isn't it?'

Nora nodded. 'Yes. Doctor Fielding.'

'Do you think,' Sara said, 'that she might have some old medical books that she doesn't want? I'd like to read some and they haven't got any in the library.'

'I don't really like to ask.' Nora frowned. She balked at anything that smacked of charity.

'Oh please, Mum. Only any old ones that she'd throw away.'

'I'll see,' Nora said. 'If I go to see her again I'll see.'

After tea Sara went up to her room again.

'You shouldn't encourage her,' Jim said. 'This being a doctor idea is crazy. You know we couldn't afford it.'

'She'd have to get another scholarship,' Nora said, 'she knows that. She works so hard. She might get a county or a state scholarship.'

Jim snorted. 'And when do they ever give them to people like us – a girl, a working man's daughter? I just don't want you to get her hopes up and then be disappointed. People like us don't go to university.'

'We never had a chance,' Nora said bitterly. 'We're both intelligent, you and me. I passed the exam to go to the grammar school but I couldn't go. My mother had seven kids to bring up. You'd have passed too if you'd taken it. We never had a chance.'

'Who gets a chance,' Jim said sourly, 'in this damn country? Not unless you're rich or one of the nobs.'

'Sara will.' Nora poured them both another cup of tea and sat down again. 'Things have got to change, Jim.' He made a dismissive noise. Her fears rose again. 'What if there's a war, Jim? What will we do?'

'I don't know,' he said.

'Do you think there will be one?'

'I don't know,' he said again. 'They don't tell us anything, do they? We're just the cannon fodder.'

'They'd attack London, wouldn't they? Like they did in Spain. Would we go back to Manchester?'

'There wouldn't be much point in that, would there? They'd bomb Manchester as well. All the factories there.'

She cleared up the table and started the washing-up, thinking, worrying.

Sara sat at the little table in her room, reading again the latest book she'd got from the library: *The Wonders of Science*. It sat before her, ready to be consumed, like a huge box of chocolates. Every word thrilled her. The first chapter was about the solar system and the planets. How wonderful that the earth rotated and went round the sun, and that explained night and day and the seasons. What was gravity, and wasn't it wonderful that Sir Isaac Newton had discovered it? Before tea she had moved on to the science of plants. They were just there, all over the place, growing everywhere, and look what they were doing – photosynthesis, changing the energy of the sun into food! And look at them inside; the xylem and the phloem carrying stuff up and down their stems; making seeds, reproducing. Tonight she was starting on zoology, beginning with the frog. She felt an excitement and pleasure that seemed to expand and fill her little room. I want to know everything, she thought. I want to learn everything there is to learn, and then I want to learn some more. The universe opened out in front of her like a flower.

'Where are you two off to?' Amy was sitting in the garden, reading *The Lancet*. The twins were stuffing rolled-up towels into their backpacks.

'Swimming,' Tessa said, 'at the new outdoor lido at Hampstead. We're meeting the gang there.'

'Can you go in together?' Amy asked. 'Isn't it segregated?'

'Mixed bathing on Saturday.' Charlie grinned. 'So we've got to be respectable and take our swimming costumes.'

Amy laughed. 'Have you got money?'

'Enough,' Tessa said. 'It's only sixpence to get in, and Mrs Parks has made us some sandwiches.'

'Have a good time.' Amy watched them leave, both so well, so contented. I've got to do what Dan said, she thought, and stop worrying. Otherwise she might set them off too. This was no time to be worrying them about anything. They were both facing perhaps the most important change in their lives – leaving school, joining the adult world. Please God, she thought, let that be all it is.

The twins took the tube to Kentish Town and walked down Highgate Road and Gordon House Road.

'Good job it's a warm day,' Charlie said. 'I bet the water's icy.'

'And I bet it's crowded,' Tessa said. 'Lots of girls in swimming costumes for you to ogle.'

'I don't ogle,' he said blandly. 'I never learnt. There wasn't much chance at school. The youngest female there was Miss Blake the French mistress, and she was at least thirty.'

Tessa laughed. 'Goodness, what an age. How ever did she survive that long?'

They paid their sixpences and went in.

'Wow,' Tessa said. 'It's lovely. It's huge.' The blue glazed bricks lining the pool sparkled in the water and the ornamental fountain glittered in the sunshine. It was crowded, young people in swimming costumes everywhere, sitting on the beige tiles around the pool or on the grass.

'Go and change,' Charlie said, 'and I'll meet you out here and we'll go and find the others.'

Tessa changed into her blue costume and put her clothes in a locker. She went out again into the sunshine, carrying her towel and a white rubber bathing-cap. Charlie was waiting in his black costume, his towel around his neck. Their friends, two boys and two girls, waved to them from across the pool and they walked round to meet them.

'Is it cold?' Tessa tucked her hair into her bathing-cap.

'Freezing,' one of the boys said, 'but it soon wears off.'

Tessa dived into the pool, enjoying the shock of the cold water. It seemed to draw her body together, concentrate her form and energy into a contained package of being young, being fit, being happy. She turned over on to her back, floating, squinting up her eyes against the bright sunshine. I'm starting soon, she thought. I'm nearly there. She had wanted to be a doctor for as long as she remembered. It was going to happen. A small cloud drifted slowly across the bright sky. It had a shape; it looked like a bird, like an eagle. Surely they couldn't stop her now, she thought, even if there was a war? They would need more doctors, more women in medicine. Her mother had once told her how the British army had refused to use women doctors at the beginning of the last war. Surely things had moved on? Surely women had proved themselves? She turned over and swam back to her friends.

'What have you been doing, Charlie?' Rob, one of the boys, was thin, with dark-brown eyes that didn't seem to focus without his thick horn-rimmed glasses. 'We haven't seen you for a week or two.'

'He's been in Germany.' Tessa took off her cap and shook out her hair. 'In Berlin.'

Both the boys sat up quickly and stared at him. 'Berlin?' Rob said. 'What were you doing there? What was it like? What was happening?'

Charlie tried to arrange his thoughts, to describe it as it was, without adding his own impressions and judgements. But there wasn't any way to avoid the reality. 'It's stiff with military,' he said, 'everywhere you go, and Hitler has got a complete stranglehold. Nobody dares to disagree with him, or you get into trouble with the police. There are swastikas everywhere and that salute. There are huge air-raid shelters and an air ministry like a fortress. They mean business.'

The boys still stared at him, saying nothing, but one of the girls gasped. 'You can't mean it,' she said. 'You're just scaremongering.'

'I didn't say they want war,' Charlie said. 'I'm just saying they're well prepared, I suppose in case anyone attacks them. They seem to be much better prepared than we would be.' He paused. 'But they look to me as if they're spoiling for a fight.'

There was a silence, a question hanging in the air. 'What would we do?' Rob said. They all knew what he meant.

Charlie shrugged. 'What we're told, I imagine.'

Rob frowned. 'I suppose we'd all have to join up.' His voice was quiet, self-deprecating, disappointed. 'I don't know what I'd do, with my eyesight.'

'I'm sure they'd find you something,' Charlie said. 'You're clever. You've got a scientific mind. We'd need brains as well as brawn.' Hitler, he thought, doesn't want his soldiers intelligent – he wants them brutal. But we'd need brains. Brains always won in the end. Britain had always had brains, always been inventive, ever since the steam engine. Surely they would come up with something...?

The atmosphere seemed to darken. Tessa looked at the boys. As she watched, something seemed to pass amongst them, a thought, a stillness.

They sat in silence, unmoving, but slowly a hardness crept into their faces, and a kind of resolution, lips pressed together, jaws clenched. Each of them seemed to change before her eyes, to grow, to age. They didn't move, but they seemed to join closer together in some kind of unspoken connection – a male connection, unavailable to the girls. Then they glanced at each other and the moment passed. They dived into the pool and raced up and down its length, laughing and splashing.

On the way home Tessa said, 'You didn't say much to me about Berlin. You just said it was fun, boating on a lake and going to a night-club. You didn't say anything much about all the rest.' Charlie shrugged. 'You won't upset me, you know,' she went on. 'I'm not frightened of it. Well, not more than anyone else.'

'I didn't want to say anything to you, or especially Mum,' he said. 'It's only my impressions, after all.' He thought for a moment. 'They seem to be thriving, getting the country together, but there's something wrong with it, Tessa. Something bad. You can't speak your mind, you can't criticize your own government, or vote them out. They're arming themselves to the teeth. It doesn't bode well.'

They walked on. 'What about Kurt?' she said. 'What does he think?'

He glanced at her quickly. 'I don't know really. He didn't say. His father's a red-hot Hitlerite, and there's this thing about the Jews. They're blaming everything on them – throwing them out or putting them in labour camps. They're all terrified. I don't think Kurt likes it, but he'll have to do what he's told. They don't stand for any opposition.'

'We'd be on opposite sides.'

'I know.' He glanced at her again. 'Did he ever say anything to you? Did he ever say that he liked you?'

She coloured a little. 'No, but I sometimes wondered.'

'Did you like him?'

'Charlie,' she said, exasperated, 'I've got six years of training ahead of me. I'm not remotely interested in anything else.'

'Just as well,' he said.

August drifted into September, and still the country held its breath. Pickfords came to take the twins' trunks to Cambridge and Amy watched them go, feeling bereft. They had to leave home sometime, she knew that, but now there was so much danger, so much rumour of war, she begrudged every day that they would be away from her.

She went to visit her father. She took a train to Bromley and walked down the familiar streets of her childhood and into the house where she had been born.

Her father came out of the sitting room and held out his arms. 'Lovely to see you, my dear.'

She kissed his cheek, the skin thin and soft. He looked well, she thought, still sprightly, doing well for his seventies. 'Are you well, dear?' she said. 'No problems?'

'I'm fine. Mrs Jones is still looking after me – feeding me up.'

They sat down in the sitting room that she remembered so well. It had never changed, still had the Victorian air that her mother had left behind.

'How's Dan?' he said, 'and the twins?'

'Very well. Looking forward to Cambridge.'

'Fancy them both going,' he said, 'and Tessa doing medicine. Family tradition now for the girls.' He smiled, a dozen little wrinkles gathering around his eyes. 'I suppose things are a bit easier for girls now – not quite such a struggle as it was for you.'

'And for you,' she said. 'I know what sacrifices you had to make.'

'I was glad to do it,' he said. 'You know that.'

'It's still a fight,' she said. 'Cambridge still won't give women proper degrees. They do all the work and the exams and then get something called a titular degree. Other universities accept the girls as proper undergraduates. I don't know why Cambridge is still holding out.'

'At least she's there,' he said.

Amy had a sudden memory of her patient, Mrs Lewis, and her little girl – Sara, was it? That little girl, obviously intelligent and studying hard and mad keen to do medicine, and hardly any chance at all. Tessa was lucky.

Her father took her hand. 'What's happening, Amy? What's going on in the world? What does Dan think?'

'He thinks nobody really knows. It all seems to depend on what Germany does.'

'Once again,' he said.

She looked around the room that held all the memories of her growing up with her father, after her mother died. It had been her home until she married Dan. But she had not been here during the Great War. She had been in France, in all that horror and pain.

She felt a sudden chill. There were ghosts here still. She thought they had gone to their rest, but they were re-emerging now, whispering and beckoning, ghosts of those dreadful years of the war, of 1914. There were ghosts of the people she had loved and lost in France, of the tears she had shed on her father's shoulder, tears for all the suffering and the dead. She took her father's hand.

'How can anyone even think of it?' he said.

She looked at him dumbly, for a moment unable to speak. She could see her memories reflected in his eyes.

She pressed his hand. 'It'll be all right; we just have to hope for the best.'

'You could leave London,' he said. 'You could come here. London would be the first place they'd attack. Sometimes I wonder whether the aeroplane should ever have been invented. It seemed such a wonderful thing at the time. We didn't know they would be used for this.'

'Let's just wait and see, shall we?'

They had tea together, then she travelled home again. Where would anyone be safe? Her father in Bromley; her own family in Holland Park? There was no hiding-place now. Perhaps her father should stay in Kent if war happened. He'd probably be safer there than in London.

She ran her usual clinics. Mrs Lewis came again.

'Doctor,' she said, 'Do you remember that I told you that I have a little girl, Sara? She wants to be a doctor.'

Amy nodded. 'Yes, of course.'

'I don't really like to ask....'

'What, Mrs Lewis?'

'Sara wonders if you have any old medical books that you don't want. She's mad keen. Only anything that you'd throw away.'

'Well yes, I have. I've an old *Gray's Anatomy* that she can have. It's falling to bits, but I think it's still readable. I'll bring it in next time I come and you can pick it up.'

'Thank you so much. She'll be thrilled to bits.' She hesitated. 'My husband says it's pie in the sky. Do you think I should put her off? My husband says it's impossible and it's not right to encourage her because she'll only be disappointed. I don't know what to do for the best.'

Amy felt her emotions rise, rebellion, fury, the memory of her own difficulties in the past, just because she was a woman. To be bright and eager and then disadvantaged by being a woman was bad enough. To be held back by poverty and class was just as bad. There should be a way for the country to use these bright young minds. 'I don't think any child should be discouraged,' she said. 'We don't know what's going to happen, do we? Let her study, Mrs Lewis. Let her at least try. If I find any other books I'll bring them in.'

After Mrs Lewis had gone she sat for a moment, reflecting. They hadn't had much, but somehow her father had raised the money for her training. He was like Mrs Lewis – determined that his only daughter should achieve her ambition. Nothing would have put her off doing medicine. Perhaps things would change, the slums, poverty, wasted lives. Things must change. No one knew what was going to happen. The future was another country.

She and Dan had dinner alone as the twins were off somewhere with their friends. 'I saw a woman today in the clinic,' she said, 'a really nice woman. Her husband works in a furniture factory. Working class, whatever that may mean. Her little girl wants to be a doctor. She asked me if she should tell her to forget it; there's no possibility that they could afford it. I told her to let her try. What do you think?'

'I agree with you,' he said. 'Let her try, let her have her dreams.' He pushed away his plate. 'I sometimes feel as if something or someone is stirring the whole damn world around like a great big mess in a great big pot and nobody knows what's going to come out at the end of the chaos. God knows, it might even be better. The little girl might get her chance....' He didn't finish the sentence. She looked at his face, serious, grim. He wouldn't voice the alternative.

After dinner she and Dan listened to a concert on the wireless, Beethoven's late quartets. Between items the concert was interrupted by the soothing voice of the announcer. They both unconsciously sat up straighter. What now? The announcer read the latest, urgent news. Mr Chamberlain, the Prime Minister, and Monsieur Daladier, the French Prime Minister, were going to Germany again to discuss the situation in Europe. Herr Hitler had also invited Signor Mussolini.

'Oh Dan!' Amy took his hand. 'At last. Surely they'll come to some kind of agreement.'

He squeezed her hand, his face solemn. 'I hope so.'

'You don't sound convinced.'

He got up and stood beside the fireplace, looking into the fire, now burning low. 'What about Austria and Czechoslovakia? I don't know what use treaties are. Hitler seems to think he can ignore them whenever he likes.'

She began to feel cold. The evening was chill after the warm day, but she knew that the chill was more than that. It came from within her. 'You're still worried, aren't you?'

'We wouldn't be ready, Amy,' he said, 'any more than we were last time. Do you know what the Germans have been doing? They were forbidden to train an air force after the war, so they've been training glider pilots – just for sport, they say. So now they've got hundreds of trained young pilots and all they have to do is convert them to powered aircraft. We haven't got anything like the number. Mr Churchill's been warning about it for months.'

Tears sprang into her eyes. 'I don't think I can bear it again, Dan.' Dreadful images of the trenches almost overwhelmed her. 'I can't bear to think of Charlie....'

He sat beside her and put his arm around her. 'He'll be all right,' he said, but his voice was grim. 'He'll be all right. Nothing has happened.' He pulled her towards him. 'Are they ready to go? Got their clothes and books and what have you?'

She took a deep breath, trying to wipe the images from her mind. 'Yes. I've been sewing nametapes on for ages. The house is going to be very quiet.'

'They'll be home for the holidays, and they're only in Cambridge. It isn't far away.'

She couldn't stop her thoughts. 'Has Charlie ever talked to you about the war?'

'Not really,' he said. 'Even if he did, how could one ever describe it? Why would one want to?'

'He told Tessa that he doesn't want to kill people.'

'No sane person wants to kill people,' he said, 'except, perhaps, for the Germans bombing Guernica. That was utterly brutal, unnecessary killing.'

'And the Spanish,' she said, 'and the Italians and the Japanese. There's killing going on all over the world. How can they do it?'

'I don't know,' he said. 'I've never been in that position. But I know one thing – if an enemy soldier had ever come anywhere near you in France I'd have put a bullet in his brain without thinking twice. It's in all of us, I suppose, to defend your own.'

'I hope to God he never has to.'

'So do I.' He held her close and kissed her hair. 'You mustn't worry so much.'

The day after was strange, an atmosphere everywhere of tension, and of hope. Mr Chamberlain was in Munich, talking to Herr Hitler. It seemed like the last chance.

'I hope Mr Chamberlain gets it right.' Amy said. 'What a dreadful responsibility. Everything depends on him.'

'I hope he kicks Hitler's behind,' Dan said sourly.

Next day Dan came home early. He was home when Amy came back from her evening surgery. He met her in the hall, holding up an evening newspaper. 'Look, Amy. Have you seen this?'

'Oh darling, I know,' she said. 'Isn't it wonderful?'

Dan looked doubtful. 'One can only hope so.'

The photograph of Mr Chamberlain half-filled the front page. He was smiling and holding up a piece of paper – the agreement he had signed with Herr Hitler. 'I believe it is peace for our time,' the headline said. Amy read the article, her eyes shining. Mr Chamberlain seemed to have pulled it off – no war. He had appeared on the balcony at Buckingham Palace with the King and Queen, to almost hysterical, cheering crowds. That night Amy slept without moving or dreaming. The dreadful nightmares didn't come. She woke refreshed and relieved.

It didn't last. That evening Dan was sombre and quiet again.

'What's happening now?' Amy said at dinner. 'What's this in the evening paper?'

'The Germans are going into Czechoslovakia tomorrow,' Dan said, 'taking the Sudetenland. That's just about half the country.'

Amy was shocked. 'Why? I thought we'd made an agreement.'

Dan looked grim. 'That, apparently, was part of the agreement. It's a disgrace. We've thrown the Czechs to the wolves. I only hope it was worth it.'

Chapter Four

1938

Sara sat beside her mother on the bus on the way to her first day at school. She was, with a little self-conscious pride, wearing her new uniform, blue dress, blue blazer, hat with a yellow hatband, and carrying her new leather satchel. The only things that were not new were her shoes, and her mother had polished those to a high shine. She glanced at her mother from time to time and Nora gave her a bright smile in reply. She was wearing, Sara noticed, her best suit and a hat with a little feather in it – dressed up for the occasion.

'Are you all right?' Nora asked.

'Yes,' Sara said. 'I'm fine.'

'Not nervous?'

'No.' Her mother looked nervous, she thought. Maybe she was herself, a little bit. She wondered how clever the other girls would be. It was a different sort of school altogether, girls who had all been clever enough to pass the exam. Where would she fit in? Would she be able to keep up?

They had both been to the school before, when Sara had been inter- viewed by Miss Jenkins, the headmistress. The headmistress was tall and thin and spoke a bit like the announcers on the wireless – what Dad called a plummy accent. Her mum's voice had changed a bit when she spoke to the headmistress, got a bit more careful, not like she talked at home. Her dad didn't seem to care, but her mum had changed the way she spoke since they came to London. She said parth instead of path and barth instead of bath, and she was getting Sara to do the same. She seemed to think it was important.

She had other things to think about. Inside her satchel were her new books, the ones they'd had to go to a special shop to buy: Maths and French and Latin. She stroked the smooth leather of the satchel. She seemed to see her way now as down a long, clear road. She didn't see any obstacles. If she worked hard enough she would get there. Surely, if you worked very, very hard, and wanted something very, very much, it could happen? She had a simple belief that she could do anything.

Her mother took her in through the gates. The school yard was thronged with girls in blue and some of the younger ones had their mothers with them. None of the other mothers seemed to be as smartly dressed as hers, Sara thought. They were just in cotton dresses and a cardigan and no hat. She saw her mother looking at them.

They went into the entrance hall. A teacher was waiting there with a list in her hand. 'All new girls come to me,' she said. She already had a small group around her – several girls, all neat and wearing new clothes. She looked nice, Sara thought, nice and smiling.

'This is Sara Lewis,' Nora said.

The teacher smiled. 'Just leave her here then, Mrs Lewis. Say goodbye to your mother, Sara.'

Nora looked as if she was going to kiss her cheek, Sara thought, but Nora changed her mind. 'I'll be here at four o'clock,' she said. 'Have a good time.' She turned at the door and gave a little, nervous wave.

Sara looked around her, breathing in the atmosphere. The old building seemed to have a sense of things happening, of purpose. It had its own smell, of a nice kind of age and chalk-dust and furniture polish. A wide staircase led to the upper floors and down into the base-ment. She glanced around the other new girls. Were they all terribly clever? Would she be the dunce of the class? She wasn't used to that.

Older girls stood in groups, talking and laughing, carrying lacrosse sticks and tennis rackets and satchels full of books. Some of them looked really grown up; sixth form girls, she supposed. One of them passed close by and she could smell the familiar scent of her shampoo. Her mother used it; 'Friday night is Amami night' was printed on the bottle. I'm here, she thought, I'm really here. They're going to teach me everything. Excitement bubbled up and made her shiver.

They were shepherded to the locker room to leave their hats and blazers and change into their indoor shoes. She had worn hers around the house at home for a bit, partly because it gave her a secret thrill, and partly to make sure they didn't creak or anything. Her mother's slippers creaked – you could hear them all over the house. That would have been terribly embarrassing. Her father had hammered little metal segs into the heels of her outdoor shoes so that they wouldn't wear out so quickly. They made a little tapping noise but she didn't mind that; that was outside and no one would hear.

'Come along, girls.' The locker doors clattered and banged and they followed the teacher to their form room. The teacher stood in front of the neat rows of desks.

'Find a desk, girls, and put your books inside.'

Sara managed to get a desk on the second row. She was determined that she wasn't going to sit at the back. Back row kids at her old school fidgeted and giggled and the boys pulled hair. At least there weren't any boys here, thank goodness. They just spoiled everything. Amidst the whispering and banging of desk lids she put her books away: English, French, Latin, Maths, History, Geography – and Science. She tucked them in as carefully as if they were newborn babies.

'Settle down, girls.' The class slipped into silence. 'My name is Miss Hunter.' She wrote it on the blackboard. 'I am your form mistress and your English teacher. If you have any problems you come to me.' She gave out timetables, a list of the school rules: no talking in class, no running in the corridors, the names of the teachers, the head girl, the prefects. Miss Butler, Sara noted, taught science.

There was no waste of time. The morning's work began with English grammar: the construction of the sentence, nouns, verbs, objects. The atmosphere was quiet and concentrated, no giggling and whispering at the back. She was given her first bit of homework – thrilling.

At break time the girls ate the snacks they had brought from home and drank the little bottles of school milk, warm from standing in crates in the sun.

The girl sitting next to Sara had a freckled face and pigtails. 'I'm Kathy,' she said.

Sara smiled. 'I'm Sara.'

Kathy sucked her milk up through the straw, gurgling up the last drops. 'Homework already,' she said.

'I don't mind,' Sara said.

'My sister can help me if I get stuck,' Kathy said. 'She's here as well. She's called Lily. She's in the Upper Fifth this year. She's nearly sixteen.'

'I haven't got any brothers or sisters,' Sara said. 'There's just me.'

Kathy frowned. 'My mum's frightened in case there's a war and Lily has to go somewhere to work, in a factory or something. My dad says that's silly, she's still a child, but my mum says they had boys fighting in the trenches in the last war who weren't any older than that. At least we haven't any boys.'

Sara didn't know what to say; she hadn't really thought about it. Her parents hadn't said much about a war, though there was sometimes something about it in the *Daily Mirror*. Dad used to start sometimes but Mum always changed the subject. Her mum hadn't liked it when she was given a gas mask at school. She'd given a shudder and put it away in the cupboard under the stairs. She wouldn't even let Sara look at it. She'd put it away in the cupboard under the stairs. She hadn't even got it out of the box.

'Where do you live?' Kathy asked.

'Near the Harrow Road.'

'We live in Bayswater. I'll ask my mum if you can come round to tea one day.'

After break they had their first Latin lesson. 'Latin is dead; bury it,' one of the girls at the back whispered, while they were waiting for the teacher to arrive.

But I need Latin, Sara thought. Doctors had to learn Latin; they wrote their prescriptions in it. It seemed like her first real, exciting step. Doctor language.

The teacher arrived and they opened the book; Latin, Part One. There was a map of ancient Europe on the first page. '*Discipuli pictoram spectate,*' the text began. The teacher wrote it on the blackboard with the translation underneath: – 'Pupils, look at the picture.' The text went on: *ubi est Britannia, ubi est Italia, ubi est Germania*? – where is Britain, where is Italy, where is Germany? So that's where Germany is, Sara thought, or where it used to be. Her last school hadn't done much geography, apart from Great Britain and a bit of the British Empire.

Nora was waiting for her in the school yard at four o'clock. She had taken off her suit and hat, Sara noticed, and was dressed in just a cotton frock and a cardigan. 'Too hot for a suit,' she said.

They took the bus home. 'You don't have to come with me, Mum,' Sara said. 'I can get the bus on my own.'

'Just for a few days,' Nora said. 'Then we'll see. How did you get on?'

'Fine. The teachers are nice and I met a nice girl called Kathy. And we did Latin.' At home she changed out of her uniform into an ordinary dress.

Over tea Jim said, 'So what's it like, Sara?'

'It's lovely, Dad,' she said. 'We did Latin.'

'I don't know what good that is,' he said. 'What are you going to do with Latin?'

'My teacher says that a lot of English words come from Latin, from when the Romans were here.' She paused. 'And doctors use it.'

He gave a grunt. 'Still going on about that?'

She nodded. 'I've got homework tonight.'

'It's a bit soon, isn't it?' he said. 'Your first day.'

'I don't mind,' she said. 'I like it.'

'Latin,' he said. 'The way things are going you'd be better off learning German.'

'Jim,' Nora said sharply, 'that's enough of that.' She began to clear the table. 'You go out and have a walk around for a bit,' she said. 'Let your tea go down before you start your homework.'

Sara slipped out of the front door into the street. A group of girls were skipping down the road to her right. She turned left. She wouldn't be accepted now. A line had been drawn between them. Going to the grammar school had separated her out. They would stare at her now and make remarks about her being la-di-da.

The streets were quiet, almost empty, and she was alone. Sometimes, back home in Trafford Park in Manchester, she would stand out in the street outside their house when the light was fading. Sometimes, then, the light would change to a soft and mysterious shining violet that would colour the long row of dull houses and the long straight, barren road, and turn them into something magic. Sometimes she would be overcome by a strange feeling, a strange yearning. She wanted something, but didn't know what it was; she had lost something that she must get back. It wasn't the same as wanting to be a doctor. It was something different; she didn't quite know what – something to do with the endless sky and all the things there were to know. She felt it briefly now, but her books were waiting, her new school, her new life. She turned back to home.

She took her satchel up to her room. It felt wonderful, important. She sat at her little table and began. Dad didn't mean it about speaking German. She opened her Latin book at page one. '*Ubi est Britannia? Ubi est Germania?*'

Amy drove the twins to Liverpool Street Station to see them off. She bought a penny platform ticket so that she could go with them to the train. They were early, but the platform was already crowded. Groups of young people, mostly young men, came through the barriers, carrying bags and suitcases, tennis rackets and hockey sticks, cramming bicycles into the overflowing guard's van, college scarves dangling around their necks. Amy smiled. There wasn't much doubt about where this train was going; they hardly needed to put up 'Cambridge' on the notice board.

The young men stood about in groups, laughing and gesticulating or jumping into the train to stow their bags and jumping out again. The platform seemed to be humming with strength and energy.

Tessa and Charlie found seats and came out again to say goodbye. They both looked excited and happy.

'Don't hang about, Mum,' Tessa said, 'we'll be all right now and we'll see you at Christmas.'

'Write to me,' Amy said, 'and telephone now and again if you get the chance, and look after each other.'

Tessa hugged her. 'We will. Give our love to Dad.' They got into the train.

For a few moments Amy watched the young people around her. They are so beautiful, she thought, surprising herself with the word, but it was true. They were beautiful. She felt an ache in her heart and in her throat; she felt as if she were mother to them all. She felt their joy and their freedom and their hopes and plans for the future.

The dark shadow touched her again. Was it true? Was the danger past? Or were these young people travelling into a future that they could never have imagined, or ever wanted.

They all began to climb aboard, doors slammed. The guard blew his whistle. At least, she thought, Tessa and Charlie were away, out of London, out of that possible danger.

The train arrived in Cambridge and unloaded, a scramble for bicycles from the guard's van, a queue for taxis. Tessa and Charlie shared a taxi and Charlie arrived at his college first. 'I don't suppose I'll see you till the weekend,' he said. 'I'll leave you a note. We could have tea somewhere.'

Tessa arrived at her college and stood in the hall with the other new arrivals, waiting to be told what to do.

They were assigned to their rooms. Tessa's was small, and looked rather bare. There was an iron bedstead with the bed already made up, a small table, a hard chair and a small easy chair, a chest of drawers and a wardrobe. A fire was laid in the fireplace and a scuttle of coal and some firelighters stood beside it. My home, she thought, for a year at least. They were to meet Miss Pritchard, their hall tutor, at five o'clock in her room.

She unpacked and hung up her clothes, then went out into the corridor to find the bathrooms and lavatory. Another girl was wandering about, looking lost.

Tessa smiled at her. 'Do you know where the bathrooms are?'

The girl shook her head. 'I've just arrived; just finding my way.'

Tessa held out her hand. 'I'm Tessa Fielding.'

The girl took her hand. 'Rita Lane.'

'I'm reading medicine,' Tessa said. 'What about you?'

Rita's face lit up. 'Medicine too. That's great. We can find our way about together.'

They found the bathrooms. 'There's tea in the dining hall at four o'clock,' Rita said. 'I'll come and get you. Which is your room?'

They found the dining hall and had a cup of tea. The room was busy with young women chatting, reading, drinking tea and eating cake.

'They all look very intelligent,' Rita whispered. 'I hope I can keep up.'

'Me too, Tessa said.

After tea they explored a little. They found the common room, furnished here and there, Tessa saw, with the kind of faded chintz that they had at home. She smiled. Very comfortable, very English. They walked a little in the garden, beginning to look wintry now, but still pretty, a nice place to study in the summer.

'We'd better go in,' Rita said. 'We mustn't be late for Miss Pritchard.'

They assembled with the other newcomers in Miss Pritchard's room. She was small and round, with grey hair pulled back into a bun. She was smiling and welcoming, but still managed to appear intimidating.

She gave them a list of college rules and went through them one by one. They were to sign out if they went out in the evening and were to be back in college by ten o'clock. They were not to leave the university boundaries without special permission. All male visitors were to be out of college by six o'clock. They were allowed to dine out of Hall twice a week; any more often than that would need special permission. Behaviour was to be ladylike and decorous at all times.

'Do remember,' Miss Pritchard said, 'that there are at least ten male students for every woman at Cambridge, and consequently you may be overwhelmed with invitations.' This produced a few giggles. 'As if we're going to have time,' Rita whispered.

They had dinner in Hall that evening, among all the older, confident-looking girls, then signed out and went for a little walk along the Backs, a walk that took them along the river behind Queens' and King's.

'What a plethora of rules,' Rita said. 'All men to be out by six o'clock. I can't see myself ever having a man in my room. I haven't worked my fingers to the bone to get here for that, although …' She didn't finish the sentence.

Tessa laughed. 'I might have my brother. He's here too.'

'Oh,' Rita said. 'How nice for you.'

They walked into town the next day and then walked through the streets with their maps, locating their departments and lecture rooms: Physiology, Anatomy, Pathology.

'That's the anatomy department,' Rita said. 'We're starting dissection on Monday.'

'I know,' Tessa said. They were to do dissection in twos. They had already decided to put their names down to work together.

'We'll stick together,' Rita said, 'then you can catch me if I faint.'

Charlie settled into his room on his staircase in college. There were two other students on the same staircase. One was a zoologist, a rather austere young man who seemed to be mainly interested in insects. The other was fair and stocky, and judging by his accent, came from the north. 'Third year engineering,' he said when Charlie introduced himself and asked him what he was reading. 'Aeronautical engineering mainly. My name's Arthur Blake. I'm just going to have a cup of tea in my room. Come and have one if you like.'

'Aeroplanes,' Charlie said later. It was a statement, not a question. 'I suppose they're the thing of the future.'

Arthur looked at him over his cup, a long, slightly surprised, considering look, as if he thought Charlie might be a creature from another planet. 'You might say that.' He took a large bite of a biscuit and then a swallow of tea. 'Especially the way things are going.'

'What things?'

'War things. What about you? What are you reading?'

'History,' Charlie said.

Arthur gave him the same look again. 'You should know the way things are going then. They say history repeats itself.'

Charlie had a sudden memory of the Air Ministry building in Berlin – huge, threatening. Nothing in history had ever been quite like this; no destructive power had ever been so huge. 'Where are you from?' he asked.

Arthur smiled. 'Manchester. We manufacture history up there.'

Charlie was startled. He had never quite thought of the Industrial Revolution in those terms. It was true, he thought. History, certainly of Britain, had been made of steel and coal and ideas and invention and taking them with them around the world, trade, building an empire. He recorded history, he thought. Arthur, perhaps, made it.

Later Charlie went to meet his tutor and got a timetable and a pep talk and a glass of sherry as it got towards time to dine in Hall.

He saw Arthur in Hall, sitting with a group of young men with the same earnest, no-nonsense look about them. Probably all bright boys, he thought, with county or state or college scholarships. They seemed to know where they were going, much more than he did.

On Saturday Charlie came to take Tessa out to tea. 'We'll go to the Copper Kettle in King's Parade,' he said. 'They do a good tea there, apparently.'

They met outside the café. Tessa looked along King's Parade, the narrow street with the grand, beautiful, ancient college buildings on the other side. 'Isn't it lovely,' she said. 'It is,' Charlie said. 'I only hope it's here for ever.'

They went upstairs in the café and ordered their tea.

'How are you getting on?' he said.

'Fine,' she said. 'I've got everything sorted out, I think, and I've met a nice girl doing medicine too. Her name's Rita.'

Charlie took a bite of coffee cake. 'I wish I could meet a nice girl, but there aren't too many women about. It's a bit like school.'

Tessa laughed. 'Give it time.'

'I've met an engineering student,' he said, 'from Manchester. Tough as old boots by the look of him. Probably plays rugby league. He says things about history repeating itself. I think he's talking about a war.'

Tessa sighed. 'Some men don't seem to be able to talk about anything else. It's all supposed to be settled, isn't it? That's what Mr Chamberlain says.'

'I expect you're right,' he said, 'but Arthur doesn't think so.'

'Do you think Arthur knows more than the Prime Minister?'

'I wouldn't be surprised,' Charlie said.

Tessa and Rita walked down Sidgwick Avenue on their way to the anatomy department and crossed over Silver Street bridge. The morning was chilly. The Cam flowed by, slowly, on the way from Granchester, a few leaves from the overhanging willows turning slowly in the stream. The punts that had been moored there when they arrived were being taken in now for the winter, all the cushions and poles already gone.

They carried their equipment in their bags – a canvas roll with little

pockets containing their scalpels and forceps, a white lab coat and a
book: an instruction manual on dissection. Tessa had looked at it the
night before. How to take a human body to pieces. How to pick it apart,
muscle by muscle, organs, nerves, blood vessels. It all looked very
clean and neat in the pictures.

'Have you ever seen a corpse?' Rita asked. She sounded apprehensive.

'No,' Tessa said. 'I've seen a few mummies in the museum.'

She remembered the first time she had ever seen what used to be a
human being, a shrivelled embalmed body, wrinkled and brown, but
still having a face that you could recognize as a face. It had given her
the creeps.

'I haven't either,' Rita said. 'Only our skeletons.' She laughed. 'My
mother won't have it in the house. She makes me keep it in the garage.
She says it gives her nightmares. She's a bit squeamish.'

Sara thought of the 'half-skeleton' she had in her room at the college,
a skull, vertebrae, half a ribcage, half a pelvis, the bones of one arm, one
leg. Her father had bought it for her, second or third hand, from some
ex-medical student, so she could get started on some anatomy. She had
inspected the skull in her bedroom at home. The top was sawn off like
a lid and attached to the rest with a pair of little hooks. She stared into
the empty eye sockets, ran her hands over the smooth bones. Who are
you, she had wondered? This person had lived, walked about, had
thoughts and feelings. Now he was kindly lending his skull to her. No
good thinking about that, she supposed. No good being sentimental,
considering what she was about to do.

They arrived at the anatomy department and walked up the stairs to
the women's cloakroom. They put on their white coats. Rita gave her a
thin smile.

'Better get it over with,' she said.

Tessa was faintly apprehensive. The frogs and the rats hadn't really
prepared her for this.

They walked down the stairs together and through the swing doors
into the dissecting room.

The room was brightly lit and smelt strongly of formalin. Several
long tables were arranged in neat rows, white-coated figures bending

over them. It wasn't what Tessa had expected. There were no bodies lying on the tables, just indefinable lumps of something, obscured by the white coats.

They stood uncertainly by the door. A small man in a brown lab coat approached them, clipboard in hand. 'Names?' he said.

'Tessa Fielding, Rita Lane.'

He ran his pencil down his list. 'You're on the arm this term,' he said, in a strong Cambridgeshire accent. 'In the chest at the back.'

Their eyes followed his pointing pencil. Two large chests stood against the wall at the back of the room. They walked up to them slowly. The lids were standing open. They peered in. One chest was full of arms, the other full of legs.

Tessa took in a breath. If she was ever going to feel queasy, she thought, this moment was surely it. It didn't happen and the moment passed. She glanced at Rita who had gone a bit pink, but otherwise seemed unmoved.

The arms had luggage labels tied around the wrist and they searched through until they found the one marked 'Fielding and Lane.' They carried it to an empty table, laid it down and looked at it. The hand was large and strong looking, worn with labour, the fingers slightly curled in. Obviously a man.

'I wonder who he was,' Rita said. 'I wonder how he ended up here?'

Tessa glanced at her. They obviously had the same thoughts. 'I expect he left his body to science,' she said. She almost smiled at the thought. Leaving one's body to science sounded so grand. It conjured up thoughts of great scientific advances, medical breakthroughs, not two nervous girls poking at it with a scalpel. 'We'd better get started.'

They got out their scalpels and opened their books at the chapter marked **The Arm**.

'Remove the skin as far as the elbow,' it began. They got to work.

Charlie began to enjoy Cambridge. He enjoyed the work he was doing. He joined a chess club and a music-appreciation society. He enjoyed the way that autumn tinted the trees along the Backs by the river and winter brought clear frosty nights and brilliant starry skies. He delighted in the ancient buildings, unchanged for hundreds of years.

He could feel the presence of his ancestors before him, the walls polished by centuries of English fingers, the stones worn by centuries of English feet. He would walk sometimes by the river at night, or stand in the soft gas lighting on Garret Hostel Bridge, watching the mysterious shadows under the gently swaying willows. In the evenings the college bells pealed together, summoning the students home to dine in Hall. To Charlie they seemed to be the voice of this ancient town. The thought that all this had been here for centuries filled him with a deep, almost spiritual contentment.

Then, sometimes, he would lie in bed at night, thinking, or perhaps trying not to think. In that first conversation Arthur had looked at him as if he knew nothing, and as if he, Arthur, had some kind of inside knowledge. Perhaps he had. In any case, Arthur had brought him up against something he preferred not to think about. 'History repeats itself', Arthur had said. History now seemed to him to be a succession of struggles for power, of wars and battles, victories and defeats; the survival of the strongest, or of those with the strongest determination. He had a sense that Arthur and his group of blunt, earnest young men, were staring resolutely into a future that he, Charlie, was trying to avoid.

One morning when they met on the stairs, he said, 'Do you really think there's going to be a war, Arthur?'

Arthur smiled, a mirthless grin. 'Read your history books, old boy.'

'What would you do,' Charlie persisted, 'if it happened?'

'What I'm training to do,' Arthur said. 'Keep 'em flying.'

Charlie stared at him. 'You think it would be a flying war?'

Arthur gave a gusty laugh. 'Where have you been? Ever heard of the German raids on Spain, on Guernica? Mussolini bombing native villages in Abyssinia? Do you think it's going to be knights in armour on horseback, waving swords and rescuing maidens?'

Charlie felt abashed and foolish.

Amy and Dan read the morning newspaper and laughed. In America Orson Welles had broadcast a radio play – an adaptation of H.G. Wells's *War of the Worlds*. Apparently hundreds of listeners thought that it was true that the Martians had invaded, and they fled into the streets in panic.

They laughed, but Amy was not really amused. What would happen if there were a real raid on London? Would the people panic, run away from the city? Would the roads be blocked with streams of refugees like those they had seen in France in the last war, women and children and old people, desperate and afraid?

'Do you think the play would have panicked people here?' she said.

Dan laughed. 'I don't think so. I think we'd be out there, hitting the Martians with our umbrellas.'

Umbrellas, she thought? Is that all we'd have?

Dan kept the smile on his face. He tried not to think about the million cardboard coffins the government had apparently stockpiled.

The news from Germany grew ever darker. They read the newspapers in horror. In November the Jews were attacked in the cities, their homes ransacked, their shop windows smashed, men beaten by mobs in the street. The Nazis launched their first aircraft carrier; they built more and more E-boats.

'It can't go on,' Dan said.

Amy thought about the boys she'd seen, getting on to the Cambridge train. Her heart ached. Such beautiful children.

Chapter Five

1938–1939

'Happy Christmas, darlings.' Amy and Dan and the twins sat down to breakfast in the kitchen. 'Don't eat too much,' Amy said. 'We've got Christmas lunch to come. The turkey's already in the oven.'

'Where's your father, Amy?' Dan said.

'Grandpa's on his way,' Charlie said. 'I heard him pottering about.'

'Can I do anything?' Tessa asked.

'There isn't much to do, really,' Amy said. 'Mrs Parks left everything ready. We only have to peel the potatoes.'

Amy's father came in, freshly shaved, looking, she thought, younger than his years. Relief after the Munich agreement seemed to have taken years off him. The thought of another war seemed to have drained him of life. 'Happy Christmas, everybody,' he said. 'A happy and a peaceful Christmas.'

Dan raised his cup. 'I'll drink to that.'

'Sit down, Father.' Amy poured him a cup of tea. 'Lunch'll be about two o'clock.'

He sat down. 'Mrs Parks gone to her daughter's?'

Amy nodded. 'Her daughter's having another baby. She always goes there for Christmas anyway.'

'You'll have to cook lunch, Grandpa,' Tessa said.

He laughed. 'Wouldn't be the first time.'

In the background the wireless was softly playing Christmas carols. Amy busied herself at the sink, washing up a few cups, putting out the potatoes to be peeled. She looked out over the garden. It had snowed a little more in the night, dusting the lawn and the trees and the garden chairs, glinting in unexpected shafts of sunlight. The garden seemed to have a heightened beauty, as if she had never really appreciated the English winter before. The colours seemed clearer, the light brighter, the bare trees showing their graceful bones against the sky. The threat, crawling through the world, diminished though it was now, seemed to have cast everything into a clearer, sharper focus. This year it brought with it an almost painful love of home. The cups and saucers in her hands, even the potatoes for peeling, seemed to have a new beauty, a new significance. This was still her home – it was still here. Her family, everyone she loved best in the world, was sitting behind her at the breakfast table, all here, all safe. The winter and the cold and the snow were welcome; anything was welcome, now that the country was its old peaceful self, now that there were to be no tearful goodbyes, no heart-rending partings.

'So how's Cambridge?' Grandpa said.

'Lovely.' Tessa grinned. 'The human body is an amazing thing, Grandpa. We took an arm to pieces this term. Leg next term. Very interesting. Such a fantastic design, the human body. You'd be amazed what's in there. You couldn't invent it if you tried. It's poetic. I should write an "Ode to a kidney", or "Shall I compare thee to a neuro-chemical transmitter".'

He laughed. 'Don't you mind,' he said, 'taking a human body to pieces?'

'No,' she said. 'We get it a bit at a time.'

He grimaced. 'Good Lord!'

'Grandpa,' she said, 'you must have had all this with Mum. Don't pretend to be shocked.'

'She's a ghoul,' Charlie said. 'I bet she sleeps in a coffin in college.'

'I hardly sleep at all,' Tessa said. 'I have too much work to do. I bet I work a lot harder than you do. We don't swan about like you people.'

Grandpa turned to Charlie. 'What about you? How are you getting on?'

'Fine,' Charlie said. 'I go to all the lectures, get my essays in on time, and I haven't been progged yet.'

Grandpa's eyebrows rose. 'Progged?'

'It means being caught by the university proctors,' Tessa said, 'for being out at night without his gown or climbing into college after hours.

Getting up to no good. They come out at night and patrol the streets. They're very spooky, creeping around those dark little streets. The Proctor is in his cap and gown and his two henchmen, bulldogs, we call them, are in striped trousers and top hats and running shoes, so they can chase you.' She pulled a face. 'Women don't wear gowns, of course. We're not full members of the university, would you believe. We're there on sufferance. Oxford took women as full members in 1920, but not Cambridge. We had student demonstrations to keep women out, and they're still holding out. Still, we can get up to no good and no one will know.'

Grandpa laughed. 'And what happens if you are progged?'

'He is fined six and eightpence, a third of a pound,' Tessa said, 'and he gets his knuckles rapped and a glass of sherry in the Proctor's rooms and a lecture about standards. He is supposed to behave with decorum and uphold the standards of the university.'

Grandpa laughed again. 'Why would you want to climb in after hours?'

'To prove a point?' Charlie said clearly. It was more of a question than a statement. 'We're all over eighteen and we're locked up at night like little kids.'

Amy smiled at him. Pushing the boundaries. Growing up. That was fairly normal. Thank God the boundaries were so innocent, the growing up so natural. Not like those eighteen-year-olds sent to France in the war, thrust into a vicious maturity before their time. The smile died. Dead before their time.

'Or spend the evening with a girl,' Tessa added.

'Oh,' Grandpa said. 'Have you got a girl, Charlie?'

Charlie sighed. 'No, I haven't. There aren't enough girls in Cambridge to go round. It's at least ten to one.' He grinned. 'And the only girls I've met are Tessa's ghoulish friends. They look at you as if they want to take you to bits. It's a bit off-putting.'

Tessa laughed. 'You ought to be used to doctors by now.'

Amy felt a little shock. More changes. Nice changes, though; Charlie with a girl, getting married some day, grandchildren. She shook her head briefly. What on earth was she doing, thinking about that? That was years away. What would they have to go through first? If God were still in his heaven, they would just be peaceful, kindly years.

After breakfast they gathered in the sitting room for presents. The Christmas tree sparkled in the corner and a bright log fire burned in the fireplace. Amy looked around her in deep contentment. Nothing had changed. The twins were easy this year – they were more than happy with a cheque, but Amy had bought them some joke presents, a teddy bear for Tessa, ('I expect she'll chop it up to see what's inside,' Charlie said), and a copy of *1066 and All That* for Charlie. Dan usually bought her a piece of jewellery. This year it was a pendant, a little ruby heart surrounded by diamonds. 'Because I love you,' the card said.

'Come and help me with lunch, Tessa,' Amy said eventually.

Dan got up. 'Do you need me?'

Amy shook her head. 'Go and have a walk or something. The sun's shining now.'

Dan looked round. 'Anyone for a walk?'

'I'll come, Dad,' Charlie said. 'I'll get my coat.'

They walked to the park. There were several people about, walking their dogs, smiling and wishing each other a happy Christmas.

'Everybody looks a lot cheerier now,' Charlie said. 'I suppose it's because things have settled down a bit.'

Dan nodded. 'Most people are beginning to think we might get through all this without any actual conflict.' He paused. 'Unlike the poor Czechs. We let them down, Charlie.'

'Do you think we will, Dad – avoid a war?'

Dan sighed. 'I hope so, but who really knows? We ought to be a lot better prepared than we are. I suppose no one can really believe that it might happen again.'

They walked on. A little dog ran up to Charlie, a ball in its mouth. It laid the ball at Charlie's feet and waited, grinning. Charlie laughed and threw the ball. The dog scampered after it, his tail wagging.

'There's a chap on my staircase,' Charlie said. 'An engineering student. He seems to have no doubt there'll be a war – a war of machines, not millions of men in trenches like last time. Mostly in the air, he says. He's probably biased, though. He's got a thing about aeroplanes. He thinks we should be concentrating on the Air Force.'

'I think he's right about the air.' Dan walked on, looking at the ground, thinking of the aircraft in the last war, of the damage they could do, the sporadic bombing in London and the coastal towns. And things had moved on. There were bombers now that could carry tons of explosives, enough to flatten any city. Where was our defence? The Germans had more planes and more pilots, more of everything. Their factories had been churning them out, while we were just marking time.

'He says we've got better fighter planes than theirs,' Charlie said. 'Spitfires and Hurricanes. He says they're better than their Me 110s, and the Spitfires are better than their 109s. And there's a man called Whittle in Cambridge developing a new kind of aircraft engine – much faster, apparently, but Arthur thinks it'll be a long time before it can be used.'

'That's reassuring,' Dan said, 'but have we got enough? Enough planes and enough pilots? We've just coasted along these last twenty years. They've just launched their first aircraft carrier, the Germans. They're going to double their U-boat fleet. What have we been doing? Nothing. Heads in the sand. We should have listened to Churchill. We have to be strong, and more than that, we have to show that we are strong, and we're not doing it. That's all they seem to recognize, these fascists – brute strength.'

Charlie had a sudden picture of the German soldiers marching at the Brandenburg Gate, faces full of strength – brute strength, if you like. If strength was all that was needed, then the Germans certainly had that. What was it that they were lacking? Their strength seemed to him to have a strange, cavernous emptiness at the core. What was it? A different attitude to life, perhaps? They believed in winning, the hubris of the conqueror, but they did not seem to have any plans beyond that. What did they really want? What did they believe in? Where were they going? They didn't seem to have the kind of implacable belief in freedom that his country had, freedom of speech, equality before the law, and based on hundreds of years of stability; a country that pulled together, one that would never even contemplate failure. He suspected very strongly that Kurt didn't like what was happening, and there must be others like him but were too afraid to say so. How ghastly must that be, not being able to disagree with your own government? And even worse, having to fight and perhaps die for something you didn't believe in. All they had was brute force. If it came to war the irresistible force would meet the immovable object. What would happen then?

'They seem to be ready for it,' he said.

Dan glanced at him. 'You sound as if you think it's going to happen.'

Charlie nodded. 'We have to face the possibility.' Dan walked on in silence. 'It wouldn't be like last time, would it?' Charlie said. 'Last time was a fiasco. It was about nothing, did nothing, got nowhere. Nobody seemed to have any faith in it. They just walked into the guns. Millions of them, just walking into the guns.'

'It changed everything,' Dan said. 'It changed the whole world. It opened Pandora's box. It let loose horrors that the world had never seen before. Killing millions of men, killing innocent women and children. What kind of war is that? What kind of mentality? And there's the dreadful thought that we might have to do the same, fight like with like. There might be no other way to win.'

Charlie's mind scrolled through history as he'd been taught it. 'I think they have been seen before,' he said. 'Perhaps it's only a question of degree, of numbers.'

'It was more than that,' Dan said. 'It opened an attitude of mind. It wasn't just numbers. It suppressed all sense of the future, of consequences. Look at the world now – there's killing going on everywhere. I sometimes wonder where the planet is going. The human race gets bigger and bigger. It learns more and more about all the wonders of science and less and less about how to use them for good.'

Charlie didn't reply. Dan noted the silence. He glanced at his son, walking beside him, looking straight ahead. He felt the beginnings of the knowledge that sooner or later must come to all men. He saw that the game was no longer his, that he must hand the torch, whatever it might become, to his son, and to all their sons. He felt a kind of humility, and enormous, heart-clenching affection. The little dog brought the ball back, opportunely, Dan thought. He could bend down and pet the dog and hide his face. The dog scampered away after the ball. 'Perhaps we'd better be getting back,' he said, 'see if the girls need anything.'

Tessa finished the potatoes and sat on the edge of the kitchen table. She looks well, Amy thought – and happy. There hadn't been a chance for a real chat since they came home. 'All well, darling?' she said.

Tessa nodded. 'Fine. I'm really enjoying it.'

'No regrets? Even after dissection?'

Tessa laughed. 'No, of course not. It's got to be done, and it isn't so bad, is it, after the first shock.'

No, Amy thought, there were worse things. Her thoughts must have shown in her face, and Tessa noticed. 'What is it, Mum?'

Amy shrugged a little. 'Oh – nothing.' She turned away and stirred, unnecessarily, the bread sauce.

Tessa got up and stood beside her. She put her arm around her shoulders. 'You must stop worrying, Mum. There probably isn't going to be a war, and if there were it wouldn't be the same as last time. Things have changed.'

Amy made herself smile. 'You're right,' she said. 'I'm being silly.' Tessa kissed her cheek. 'Are the students nice; are you making friends?'

'Yes,' Tessa said, 'but you'd be surprised how much male opposition there still is. There are still some diehards, even among the students.'

I'm not surprised, Amy thought. Even with all the things that women did in the last war, there were still some men who clung for dear life to their God-given superiority. How many girls were there, in Tessa's year, reading medicine – ten, perhaps? Ten out of how many? A couple of hundred? And what about girls like little Sara Lewis? Good minds wasted. She was female and she was poor.

'How's Charlie getting on?' she said. 'Do you see much of each other?'

'Not really,' Tessa said. 'I haven't got the free time that he has. I seem to have every minute accounted for. But we meet at weekends quite often.'

Amy took the turkey out of the oven, basted it carefully, and put it back. 'Has he got a girlfriend?'

'I don't know.' Tessa laughed. 'I don't think he'd tell me about it anyway. I think he's rather shy with girls. That's boarding school for you, I expect. They don't get much chance to meet girls, do they?'

'What about you?' Amy said.

'No chance.' Tessa put some dishes in the sink. 'I've got too far to go. I'm not going to go all wobbly about some male. I might think about it when I'm about fifty.'

Amy laughed. She looked at Tessa's bright head bent over the sink, washing up the dishes. She has so much to learn, she thought, her heart aching a little. Tessa was just at the beginning. She saw medicine as a clinical science: note the symptoms, make a diagnosis, apply the treatment, job done. She hadn't yet had to watch someone die because there was no way to treat them: no cure for septicaemia, pneumonia, TB, and many other diseases. She knows nothing of love, she thought, of driving passion. And she knows nothing of loss, of the pain of it. Her heart ached more, with the hope that her daughter would never know the latter, never have to go through what she had gone through, never have to see what she had seen.

How do you accommodate to it, she thought? How do you change from a carefree student who knows nothing of the world, to someone who can bear the suffering and pain of other people? How do you learn not to be overwhelmed by it, and stay steady and useful and do your job?

She remembered the shock of her first day on a ward as a clinical student. There she had seen a woman in dreadful pain, longing for death, and no one had been able to help her. The next day, mercifully, she was dead. It was her first brush with such suffering. And then came the shock and horror of the outrageous, inhuman suffering in the trenches in France, and the deadening pain of loss for those who loved them. Johnny, her first love, had died, killed in the Royal Flying Corps. There was joy too – joy of a new life beginning, of a patient getting better, defeating death.

Tessa was humming a dance tune – something of Fred Astaire's, probably, shrugging her shoulders to the rhythm. Life, Amy thought. You can't put life into a test tube, my darling Tessa. Life you have to learn with your heart, not your brain.

Tessa turned to her and smiled. 'You look very thoughtful, Mum.'

'It's nothing,' Amy said. 'I was just thinking how lovely it is to have you all at home again.'

Amy's father sat alone in the sitting room, sipping coffee, and listening to the carols on the wireless. He knew Amy so well. He could read her face, more or less knew what she was thinking. She was still worried, he knew that, even though the Prime Minister seemed to have sorted things out with Germany. He had to admit to himself that he was worried too. You couldn't trust the Nazis to do what they said. Look what they'd done already, bombing Spain. This Czechoslovakian thing was a disgrace. The Nazis did what they liked and no one attempted to stop them. What would they try next? If they did anything, it would be Poland, for sure. They were already making noises about Danzig. And what would the rest of Europe do about that? He feared, as Amy and Dan must, for his grandchildren, for all the young ones.

He got up and walked around the room, touched a silver bauble on the Christmas tree, making it swing, glinting in the firelight. He remembered all those bleak Christmases without Amy when she went to the hospitals in France in the Great War – year after year of appalling work for her and appalling worry for him. He remembered her pain and her tears, sobbing on his shoulder. She lost her first love, Johnny Maddox, shot down in an aeroplane. Then she lost her best friend, Helen, blown up by a bomb in the hospital encampment. What she must have seen and endured! Things he could scarcely imagine. He was suddenly angry, outraged. Surely she had suffered enough pain and loss? Surely they all had, the Germans too? How, in the name of God, could anyone contemplate another war? He didn't know how she could bear it if it happened again. Human beings could only take so much without breaking. The last war had proved that, there had been men with broken minds as well as bodies.

She had never really told him about her war. Whenever he asked her questions she avoided them, laughed them off, or brushed them aside. But he had seen her war in her face, in her eyes, heard it in her silence. How could one possibly know or feel what it was like? No wonder she was terrified that it might happen again. Where could she go for comfort? He assumed that she talked to Dan about it. Thank God for Dan. He had been there with her. He knew. He understood.

Nora laid the table in the kitchen for Christmas dinner. She spread a spotless white cloth and decorated it with a sprig of holly and some Christmas crackers. At least they were going to have a real Christmas dinner this year – a roast chicken. Last year had been terrible; Jim had been out of work again and it was a struggle to feed them and pay the rent. They'd had a rabbit pie. No Christmas tree, just some paper chains she and Sara had made. This year the kitchen was warm, a big fire burning in the grate. Jim had bought a treat – a bottle of sweet sherry and some cider to have with dinner. The delicious smell of roast chicken filled the house, and the tangy scent of the onions and the dried sage leaves she'd rubbed between her hands to crumble them into the stuffing. The Christmas pudding, with a few silver threepenny bits inside it, to be discovered with feigned but delighted surprise, bubbled in the simmering water at the back of the stove.

Sara hovered in the kitchen, savouring the scents. She touched the holly, bright with berries. 'It looks lovely, Mum,' she said. The berries gleamed red, almost too perfect to be real. Funny to think that inside each berry were the seeds, tiny little things you could hardly see that, amazingly, were going to be the next holly trees. How did they do that? How did they know that they were holly trees, and not roses or rabbits?

'That smells good,' Jim said. 'It's a long time since we had a chicken.'

Sara had watched her mother preparing the chicken. It had been bought from the butcher ready plucked of its feathers, but her mother had to pull out its innards, saving the neck and the heart and liver to make the gravy.

Her mother made a face. 'I hate doing this,' she said, 'putting my hands in here, all cold and slimy.'

'I'll do it,' Sara said. 'I'd like to,' but her mother shook her head.

'I don't know why you want to be a doctor or a nurse,' Jim said. 'It'd be worse than chickens, putting your hands inside people.'

'Not a nurse,' Sara said. Jim gave an exasperated sigh and Nora glanced at him and shook her head. Sara only had time for a brief look at the heart and liver before they went into the saucepan.

When she woke that morning her stocking had been on the end of her bed, as usual. She still had a stocking, though she didn't believe in Father Christmas any more. There was the usual orange and a few nuts in the toe. There was a pair of warm woollen gloves that her mother had knitted, and some new pencils and a notebook, and a new pencil-case that her father had made for her, beautifully veneered in soft, silky wood. Her real present had been unexpected. Nora and Jim handed it to her in the sitting room, a small box, longer than it was wide. They waited, expectantly, for her reaction. She opened it carefully. Inside was a fountain pen, dark blue with a gold band round the middle. She gave a little gasp. A fountain pen! She could fill it with ink and write and write without dipping her pen in the ink all the time. It was perfect. She filled it from the ink bottle and wrote her name carefully in the notebook. The writing looked different already, firm and even and grown up.

After Christmas dinner she sat at the table, writing with her new pen in her new notebook. What should she write? *My autobiography*, she wrote at the top of the page. As she wrote, she remembered quite a lot of her early childhood, before they came to London. She remembered the long, straight road in Trafford Park, grey and unrelenting: no trees, no gardens, not a flower or blade of grass. She remembered the back yard with the outside toilet, freezing on winter nights. She remembered the lamplighter coming to light the streetlamps with his pole and his ladder, and how she had been afraid of the Sisters of Charity with their great white headdresses, going about the streets among the really poor. When she was little she thought they had no faces. This street wasn't that much different, but at least the toilet was inside and they had a proper bathroom. Things were better here, and her father had a proper job. She knew how important that was.

She remembered her father coming home with his eyes red and streaming when he'd had a job for the day, loading lime on to lorries at one of the factories. She remembered him pulling up the grate over the drain in the street because he'd dropped a half crown and it had rolled, almost purposefully, into the drain, and sat there, glittering. He had lain down in the gutter to fish it out – half a week's rent. She remembered her mother's desperate tears when he lost his job again. He had a job now, but she knew that her mother was always worried. She never felt safe.

There was one other memory that she found very hard to put into words. It seemed to have a meaning for her that she couldn't quite describe. One summer's day, when she was quite small, she had been in the back yard playing on her own, her mother busy in the kitchen. It was summer. She looked up into the intense blue sky and she saw a little aeroplane turning and looping, making a noise that sounded almost like words, coming from far away. It was beautiful, dancing in the sky, glittering in the sun. As she watched, fascinated, it came to her quite suddenly that this was not just a thing that happened to be in the world. It was not a bird, flying on its own. There was a man inside, making it fly, and somewhere, somehow, a man had made it. She had realized, with a shock of amazed excitement, that people could do this – they could make things and change things and make things happen. All kinds of things; there were all kinds of things to think about.

Looking back, it seemed to her that it was the first time that she had ever felt separate, a person on her own; as if, for the first time, the world had revealed itself and she was looking out into it with her own mind and her own self. She was her own person. She ran inside to her mother, to tell her this amazing thing, but she was too little, she didn't have the words. 'I saw an aeroplane,' she remembered saying, and her mother smiled and nodded. There was so much more to it than that. She wrote it down now because it seemed important. She didn't really know why, but it was something that she always remembered.

My mum is still worried, she wrote. *She still thinks my father is going to lose his job and we'll have no money and have to go on the dole, or she thinks there's going to be a war with the Germans.*

She wrote on a new line, *I am going to grammar school now and I'm going to be a doctor when I grow up.*

Even as she wrote, she didn't connect the reality of the world she lived in with the reality of the words on the page. They seemed, somehow, quite separate, as if one had no effect on the other. She was nearly twelve. Her father, he had once told her, had a job in a steel works when he was twelve, and her mother had been in domestic service when she was fourteen. They didn't know anyone who hadn't left school at fourteen. They certainly didn't know anyone who had been to a university. She worked hard at school – she loved it, but she had no idea how she was going to get where she wanted to go. Medical school. She didn't even think about it, or what she was going to do if it didn't happen. Childlike, she just saw the goal as a kind of reality, already achieved.

Chapter Six

1939

A my drove the twins to the station when term began again. The
platform was crowded with young men with the same rowdy
energy, squash rackets, hockey sticks, flying scarves – all the parapher-
nalia of being young, being free from responsibility. But she sensed a
change. They seemed to her to be more subdued, the laughter and the
jumping about and the energy not so free. Perhaps it's me, she thought,
perhaps it's all in my mind.

She was trying to suppress the memory of standing on the platform
at Victoria Station in 1914, watching endless streams of innocent,
untried young men on their way to the killing fields of France. There
had been laughter then, and jokes and calling voices and backslapping
camaraderie, but behind it all there was a reservedness, an apprehension. Those were young men, many of them just boys, going into
unknown dangers, not knowing what waited for them in France,
unable to imagine anything so terrible. She shivered and tried to shrug
off the thought.

Tessa noticed. 'Are you cold, Mum?' she asked.

'No,' Amy said. 'Just a goose walking over my ...'

Tessa kissed her cheek. 'Got to go. See you at Easter.'

Amy watched the train pull slowly out of the station. She understood now how her own father must have felt, watching her leave for
France at the beginning of the war, wondering whether he would ever
see her again.

Charlie and Tessa settled down in a crowded carriage. One of the
young men smiled at Tessa. 'Are you a student,' he asked, 'or just
visiting?'

73

'She's a student,' Charlie said, before she could answer. 'A medical student. She's got someone's leg in her suitcase.'

The young man flushed, looking shocked, bemused.

'I've only got the bones,' Tessa said hurriedly. 'I've been studying them in the vacation.' The young man looked away and didn't speak to her again. He looked, she thought, thoroughly disgusted.

When they got out at Cambridge she dug Charlie in the ribs. 'What are you trying to do?' she said, laughing. 'Ruin my marital prospects?'

Charlie grinned. 'Merely revealing that he was a complete twerp. You have to admit that I was right.'

'Yes,' she said. 'You were right. Obviously an anti-woman-doctor diehard. Anyway, I'm not in the market. Five years and three quarters to go.'

Charlie carried his suitcase up the staircase to his room and unpacked. He realized that he had a certain amount of envy for Tessa. He envied her complete assurance about her future, her determination about where she was going. What was his future? The Civil Service, perhaps, or the Colonial Service, or teaching. He couldn't quite see himself spending the rest of his life as a housemaster in some minor public school, or swatting flies under a solar topee in some remote part of the Empire. He had no idea where he was going, no matter how much he thought about it. It was like an itch that he couldn't scratch. Most of the acquaintances he'd made seemed to be the same, but most of them didn't seem to worry about it. That was OK he supposed, if you came from a rich family and didn't have to work for your living.

The exception, he thought, was Arthur. Arthur seemed to know where he was going all right. He seemed to know where the whole world was going. Was he right? If so, then he, Charlie, and all the others, would have no decisions to make.

He walked to the window and looked out over the quad. It had not changed much since it was built, some of it in the sixteenth century. Would it survive now? Or would some vicious German bomber wipe it out in an instant, intent on destroying everything the British held dear, intent on breaking their spirit, wiping out their history? Frightening us to death.

Students were arriving, talking in groups, silently watched by the ancient stones, by mullioned windows that had looked out on the same scene for hundreds of years. All-out war would make no differences amongst them. The scholars and the dilettantes, the swotters and the time-wasters, those who studied every day in their rooms and those who spent the day messing about on the river, would all have the same future. For God knew how long. And a sizeable number of them would never have to think about it again. They would not be here. They would be a name on a village war memorial, a photograph on a cottage sideboard. Would he be one of those? These ancient stones, God willing, would still be here, a reminder, watching over the generations to come. The thought was a kind of comfort.

He remembered Arthur's amused remark about knights on horse-back. In a way, Arthur was right; that was how he felt. If it came to it, that would be what he wanted. Face-to-face combat with another man – not firing a huge gun, or scattering machine-gun bullets, or dropping bombs, not knowing who or what it might wipe out at the other end. When they were settled in he would go to see Arthur again.

'Hello Tessa.' Rita bounded into Tessa's room. 'Good Christmas?'

'Yes,' Tessa said, 'it was lovely. Just the family.'

Rita sat down on the bed. She looked excited, bursting with news. 'Guess what I did in the vacation.'

Tessa smiled and shrugged. 'What?'

Rita held out her left hand. 'I got engaged.' Her third finger bore a small diamond solitaire.

Tessa was almost shocked. 'But – how can you?' she began. 'You've got all this to do ...' Her voice tailed off.

Rita looked pensive. 'I can still do it,' she said. 'Being engaged won't stop me.'

'But when are you thinking of getting married? You know they might not let you stay here if you are married.'

'We'll wait,' Rita said defensively. She turned the ring on her finger. 'He's in the army, you see – a lieutenant. We wanted to make it official.'

'But you've got three years just at Cambridge, and then there's the clinical training,' Tessa said. 'It's a long time.'

'It doesn't matter.' Rita was even more defensive. 'If he has to go away, if I don't see him for months at a time, I want him to know that I'm here and I'll wait, no matter what happens.'

Tessa stared at her. She couldn't imagine anything that might divert or distract her, but then, she couldn't imagine having those feelings, having those dreadful worries. She sat down on the bed and smiled and gave Rita a hug. 'Well, congratulations,' she said. 'It's great news and I hope you'll be very happy.'

Rita slipped off her ring and hung it on a chain and put it around her neck. 'I just hope he doesn't have to go,' she said. 'I don't know what I'd do if …' Her eyes glistened.

Tessa took her hand. 'Why does everybody think that war is inevitable? Mr Chamberlain has sorted that out.'

'My fiancé thinks it is,' Rita said, 'and he ought to know.' She touched her ring with her fingers. She coloured a little. 'Tessa,' she said, 'do you know anything about sex?'

'What do you mean?' Tessa said. 'I know how babies are conceived. You must know that. You must have done biology at school and we've done human reproduction in physiology lectures here.'

Rita coloured even more. 'I know that,' she said. 'But it's sort of skimmed over, isn't it? They don't tell you anything about feelings. I always thought you only did it if you wanted a baby. You know – you got married and did it and had a baby and then if you wanted another one you did it again. My mother never told me anything. It was absolutely taboo. I thought perhaps, with your mother being a doctor....'

'Well, what is it you want to know?'

Rita bit her thumbnail. 'My fiancé says people do it all the time, whether they want babies or not. He says they do it to show they love each other.'

'You mean he wants you to have sex with him before you're married?' Rita nodded. 'But you might get pregnant before you're married.'

'He says there are ways of preventing it. And he says he'd marry me at once if I did.'

'I see.' Tessa said. She knew about contraception, from her mother, but she didn't really see. She had never imagined herself having this problem. Her mother had explained it to her as far as she could, but it had all seemed theoretical to her. Marriage and sex could wait. That was somewhere in the future.

'Have you ever done it?' Rita said.

Tessa, despite herself, was shocked. 'No,' she said. 'Of course not.' She paused. 'But then, I've never been in love with anyone.'

Rita sighed. 'I don't know who to ask.'

'Whoever you ask,' Tessa said, 'they'll say no. If you're asking me, I'd say it's not a good idea.'

'I just wish he wasn't going away. I wish there wasn't all this about war. If we got married I suppose I'd have to give up my training.' Rita got up. 'I'd better go and unpack. You won't say anything to anyone, will you?' She left, closing the door gently behind her.

Tessa crouched before the fireplace and put a match to the fire. There's so much I don't know, she thought. I'm going to be a doctor; I ought to know about these things. She remembered her mother's anger one day, when she came home from work. She heard her telling her father. One of her patients, a girl of sixteen, had become pregnant outside marriage. 'They've locked her away,' her mother said, 'the authorities. She's been put in a mental hospital with a "diagnosis",' she pronounced the word with utter scorn, 'of moral insanity. God knows what that means and God knows when they'll let her out. And she's not the only one. And the man gets away scot free. He's only got to deny it and there's no way of proving that he's the father. Moral insanity! Good God. It's ignorance. If these girls were given a bit more information, it wouldn't happen so often.'

How had Rita got herself into this situation, she thought? She couldn't allow herself to be involved with a man if there was going to be a war. How could you live with that kind of fear and worry? It would be nightmare enough worrying about Charlie. How would she manage her feelings? Am I a coward, she thought? Would I falter and break if it all got really bad? Handling bits of the human body were one thing if they were long dead. How would she cope with those other realities, with violent pain and death? I'll ask my mother, she thought. She'll know. She's been there. She had never talked about it, but she knew. There were a lot of things she needed to know.

*

Arthur was in his rooms when Charlie went up to speak to him. He was making one of his innumerable cups of tea. 'Hello Charlie,' he said. 'Come in and take a seat.' He poured and handed Charlie a cup of tea. 'Just a social visit?'

'Not exactly,' Charlie said. 'I wanted to ask you something.'

'Fire ahead.'

'I believe you're in the University Air Squadron,' Charlie said. Arthur nodded. 'Done my first solo and short cross-country. Not far off a private licence.'

'Do you have to be an engineer or something to get in?' Charlie asked, 'or will they take anybody?'

'They won't take just anybody,' Arthur said. 'You'd have to show some kind of ability. Why? Are you interested? Do you see yourself having a nice little hobby playing with an aeroplane?'

'Arthur,' Charlie said, annoyed, 'I'm not a complete wet. I'm prepared to fight if it comes to it. I just think I'd rather do it in the Air Force.'

Arthur smiled a grim smile. 'Why? Do you think it would be an easy option?'

Charlie stared at him for a moment. Did he, he wondered? Did he think it was an easy option, spending a war living in England probably, or at least sleeping in his own bed at night? 'It isn't that,' he said. 'I don't quite know what it is. Perhaps I just want to see my enemy – one to one, man to man.'

Arthur grinned again. 'See yourself as a fighter pilot, do you? Only kill the man who's trying to kill you? The old white knight again. What if they put you on bombers? What if you had to fly over Germany and drop your bombs on cities full of civilians? What then?'

Charlie hesitated. It was something he had not been able to decide about. Not that he would have the choice. 'I expect I'd have to do what I was told,' he said.

'Too damn right.'

Charlie said nothing, watching Arthur's face.

'Why do you want to talk to me about it?' Arthur said softly. 'You're not like me. You've never had to fight for anything, have you, Charlie? You've just been given everything. Most of the men at this university are the same. Born with silver spoons. Just look at them. Dawdling dandies, most of them, come here to finish off a gentleman's education, and then out into the tight little world of the old-boy network. Most of them look down on people like me with scholarships – working-class upstarts.'

'I don't,' Charlie said, irritated. 'My parents aren't like that; they're both doctors. My mother does a lot of work in the slums.'

'Maybe she does,' Arthur said, 'but it's charity, isn't it? Charity hospitals, soup kitchens, hand-me-downs from charitable ladies. It's disgusting. These people have a right to a better life. They thought they'd get it after the last war, but they didn't.'

Charlie didn't know what to say. He had a flash of memory of Germany, of their heartless strength. They seemed prosperous enough, but surely that couldn't be the way to go. There was a better way of living, of thinking. 'Is there going to be a war, Arthur?'

Arthur gave his gusting laughter. 'There's a breathless hush in the close tonight, Charlie, and it isn't going to last. And who's going to be fighting? Blokes like me. Have you forgotten those blokes at the Oxford Union who said they wouldn't fight for King and country?'

Charlie was stung, annoyed. 'We're not all dawdling dandies,' he said. 'Some of us do think, you know. And sometimes diplomacy is best. The pen is mightier than the sword.'

'I know that,' Arthur said. 'Strangely enough, some of us think so too, but sometimes only the sword will do.'

'Can you get me into the Air Squadron, Arthur?' Charlie asked, 'without the rhetoric.' His voice held an edge that Arthur seemed to recognize.

'I can take you along,' Arthur said, 'but I can't guarantee anything. I'll take you on Saturday. Meet me here at eight o'clock. Wear something warm.'

Charlie went back to his room. Them and us, he thought. Why is it like that? Maybe part of the German strength was the way they had united the people, made them feel that they were all equal, even if it was in some kind of oppression. Why were his countrymen only equal when they were fighting, and mostly not even then? The equality didn't seem to last. Kipling had it in a nutshell: 'Tommy' was almost an insult in peacetime, but 'Tommy' was a hero when the drums began to roll. No wonder Arthur was so cynical.

On Saturday afternoon Sara arrived at Kathy's house. The street was very different from what she was used to. The houses looked big and had big pillars at the doorways and steps that went down into a sort of basement. They were all nicely painted and there were one or two cars parked in the road. No one had had a car in Trafford Park except the doctor and his looked a bit old and shabby. Her dad went to work on his bike – when he had a job. There had been a few big houses at the top of their street, but they didn't look like this. The doctor lived in one, and the headmistress of her school in another, and someone her father called 'that useless councillor'. They might have been big but they looked all gloomy and neglected. She had never been inside a house that looked like this.

She rang the doorbell. After a few moments the door was opened by a maid in a white apron. 'I've come to see Kathy,' Sara said. The maid opened the door and gestured for her to come in.

She stepped into a long, wide hall paved in black and white tiles, with a long, silky-looking rug down the middle, deep red and blue. Somewhere in the house music was playing. It wasn't the kind of music her mother listened to on the wireless, or sang about the house, or her dad sometimes strummed on the piano: 'Alexander's Ragtime Band', or something like that.

The maid disappeared and then Kathy came running into the hall. 'Come in,' she said. 'My mum's in here.'

Sara looked about her. The sitting-room was big enough to have two sofas and there was a marble fireplace with a log fire burning brightly. She could see the laid wooden floor round the edge of the carpet. Parquet, her Dad had told her once. He put it down sometimes for someone as an extra job. They had lino at home.

'This is my mum,' Kathy said. Her mother was small and round and her hair was going a bit grey. She held out her hand. 'How do you do, Sara.' Sara shook her hand and just smiled. She was a bit overcome by the poshness of it all: the marble fireplace and the big windows with big curtains and the cabinet with little figurines in it. She tried to tuck it all into her memory. She knew that her mother would want to know all about it when she got home.

'Come up to my room,' Kathy said. They climbed the staircase, with its polished rails and banisters and brown carpet held down by gleaming brass rods.

Kathy's room was bigger than hers at home, but not different, really. It had a bed and a desk and a table and there was a teddy bear on the bed. That rather surprised her. She had given up teddy bears long ago. As her eyes took it all in she realized that there were a few differences. Kathy had her own wireless, and, wonder of wonders, there was a radiator giving out heat, just like they had at school.

Kathy shut the door with a little bang. 'Beethoven,' she said. 'Lily's always playing Beethoven on her gramophone, but I'd rather have dance bands. My mum say I'm a philistine.' Sara wasn't really sure what that meant, but she didn't like to ask. Kathy did a few dancing steps. 'Can you do the quickstep?'

'No,' Sara said. 'I don't know how to dance.'

'I've got a book,' Kathy said, 'that tells you how to do it.' She turned on the wireless. 'Sometimes there's Victor Sylvester's band on in the afternoons.'

There was no music, only some man talking about Italy and Mussolini. 'I do wish they'd stop going on about it,' Kathy said. 'They never seem to talk about anything else. It's so boring.'

She showed Sara her clothes. Sara had never seen her in anything but her school uniform. They're not much different from mine, Sara thought. Her mother always made sure that she was nicely dressed – neat and tidy. 'What does your dad do for his living?' she asked.

'He works in a bank,' Kathy said. 'I don't know what he does there. Counts the money, I expect.' Sara could see and feel the money all around her. She didn't suppose that Kathy's father had ever been out of work.

A bell tinkled down below. 'That's tea,' Kathy said. 'We'd better go down.'

Tea was bread and butter and cake and a cup of tea in a flowery china cup. There wasn't anything like real food, Sara thought, and anyway, it was too early. She'd have to have her proper tea when she got home.

She left at half past five and took the bus home. Her mother was getting tea ready – no, not tea, she'd have to learn to call it dinner – sausage and mash today. Her father was sitting at the kitchen table reading the paper. 'Have a good time?' her mother asked.

Sara nodded. She had a strange reluctance to go into it all, all the descriptions of the house that her mother would want, but she knew she'd have to do it after tea – dinner.

'We had tea,' she said, 'but it was only bread and butter and cake.'

Her mother nodded. 'Afternoon tea,' she said. 'That's different.' She turned back to her potatoes, her back to Sara.

'They had a maid,' Sara said. 'She brought in the tea.'

Her mother said nothing for a moment, but Sara could see the sudden tenseness in her shoulders and the momentary halt in her peeling of the potatoes. 'Oh, did they?' she said.

When Sara went up to her room Jim put his paper down. 'Now look what's happened,' he said. 'What's she going to think when she goes into these houses with these people? We're not going to look very good, are we? She's going to be ashamed of us, isn't she?'

'No she isn't,' Nora said. 'She's not like that.'

'You're going to lose her, that's what,' he said. 'If she ever gets what you want you'll probably never see her again.'

'Don't be daft,' Nora said. 'She wouldn't do that. She'd never be that sort of snob.' But she felt a little chill. I don't care, she thought. Just as long as she gets it.

'You'll see,' he said. 'That's if we're not taken over by the Germans.'

'Just let them try,' she said.

At eight o'clock on Saturday Charlie met Arthur in his room. 'The airfield's at Duxford,' Arthur said, 'but I believe there are plans to move to Marshall's.'

They took the bus to Duxford and walked into the airfield, towards the hangars. Arthur took a deep breath. 'Smell it,' he said. 'It's the best smell in the world, oil and aircraft dope and all the rest. You can keep your posh perfumes.' Charlie glanced at him and smiled. He hadn't suspected Arthur of having a poetic soul. Flying seemed to bring it out.

There were three aircraft parked on the grass. 'That one's an Avro, and those two are Tiger Moths,' Arthur said. His voice held a tone of pride and satisfaction. 'One of the best aircraft ever made.'

He took Charlie into the office. 'Another recruit, Bill,' he said. 'I'll have to go. I've got a flight booked this morning.'

Bill was tall and thin, wearing a flying suit. 'Have a seat,' he said. 'So you want to fly. Have you any experience?'

'No,' Charlie said. 'I've never been up before.'

'I see.' Bill looked at him for a moment. 'What are you reading?'

'History.'

'Any hobbies or sports?'

'I play cricket, and club tennis,' Charlie said. He hesitated. 'And I play the piano.'

To his surprise Bill's face brightened. 'Play the piano? Good. You might have a light touch on the controls.' He looked at Charlie: a speculative look, Charlie thought, weighing him up. 'Why do you want to fly?'

'If there's a war,' Charlie said, 'I'd like to join the Air Force.'

'Do you think there's going to be a war?' Bill said.

Charlie shrugged. 'Who knows? But it sounds as if it's getting more likely.'

'Our wing commander would agree with you,' Bill said. 'He's pretty convinced. Very keen on training more pilots. You'd have to have an interview with him, but I can take you up this morning if you like – see how you get on. No point in being interviewed if you're sick as a dog or terrified.'

'I'd like that very much,' Charlie said. 'Thanks.'

Bill got up and took two flying helmets from hooks on the wall. 'Come on, then.' They walked out to one of the Tiger Moths. 'You sit in the back,' Bill said, 'and be careful where you put your feet.' He hung over the cockpit and showed Charlie how to strap himself in. He grinned. 'Don't want you falling out, do we? And don't undo it till we're back on the ground and stopped. And if by any unlikely chance we turn over on the ground don't undo them at all, or you'll fall straight on your head and break your neck. Wait for help.' He pointed around the cockpit. 'Control column or stick, rudders, speaking tube. And don't touch anything unless I tell you to.'

'Yes, sir,' Charlie said.

They taxied into the wind and Bill took off.

Charlie watched the ground fall away beneath him. For a few moments he felt a kind of stillness, as if he were waiting to find out how he felt. He watched the stick move and felt the pressure on his straps as Bill put the plane into a gentle turn. He looked down over the airfield, the roofs of the hangars, the woods and fields beyond. Slowly, stealing over him in the clear air, he felt a kind of exultation, a sense of extraordinary freedom. They flew through a patch of cloud and came out above it, the sun gleaming and casting rainbows on the white billows below. I'm so lucky, he thought. Fifty years ago no man had ever seen such beauty; this unknown world.

They came out again into clear air. 'All right?' Bill said, through the tube.

'Yes.' Charlie found himself nodding vigorously.

'Fancy doing a loop?'

'Yes,' Charlie said again. He felt himself pushed back in his seat as the aircraft climbed. The earth disappeared, and then slowly revolved in front of him until they were straight and level again. It was extraordinary. He didn't feel that he had moved at all. It was as if the world had moved around him.

'All right?' Bill asked again.

'Yes,' Charlie said. 'Fantastic.'

'Put your hand on the stick and your feet on the rudder bars,' Bill said, 'and don't do anything. Just feel what I am doing.'

They did a gentle turn to the left and Charlie felt the movements of the controls. I can do this, he thought. I know I can. He wanted to do it more than anything he had ever wanted in his life.

'I'm going to do a spin,' Bill said. 'That's the one aerobatic manoeuvre you'd have to learn before you went solo. You can get into them by accident. You need to know how to get out.' Charlie saw the stick move back and then they seemed to flip into a turn. The plane began to spin, round and round, and the ground came rushing up to meet them. 'Stick forward and full opposite rudder,' Bill said in his ear. The plane came magically out of the spin, flying straight and level. 'All OK?'

'Brilliant,' Charlie said. 'It's brilliant.'

Bill did a circuit of the airfield, landed and taxied back. They went back into the office. 'What do you think?' Bill said.

Charlie firmly suppressed his emotional reactions and tried to be practical. 'I think it's great,' he said, 'and I want to do it.'

Bill grinned. He knows, Charlie thought. He knows how desperate I am to get in.

'We'll make an appointment with the wing commander,' Bill said. 'You might do.'

Charlie stayed at the airfield for an hour or two, ostensibly waiting for Arthur, but in reality just watching, watching the aircraft come and go, doing take-offs and landings, circuits and bumps. He had a sense of extraordinary peace and contentment. He watched someone apparently doing a first solo, the instructor standing on the grass, his body tense, watching the aircraft circling the field, watching it land, bumping a little but landing safely. He watched him greeting the new pilot, shaking his hand. I can do this, he thought. I will do it. He felt as if he's been handed a huge gift, a goal, a reason for being alive. He knew that he would be back.

'It's spring,' Amy said, 'March already.' The garden was waking up again, snowdrops gleaming.

'Look at this,' Dan said. He held up a cartoon in *Punch*, showing John Bull, who seemed to be waking up from a nightmare – the nightmare of another war.

Amy didn't smile. Dan put his arm around her and held her against him. 'I don't believe it,' she said. 'It isn't over. It's like living on top of a time bomb.'

He kissed the top of her head. 'We'd get through it,' he said. 'Whatever happens, we'd get through it, together.'

'We shouldn't have to,' she said, agonized. 'We shouldn't have to go through that again. Twice in one lifetime. It isn't fair.' There was nothing he could say.

She did her normal clinics and surgeries, meeting every day other women with stricken faces and frightened eyes. 'My son ...' they said, 'my husband, my son, my children....' She tried to be reassuring, but she knew that there was nothing that would really help. How could there be when she felt the same?

She opened the morning paper one March morning, and gasped. Hitler had invaded and taken the rest of Czechoslovakia. There was a picture of jeering, weeping crowds in Prague, of crowds of Jewish people storming the railway stations, trying to get away, knowing too well what the future held for them. Dan took her hand, not knowing how to comfort her, knowing, as she did, that the future was now decided, whatever the politicians might say. She telephoned her father. He sounded older, more tremulous. She thought, perhaps, that he had been crying.

The twins came home for the Easter vacation, Tessa worried and strained about the news from Europe, and Charlie strangely calm and cheerful.

Tessa sought him out in the garden. 'You seem very calm about it all,' she said. 'You're up to something, aren't you? Have you joined up or something?'

'No,' he said. 'I wouldn't do that without telling the parents.' He hadn't told her, or his parents, that he was learning to fly. He didn't want to tell them until he'd got his wings, and he didn't want his mother worrying herself to death. He'd tell them when it happened. He had another reason. It was a new and private joy. He didn't want to tell Tessa that flying had answered his prayers, had opened the door to his own new world, that he felt about it the way she seemed to feel about medicine. He had to prove himself first.

The twins went back to Cambridge. The year wore on. It seemed to Amy that the whole world was taking one irrevocable step after another, as if pacing steadily and meaningfully towards another war. A new aircraft carrier, HMS *Illustrious*, was launched at Barrow-in-Furness, Italy invaded Albania, conscription of young men was begun, plans were made for the evacuation of children from the major cities. One step after another, relentless, destroying all hope. Germany and Italy formed the 'Pact of Steel'. It was as if the monster, death, had been resurrected and had planned it all – do this, do that, run about like chickens with their heads cut off, but you can't escape me. Everything you do will bring the horror nearer.

'We'll get through this,' Dan said.

There was nothing that Amy could say.

Chapter Seven

1939

The twins came home for the summer vacation. On their first evening they sat in the garden, having sherry before dinner.

'Nice to have you home,' Dan said, 'have the family together again.'

'Have a good term?' Amy asked.

'Yes,' Tessa said. 'It was lovely. I've got some snapshots to show you. I've got very good at poling a punt. I only fell in once.'

Amy laughed. She looked around the garden, at the height of its summer beauty, the finest summer for years. How could one imagine that all this would ever change? Surely nothing was going to happen? The King and Queen were back home from touring America. They had come back. They obviously hadn't intended to send for the Princesses and stay in America or Canada, out of danger. That wouldn't be very good for morale. She looked at the children, half-closing her eyes against the evening sun. They looked well. Charlie especially looked cheerful and full of energy. He must have found Cambridge very much to his liking. If it wasn't a girl, perhaps he was finding his way, something he wanted to do with his life – if…. The terrible thoughts would not go away. If he was allowed to do anything.

'What are you going to do in the holidays?' she said.

'I'm going to see if I can do a first-aid course,' Tessa said. 'I'm not much use as I am now, am I? I can't actually do anything.' Amy glanced at her quickly, but Tessa was calmly sipping her sherry. 'Do you know if any of the hospitals are doing them?'

Amy forced down the immediate spike of fear. 'I don't know,' she said, 'but I can find out.'

'I might go up to Cambridge now and again,' Charlie said.

Amy's ears pricked up. 'What for?'

'Oh,' he said, 'just to see some chaps.'

Amy wondered again whether he had a girl. Neither of them had said anything.

'I can take you to the hospital, Tessa,' Dan said. 'I'm sure the casualty officer would help you. He would probably be a better instructor than your mother and me. He does that sort of thing all the time. And the nurses could show you a thing or two.'

Amy looked at him sharply, but he merely raised his eyebrows, signalling her to say nothing.

After dinner Dan followed Charlie back into the garden. He lit his pipe, puffing to get it going. He blew out the match and flipped it into a flower-bed. 'Why are you going back to Cambridge, Charlie,' he said. 'Anything we should know about?'

Charlie leant back, looking up into the sky, blue and cloudless. 'I wasn't going to say yet,' he said. 'Especially to Mum.'

'What then?'

Charlie looked back at his father, smiling a little. 'I've been learning to fly, Dad, in the air squadron. It's absolutely terrific. I'm about to do my first solo. If the balloon goes up I want to join the Air Force.'

For a long moment Dan was silent. It was all too easy to bring back the last war – those young men in the Flying Corps. Many of them died just a few weeks after they got their wings, shot down, killed, or worse. 'Perhaps you're right,' he said. 'Don't tell her yet. Nothing has happened yet. Get over your first solo.'

'How do you think she'd take it?'

'Your mother,' Dan said, 'is one of the bravest women I know. Women are tough, Charlie, when the chips are down. She did her surgery all the way through the last war in France, through the bombing and the danger. She went out with an ambulance picking up the wounded from God knows where. She'll love you and support you whatever you do.'

Charlie grinned. 'I think at one time she thought I might be a conscientious objector.' He looked into the sky again. 'I want to fly fighters, Dad. If I have to fight I want to see my enemy, face to face, man to man.'

Dan sighed. 'If what we are hearing about Germany is true, our enemy would be far more profound than fighting only men. We'll be fighting something much worse, a philosophy that could poison the world for hundreds of years. We will have to win, whatever it takes. We will all have to do what we're told, whatever it is, no matter how much it goes against the grain.'

'But women and children, Dad?'

'They won't care about women and children,' Dan said. 'Look what they did in Guernica. They're very powerful, Charlie. They have enormous military strength. They'll try to frighten us to death.'

Charlie smiled. 'No chance.'

'Could I come?' Dan said. 'Could I come to see you do your first solo?'

'That would be great,' Charlie said. 'I've brought a paper for you to sign. You have to give your consent, as I'm not twenty-one yet. I suppose we'd have to tell Mum.'

'I'll do that,' Dan said. 'I'll tell her afterwards, when you've done it and it's all over. She'll be fine.'

They arrived in Cambridge and Dan booked into the University Arms Hotel. They had dinner in the restaurant.

'You'd better get back to college early,' Dan said. 'Get a good night's sleep. I'll pick you up tomorrow in a taxi. Get you there calm and collected.'

Charlie smiled. 'I think it's you who has to be calm and collected. I'm going to be busy.'

Dan lay in bed, thinking of Charlie, up there alone for the first time. He wasn't worried – well, not too worried. Charlie was sensible and reliable. He wouldn't be doing it if he didn't think he was ready. Hundreds of people did it. Girls did it. What about Amy Johnson? He deliberately closed his mind to the images of the air battles in the so-called Great War, aeroplanes a new weapon then. At least the RAF gave their pilots parachutes now. He would not think of Charlie in a fighter, turning and weaving in that desperate game.

They drove to the airfield the next day. Dan stood at the perimeter, out of the way. Why did I come, he thought? Was it just because he wanted to be here to watch his son do something rather important, or was it because he wanted to be here in case something went wrong, so that he, and his medical expertise, would be on immediate hand? He shook his head briefly. He must dismiss that thought. He could not always be there. That responsibility would belong to someone else. The risk of impending war could so easily lead to black, negative attitudes. As he got older, he had begun to believe that thoughts were things, and that even unexpressed they could influence reality, one way or another. Positive. Be positive.

He watched as Charlie climbed into the Tiger Moth with his instructor and they took off. The aircraft did one sedate circuit of the airfield and then taxied back. He saw the instructor get out, have a brief word with Charlie, and walk away. His throat tightened. He watched as Charlie, alone now, turned the aircraft into the wind, watched as the aircraft trembled on the edge of the grass runway, gathered speed, and then as it rose, steady and graceful into the air. His throat tightened more. Is this what it's like, he thought? Is this what it's like, watching your son go off to war, into danger, into some steadfast resolve that you couldn't share? The instructor, he saw, was standing as motionless as himself, watching the sky intently, waiting.

Charlie did his cockpit checks in a kind of tense calm – fuel, trim, magneto, compass, harness. All seemed well. Remember how to get out of a spin – stick forward, full opposite rudder – not that he'd have enough height. Air speed. Don't stall. The green signal appeared. 'Here we go,' he said aloud. He pushed the throttle forward, his heart pounding. The Tiger began to move, gathering speed over the grass. He reached flying speed, eased gently back on the stick. The aircraft rose, steady and true into the still air. This is it, he thought. I'm off. There was no turning back now.

The ground fell away. He glanced down, then upwards into the clear sky, and felt a sudden kick of pure joy, of pure exhilaration. I'm on my own, he thought – there is no one here with me. It is all mine. He knew that for the first time in his life he was totally reliant on himself, that whatever happened now was entirely in his own hands and that nothing and no one could help him. The thought filled him with the deepest satisfaction.

He reached 800 feet and made the first of the gentle turns that would take him in a circuit around the airfield – stick and rudder together; watch the airspeed, nose attitude, come out of the turn straight and level. It felt absolutely meant, intended, that he should have the power of this wonderful machine in his hands. It felt right, as if the aircraft had settled with intention into his safe control. It felt like part of him.

He flew round the square circuit, maintaining his height, until he was on final approach. He had no doubts now, no uncertainty. He was in his element, and that element, he knew now, was the air. He felt that he had found something that he hadn't even known he was looking for. He made his careful approach to the grass runway: flying attitude, airspeed, flaps, throttle. He watched the ground coming up gently to meet him, watched the yellow dusting on the grass turn into buttercups – throttle back, stick back into his stomach, the little bump. The aircraft rolled to a halt. I'm down, he thought. I've done it. I'm a pilot.

He taxied back and parked the aircraft. He got out and shook hands with his instructor, and walked back to his father.

Dan watched him coming towards him over the grass. He's different, he thought. Something is different, some assurance, some strength. He shook Charlie's hand. 'Well done,' he said.

Charlie gave a huge grin. 'It's fantastic, Dad. I wish I could show you. Perhaps I will, one day.'

'I'll look forward to that.'

'I'll have to stay for a bit,' Charlie said. 'De-briefing with my instructor. I'll meet you back at the hotel in an hour or two.'

'Fine,' Dan said. 'Then I'll make my way home. I'll give your mother a call and tell her what you've done and that you're still alive. She'll be much relieved.'

His instructor seemed unmoved by Charlie's pleasure. He'd obviously seen it all before. 'Now you've got to do it again,' he said. 'Then we'll have to start on some aerobatic manoeuvres. Can't have you flying just straight and level, can we? Not a good idea.'

Charlie felt a moment of shock. He had been so engrossed, so filled with his achievement, that he had forgotten everything but the joy of the moment. He hadn't imagined the obvious – that he was being trained to dive and twist and weave with a hungry German fighter on his tail. He was instantly sobered. 'Yes,' he said. 'Of course.'

His mother hugged him when he got home, smiling, but he could sense her tenseness. 'Well done, darling,' she said, but her mouth trembled.

'I've had a letter from one of the chaps at college,' he said. 'Arthur Blake. He's asked me if I'd like to go and stay with him in Manchester for a few days.'

'Of course,' she said. 'I suppose he flies too?'

'Yes,' Charlie said, 'but he's doing it just to get more experience with aero engines. He's an engineer. He knows how everything works. He's offered to give me a few tips.'

'I see,' Amy said, keeping her voice carefully neutral. 'I suppose that would be very useful.'

'Yes, it would.' It was time to tell her, he thought. Things didn't look good. No point in hedging now. 'It would help me to get into the RAF.' He saw the colour drain from her face and put an arm around her shoulders. 'That's what I want to do, Mum, if war breaks out.'

She leant her head against him 'I know, Charlie. Why else would you be flying?'

'It's great, Mum,' he said. 'The best thing I've ever done.'

She reached up and kissed his cheek and he saw the tears in her eyes. 'I know, darling. Go and see your friend. The more you know the safer you'll be.'

'It'll be all right, Mum,' he said. 'We're better than they are.'

She didn't reply. For a few moments he hung about, awkward, not knowing what to say, then he went up to his room and sat on the bed. He hadn't thought much about death. Life had been unquestioned and unquestioning. But if war came, the possibility was there. The possibility was always there, but war was different. So far no one had actually been trying to kill him. If he died, his parents would still have Tessa, and she would see them through, she was the practical one. He smiled. Practical to a fault in some ways. As far as Tessa was concerned, if you couldn't get it into a test tube, it didn't exist. It wouldn't occur to her to question the morality of this war. Enemies were there to be defeated, be they disease, or want, or Germans.

We're the wrong way round, he thought wryly, Tessa and me. But ever since his first solo, he had felt an absolute and pure determination to defend what he loved. He was under no illusions. War was a bloody and cruel business. History had taught him that. He did not see Agincourt or the English and the American civil wars as a kind of sanitized Hollywood adventure. He was aware of the cost and the pain. You couldn't spend your life with two doctors and not be aware of those two realities. Pain and death could not be romanticized. And yet, in a way, he thought that Arthur was right. If he wanted to see it that way, he had been handed his steed and his sword.

He took the train from Euston. It was crowded, even more crowded than the Cambridge train when term started. There were uniforms everywhere, mostly army, and a few navy and RAF. There was conscription now, he remembered, for men over twenty. He was only nineteen. It doesn't matter, he thought. I'll volunteer – get in on the ground floor. He looked at the faces of the young men in their new uniforms and boots. They seemed mostly to be unperturbed. The older men in uniform – regulars, he supposed – looked, not pleased exactly, but confident, determined, casting steely, sardonic eyes on the raw recruits.

The train got more and more crowded as they travelled north. The voices changed, to accents he sometimes had to strain to catch. Homburgs and trilbies gave way to flat caps. They rolled through beautiful countryside, and then, at intervals, through the cheerless back streets of city suburbs.

They arrived at Manchester Piccadilly station in the early afternoon. Arthur was waiting for him. 'We'll get the bus to Trafford Park,' he said. 'There's a bus station just down the road.' Charlie looked about him. It looked much the same as any other big city, he thought, greyer than London perhaps, and the streets not so wide. There were a few fine buildings, big department stores, well-dressed women. Then as the bus took them away from the city centre the scene slowly changed. The streets became narrower and grubbier. There were groups of men standing on street corners, doing nothing, smoking, watching the bus go by with empty eyes.

They got off the bus at the end of a long, grey street and walked to
Arthur's house. The front doors of the houses opened directly on to the
street. Here and there, women in flowered aprons sat on stools or hard
chairs on the pavement, chattering, laughing, fanning themselves with
bits of paper. There seemed to be children everywhere, some of them,
he saw with surprise, hardly more than babies. No cars, he saw; not
even a bicycle. The children seemed to be alone.

'Where are their mothers?' he asked.

'Inside,' Arthur said, 'doing their housework or baking or something. The older kids look after the little ones, and there's always an
adult about somewhere. It's very neighbourly.'

They arrived at Arthur's house and he opened the door. 'My mam'll
be in the kitchen,' he said. 'Come through.'

They walked down a short narrow hallway to the kitchen at the
back. Arthur's mother was making bread. She wiped her floury arms
on her apron and shook Charlie's hand. 'Pleased to met you, Charlie,'
she said, smiling broadly. 'I expect you'd like a cup of tea.'

'Thank you,' Charlie said. 'I'd love one.'

'Sit down then.' She bustled about, pouring water into a teapot from
a black iron kettle on the range. 'Have a piece of currant pastry,' she
said. 'I've just made it.'

'Thank you,' Charlie said again. They sat down at the kitchen table.
Charlie took a bite of the currant pastry, aware that Arthur was
watching him. It melted in his mouth, crumbly and sweet. 'That's the
best pastry I've ever had,' he said.

Arthur's mother smiled delightedly. 'Good lad. Always had a good
hand with pastry. Have some more.'

Arthur laughed. 'You've made a good impression, Charlie,' he said.
'Praise my mam's pastry and you're a friend for life.'

When they had finished, Arthur took him up to his room. It was
simply furnished, brown lino on the floor and a rag rug by the bed.
There was an iron bedstead with spotless white sheets and in the
corner, a washstand with a large jug and a bowl.

Arthur picked up the jug. 'I'll get you some hot water,' he said. He
looked about him. 'Not what you're used to, I expect,' he said.

'It's grand,' Charlie said. 'I'll be very comfortable.'

'The lavatory is out in the yard,' Arthur said, 'and there is a bath in one of the bedrooms. My dad put it in, in one of his flush periods. I'll be back in a minute.'

Charlie sat down on the bed, looking about him at the gleaming lino and the sparkling window. This, he thought, must be the cleanest house he'd ever seen.

Arthur came back with the water. 'Arthur,' Charlie said, 'I'm very grateful for this. It's very kind of your parents to have me. If there's anything I can do....'

'If you mean money,' Arthur said, 'forget it. My dad's in work, and my mother would be upset.' Charlie nodded and coloured a little. 'Come down when you're ready,' Arthur said, 'and I'll show you round.'

Charlie washed his hands and face, and brushed his hair and went downstairs.

'We'll go and have a walk round,' Arthur said. 'Show you the sights.'

They walked down one long, grey street after another. The doorsteps, Charlie noticed, looked scrubbed clean, many of them edged with a neat white band.

'White stone,' Arthur said. 'The women put it round the steps after they've scrubbed them. 'Makes it look neat.' He gave a short, humourless laugh. 'They often scrub their bit of the pavement as well,' he said. 'Cleanliness is next to godliness, you know.' He paused for a moment. 'It's the only way most of them have of keeping their dignity.'

They walked on. 'Do you have any brothers or sisters?' Charlie asked.

'My sister's married and my brother's just joined the army,' Arthur said. 'Just in time to get his head blown off.' He smiled. 'You'll meet my father tonight. You'll have to be prepared for my father. He's Labour to the bone. You'll be getting a party political lecture probably.'

A group of children ran shrieking along the street, many of them, Charlie noticed, in ill-fitting old clothes, and some of them without shoes. 'Look at them,' Arthur said. 'It's a disgrace.'

'Yes,' Charlie said. 'It is.' He was aware of a deep shame.

They came to a small municipal park, some green lawns, sparsely planted flower-beds and a tree or two.

'Here we have the only breathing space,' Arthur said with heavy sarcasm, 'for the workers to relax. But can the children play here? No.' He pointed to the signs: KEEP OFF THE GRASS. 'And there's a park keeper employed to make sure that they do. Can't have the workers' children running about on the grass or climbing the trees, can we? They might get above themselves.'

Charlie felt the isolation of the place. This empty park seemed to encapsulate the whole poverty-stricken desolation of it all. Instead of being a place of peace and beauty and colour and childhood joy, it seemed only to be an open wound in this grey place, a sop, grudging and ugly. It seemed significant to him that there was no one there. He thought of the Round Pond at home in Kensington Gardens, of the children with their mothers or their nannies sailing their little boats, riding their little tricycles, running on the grass. Truly a different world. And still the women cleaned and baked and strove to keep up standards, and the children laughed and played with whatever scraps they could find. It shouldn't be like this, he thought. It shouldn't be like this.

'We'd better get back and do some work,' Arthur said. 'That's what you've come for, isn't it? We'll start with Bernoulli's theorem and the theory of flight, construction and function of controls, and then we'll do the engine. I've got an old motorcycle engine in the yard that we can take to pieces. Give you some idea.'

'I'm very grateful, Arthur,' Charlie said. 'I've got to get into the RAF.'

'Oh, you'll get in,' Arthur said. 'That's what the university squadrons were for. They'll bite your hand off.' He kicked a stone and it went bouncing down the street. 'They'll go through pilots like a hot knife through butter.'

Charlie glanced at him, wondering if he meant what he said. 'You sound very pessimistic.'

'Realistic, Charlie. But knowledge is strength, so they say. So we'll give you a bit extra.'

Arthur's father came home from work in the evening. He was short and stocky, his hair cut very short. He shook Charlie's hand vigorously. Arthur's mother produced a large meat-and-potato pie and peas. She gave a smaller one to Arthur. 'Just go and give this to Mrs

Green,' she said. 'She's the old lady next door,' she said to Charlie. 'She hasn't got much.'

They sat at the kitchen table and Arthur's mother gave them each an enormous piece of pie. Charlie was suddenly very hungry. The scents of meat and potatoes and gravy and Mrs Blake's excellent pastry rose up.

'So you're going to join up, Charlie?' Mr Blake said. 'Going to be a flyer.'

Charlie nodded. 'If I can get in. Arthur's giving me some tips.'

'Your parents are doctors, are they?'

'Yes, both of them. They were in France in the last war.'

'War,' Mr Blake said. 'There's one thing if it happens – everybody will have jobs, even if it's only killing Germans.'

'That's a horrible thought,' Charlie said.

'Aye, it's a horrible world, Charlie. Look at the state we're in. I'm lucky, I've got a job, but thousands haven't. Look at the old lady next door. Wouldn't get enough to eat if the neighbours didn't help. And on this other side of us,' he pointed with his fork, 'eight children and out of work. Do you know what goes on?'

Arthur caught Charlie's eye and smiled, but his eyes were dark and thoughtful.

'The means test people come round,' Mr Blake went on, 'to see if there's anything they can be forced to sell to reduce the dole. They ask if the baby's breast fed, and if it is they knock off two shillings a week. Hundreds of boys try to get into the army to get fed, and a few years ago sixty-six per cent were rejected on medical grounds. Medical grounds! Starvation, more like.'

'I think Charlie's had enough of that, William,' Mrs Blake said.

'It's all right,' Charlie said. 'My parents feel the same and so do I. There has to be a better way. I was in Berlin a few months ago. There didn't seem to be much poverty, but I suppose I wouldn't have been shown that. They seem very prosperous, but there's something wrong there, something nasty.'

'I know,' Mr Blake said. He held his knife and fork upright on the table. 'The British aren't like that. We don't go in for extremes. We'll never be communist and Mosley and his blackshirts just make us laugh. But we want justice, and by God, after this war is over we'll get it, or we'll know the reason why.'

'Well, there's Arthur,' Mrs Blake said quietly. 'And boys and girls like him. They're going to change things.'

Mr Blake looked at his son, his face filled with pride and affection. 'That he will,' he said. 'Clever. First person in the family to go to university, and Cambridge at that. He'll change things.' Charlie glanced at Arthur's mother and saw her face fall and twist, love and pride replaced by raw, terrible fear.

Tessa arrived in the casualty department and was introduced by her father.

'We haven't much in at the moment,' the casualty officer said. 'A lady with a broken wrist – classic Colles fracture, fall on the outstretched hand. You can help me put on a back slab.' He showed her the X-ray.

'I've only just finished first year,' Tessa said, 'so I don't know anything really. But I would like to be of some use if there's a war.'

'You're at Cambridge,' Dan said. 'You won't have to do anything except get on with your work. No one would be depraved enough to bomb those irreplaceable old buildings.' Why are we talking about this, he thought, as if it's real?

'You don't know that, Dad,' she said, 'and I'll be at home in the vacations.'

'No,' was Dan's first thought. 'Not Tessa. Not both of them. She was just starting her life. Did it have to start like this? He thought of those girls in 1914, the things they had done, things they could never have imagined in those pre-war years; Amy had been there beside him, operating on the endless streams of men with ghastly wounds. He thought of the gently raised girls nursing in France, driving ambulances, carrying messages on motorbikes through the soaked and shell-rutted lanes, of the horror and the carnage. Did Tessa have to see that? He glanced at her. She seemed so calm. He comforted himself with the fact that she was only in the pre-clinical part of her training. She would be in Cambridge for the next two years. He would not even think of what might happen if the Germans invaded.

'I think we'll start with the basics,' the casualty officer said cheerfully. 'Controlling haemorrhage. How much anatomy have you done?'

'Only the arm and the leg,' she said, 'and a bit of head and neck.'

He smiled. 'That's a good start. 'You'll have a good idea where most of the major arteries are.'

Sara went to tea with Kathy again. They sat in the garden in the sunshine, drinking Kathy's mother's home-made lemonade.

'My mother says she's going to send me away if there's a war,' Kathy said, 'so I won't get bombed.'

Sara stared at her, round-eyed. 'Away where?'

'I've got an aunty in the country,' Kathy said, 'in Kent. My mum says there won't be any bombs there.'

Sara felt a moment of panic. 'But what about school?'

'My mum says that doesn't matter – I can go to school there. She just wants me out of London.'

Sara was shocked. She had never even thought of this possibility, that she might be sent away, deprived of her school when she had only just started, of everything she wanted to do. 'Well, I'm not going,' she said, 'whatever they do.'

'You might have to,' Kathy said. 'They might make you. I could ask my mum if you could come with me to Kent. That would be nice, wouldn't it?'

Sara went home on the bus, deeply upset. 'Mum,' she said, as soon as she stepped into the house, 'You won't send me away, will you?'

Nora looked puzzled. 'What are you talking about?'

'Kathy says her mother is going to send her away if there's a war. You won't send me away, will you?'

Nora paled. 'I don't know yet, dear,' she said. 'It depends what happens.' She looked at Sara for a few moments. There was no use any more in pretending that nothing was happening. The child seemed to have grown up suddenly, her face set and resolute.

'I'm not going,' Sara said. 'I'm not leaving home and I'm not leaving school.'

'I just want you to be safe,' Nora said. 'If the government thinks the children ought to be sent out of London, you'll have to go. They know more than we do. I won't have you being in danger. I couldn't live with that.'

Sara went up to her room. She laid her books out in an orderly row on her little table. For the first time, she felt frightened, not of a war or anything the Germans could do, but of the possibility that she would have to leave her school, be prevented from doing her studies, from getting to university. 'I'm not going,' she said out loud. 'They can't make me.'

Chapter Eight

1939

'Could I speak to you for a moment, Doctor?' Mrs Parks looked stressed, Amy thought. Of course she did – everyone was stressed.

'Of course you can, Edith,' Amy said. 'Come into the kitchen and we'll have a cup of tea.' They sat down at the kitchen table.

'It's my daughter,' Mrs Parks began. 'She's so worried about a war. She's writing to me nearly every day.'

'I know,' Amy said. 'We all are, Edith, aren't we? What can I do to help?'

'She says her husband will be called up for sure. He's only twenty-seven and he works in a chair factory in High Wycombe. That's not a reserved occupation. He'd have to go for certain.'

Amy thought she knew what was coming. 'I'm so sorry, Edith,' she said. 'It's a dreadful time.'

'She wants me to go and live with her if war breaks out,' Mrs Parks said. 'She says she can't manage the children on her own, especially with the baby.'

'I understand,' Amy said. 'Of course she can't.'

'She says she might have to get a job. She won't be able to manage on army pay.'

Oh God, Amy thought, every little thing, every life disrupted and spoiled and possibly ended. And for what? Her eyes filled with tears. 'Oh Edith,' she said. 'It's all so awful. How can anyone even contemplate it? Hitler must be mad.' Mrs Parks reached out and took her hand. For a few moments they sat in silence, hands joined, both mothers, both afraid.

'I'm so sorry,' Mrs Parks said. 'I don't want to leave you at a time like this. I've been really happy here, helping you, watching the children grow up. They've been good years.'

Amy wiped her eyes with her fingertips. 'I know, Edith. We'll miss you terribly, but you have to look after your own family.' She paused. 'Charlie says he's joining the air force if it happens. He's been learning to fly at Cambridge.'

'Oh. Little Charlie. It doesn't seem five minutes since ...' Mrs Parks closed her eyes for a moment. 'It hardly seems possible. All the children. I wish she hadn't had another baby. What a world to bring a baby into.'

'They'll be all right,' Amy said. 'You'll all be in the country. They won't be bombing there.'

'But suppose they get here – those Germans? They seem to go anywhere they want.'

'They won't.' Amy said firmly. 'We just have to believe they won't. We haven't been invaded since 1066 and we're certainly not going to let it happen now.'

'I lost my husband at the very end of the last war,' Mrs Parks said. 'Almost on the last day. All for nothing. My daughter never had a father. And now my grandchildren ...' Amy could find no words to comfort her. 'What would you do, Doctor? How would you manage?'

'Don't you worry, Edith,' Amy said. 'I'd have to find someone else. I'd miss you more than I can say, but I'll find someone.'

Mrs Parks got up. 'Maybe it won't happen. Maybe I won't have to go. We'd better get those blackout curtains made, though, just in case. I believe they've still got some stuff at John Lewis's. And we should lay in some candles and matches and some torch batteries.' She sighed. 'I'd better go and finish the dusting.'

Amy sat on for a few moments. She rubbed her brow with her fingertips. Edith was the kingpin of the house; she'd been a fine housekeeper and a reliable friend for ten years. She would have to find someone else who perhaps would live in, in Edith's little flat at the top of the house. Otherwise she wouldn't be able to work, and God only knew how bad it might get, how much and how many doctors might be needed.

*

The days wore on through August. Dan went off to work each day, Amy did her surgeries and clinics and visited her patients with a kind of mechanical efficiency. The atmosphere was extraordinary, tension and apprehension were everywhere. Some of the mothers in her clinics were close to panic. 'What will we do? We'll have to send the children away, to the country, Canada, Australia, anywhere away from here. Will we ever see them again?' She could share the pictures that were in their heads, the pictures that had been in the papers of dying men and women and children in Spain after the German bombing. She thought of the Jewish children, sent alone to England by their agonized parents to escape the horrors of Germany. Surely it couldn't happen here?

Not knowing was the worst thing, she thought. If you knew what was going to happen, you could prepare yourself; prepare your mind and your actions. Otherwise imagination could run riot. She saw the physical preparations all around her – trenches dug for air-raid shelters in the parks, barrage balloons tethered, ready to be raised, shops running out of heavy black fabric for blackout curtains and sticky tape for the windows to stop flying glass. There were already men in the streets with bells and rattles and tin hats, ready to give the alarm if there was poison gas. That frightened her the most. She remembered all too clearly the men in the last war, gassed horribly in the trenches. Surely to God they wouldn't do that to the children? The country seemed to be moving steadily to an inevitable and terrifying future.

The twins seemed to be extraordinarily cheerful, Charlie now as obsessed with flying as Tessa was with medicine. Of course they saw the danger; they must. But they were so full of life, of optimism, of the absolute youthful certainty that life would go on for ever. They put me to shame, she thought. I must be as they are. I must forget the last war. This is a new challenge. It will not be the same. But why? Why, twice in one lifetime?

'We're going out on Friday night,' Charlie said one day. 'We're going to the Café de Paris. It's Rob's birthday.'

They came downstairs that evening, looking so young and so happy and so handsome that Amy's heart turned over; Charlie was in a dinner jacket and Tessa in her blue evening dress, silky, bias cut, clingy around the hips and swirling out below. They are beautiful, she thought, as all young people are – beautiful in their promise, not children any more, and not quite adults either – somewhere in between. How was that bridge to be made? Gently, with time, or a bitter wrench from one to the other?

'You both look lovely,' Amy said. 'Have a good time.'

'Oh, we will.' Tessa kissed her cheek. 'Don't worry, if they drop a bomb on us, we'll be all right – the C de P is underground.'

Amy paled. 'Don't joke, darling.'

Tessa grinned. 'What else can you do? Come on, Charlie. The taxi's waiting.'

They arrived at the Café de Paris and walked down the long steep staircase to the small dance floor with the tables around it. The band was playing a version of *Moonlight Serenade*. Their friends were waiting. 'Good band,' Rob said.

'I love Glen Miller,' Tessa said. 'Cheers you up like mad.'

Rob grimaced. 'We could do with cheering up. I hope I actually live to see my next birthday.'

'None of that,' Charlie said. 'Of course you will. You can come and live here, underground, like a mole. Spend the whole war safely tucked away in the C de P.'

Rob laughed. 'Hope they've got enough champagne to last.'

'Well they've got enough for tonight,' Charlie said. 'Let's dance. Eat, drink and be merry.'

'Shut up, Charlie.' Tessa said. 'Don't finish it.'

Amy and Dan sat over their coffee in the sitting room. Dan looked grey and drawn. He looks older, Amy thought. Weary.

'What's happened, darling?' she said. 'Something new?'

'We've been ordered to clear all beds of chronic cases,' he said, 'move them out of London. They want those fifty thousand beds for civilian casualties, just for a start, and God knows if that will be enough. Some people seem to think we'll need hundreds of thousands. They're putting huts up in the hospital grounds to make more wards.

It doesn't bear thinking about.' He took Amy's hand and drew her close. 'Do you want to leave London, darling? You could go to your father in Kent. He'll be safe there, in the country. I'd feel better if you did.'

'Not on your life,' she said. 'I'm staying here. I'll be needed, and anyway I think we should stay together. I'm not leaving you, whatever happens. We've got to be here, always, for the children – when they come home.'

'Yes,' he said. 'I thought you would say that.'

She looked up at him. 'Do you think I should go back to surgery? I could do some retraining.'

'No,' he said. 'If it happens, this time it'll be a civilian's war as well. We'll need the family doctors. The common things will still go on – people will have babies, the kids will still get sticky ears and measles and chickenpox. They'll all have to be looked after even more.'

She leant against his shoulder, solid and comforting. 'The Ministry's survey of London GPs is in,' she said, 'about whether we'd work under emergency conditions. Ninety per cent of them say they would stay. I'm not going to be among the bolters.'

He kissed the top of her head. 'We'll do it together then, like we did before.'

Charlie came home from a weekend in Cambridge looking very pleased with himself.

'I've done it, Dad,' he said, 'I've done my cross country and passed the papers. I've got my licence. I am a pilot, of sorts.'

Dan shook his hand. 'Well done, Charlie. Very well done. We'll tell your mother. I think it's an occasion for a glass of champagne.'

'Clever old you, Charlie,' Tessa said. 'You're a star. Old Biggles Charlie.'

Amy hugged him. 'What did you have to do, darling?'

'Some papers,' he said, 'about navigation and weather and air law and stuff. And a flying test and a cross-country flight.'

'Where did you have to fly to,' Amy asked, 'on your cross country?'

'Birmingham,' Charlie said. 'There and back.'

'How do you ever find your way?'

Charlie laughed. 'I've got a compass, Mum,' he said, 'and a map.' He grinned. 'And you can't really miss Birmingham.'

She raised her glass. 'Here's to you then, Charlie.'

'Flying's wonderful, Mum,' he said. His face was alive, alight. 'I'd like to do it for the rest of my life, for my job.'

Yes, she thought, yes. He's found what he wants. 'Would they let you do that in the RAF?' she said, 'as a career?'

'No, not as I got older. You have to be young to fly combat planes, but Arthur says there'll be a lot of commercial flying in the future, passenger planes all over the world. Especially if this man Whittle develops his new engine. I'd like to be a commercial pilot.'

Amy deliberately formed a picture in her mind of Charlie, dressed in a smart uniform with a peaked cap, not a flying helmet, walking out to a great aircraft, settling himself into a comfortable cockpit, flying between peaceful countries in safety and pleasure. She made the picture as real as she could. She saw him as older, more mature, a family man. This was the picture she would hold in her mind, whatever happened. Thoughts were things; thoughts were things.

Later, Charlie managed to get his father alone. 'I'm joining the RAF Volunteer Reserve, Dad. That's what its all been for.'

Dan took him in his arms and held him for a moment. 'I know, son,' he said. 'We're both very proud of you – your mother and I.'

On the twenty-first of August Dan came home early. 'You know what's happened?' he said.

Amy nodded, holding out the evening paper, the headlines stark and bleak. The Russians had signed a non-aggression pact with Hitler – the last thing anyone had expected.

'That'll leave Hitler free to do what he likes in Europe.' Dan said. 'Now that he won't be fighting the Russians. It doesn't get any better, does it?'

'There's something else,' Amy said. 'I've had a letter telling me to be prepared to go to Paddington Station at short notice to help with the evacuation of the children.' She bit her lips. 'Short notice, Dan.' He took her in his arms and held her close.

*

The family was in the kitchen, having breakfast; Mrs Parks was frying eggs and bacon. The wireless was on, as usual. It was on all the time these days. For Amy it held a kind of fascinating horror – she had to listen, but dreaded what she might hear. September the first, she thought; the year was dragging on. The appalling news was given in a very calm, very unemotional way. At dawn, the German army had invaded Poland. The Prime Minister had ordered the mobilization of all forces.

Dan turned the wireless off. For a few moments no one said anything, then Charlie blew his breath out through his teeth. 'That's it then,' he said. 'It's started.'

'Not yet,' Amy said, her voice cracking. 'Not yet. There might still be some way....'

Charlie put his arm around her shoulders and gave her a squeeze. Then he went out into the sunlit garden. He wasn't sure how he felt. His mother, he was sure, was wrong; there was no way out now. In a way it was a kind of relief – better to know what was to happen and be prepared. Was he prepared? It wasn't the flying. He was more than prepared for that. Was he prepared to kill? Now it was not theoretical; it was real. He turned back to look at the house. He could see his family through the window. He could see his father with his arm around Tessa's shoulders; he could see Mrs Parks with her face in her hands, and his mother bending over her, speaking to her. His family. His home. Yes, he thought, yes, I would be prepared. I will have no choice.

Tessa came out to join him. She gave a hesitant smile. 'What happens now, Charlie?'

'Nothing for you, Tess,' he said. 'Go back to Cambridge, carry on as normal. I'm going to be called up, of course. I'll still have a lot of training to do. Flying a Spit or a Hurricane is a bit different from flying a Tiger Moth.'

'I wish I could do more,' Tessa said. 'I feel so useless.'

'Don't be daft,' he said. 'You'll be of enormous use when you're trained. Vital. We'll always need doctors. You'll have to put it all together again – after the war.'

'And when do you think that will be?'

'God knows,' he said. 'It isn't going to be easy, not if what I saw in Berlin is anything to go by.'

'What will we do, Charlie? What will they do?'

He smiled. 'They'll lose, of course. They're far too nasty to win. We can't let them do that.'

'Oh Charlie,' she said.

He took her hands in his. 'Listen,' he said. 'I've every intention of coming through this, but if I don't …'

Her eyes filled with tears. 'No Charlie,' she said, 'don't even say it. We're not at war yet.'

'If I don't, you'll look after the parents, won't you? Especially Mum.'

'Charlie. Please!'

'It's all right,' he said. 'It won't happen. I only said if.' She let go of his hands and walked down to the bottom of the garden. He could see her shoulders shaking. He went after her and put his arm around her. 'I'm sorry,' he said. 'It was a daft thing to say. It won't happen. Come on, no tears. Let's go in. Don't let Mum see you crying.'

He thought suddenly of Kurt. What was he doing now? Joining up probably, like everyone else. What service would he be in? The German air force, perhaps? He'd be fighting Kurt – what a crazy thought. What a bizarre, stupid world.

His parents and Mrs Parks were still in the kitchen. 'There's no point in me going back to Cambridge,' Charlie said. 'Even if I'm not called up yet.' His mother was about to protest, he could see that, but his father intervened.

'I think you're right, Charlie,' Dan said, 'unless there's a miracle. You'd better write to your college. I expect they'll have some system of letting you finish your degree afterwards.'

'If I want to go back,' Charlie said.

Nora and Sara took the bus to Paddington station. 'I don't want to go, Mum,' Sara said. 'The school isn't closing. The teachers are going to carry on.'

Those that will still be there, Nora thought darkly. Those that haven't been called up.

'Your friend, Kathy, is going away, isn't she?' Nora was trying very hard not to cry, but it was a struggle. She could feel the tears pricking, and she didn't want Sara to see. 'I'm not having you in any danger. I wouldn't be able to go on.'

Sara stared out of the window. She was filled with an overwhelming anger, anger at the Germans, anger at the thought of having to leave her mum, losing her place at school, and dread that everything was so messed up that she could never get it back. Other dreads she couldn't really imagine – bombs dropping, houses falling down, people being hurt or killed. That didn't seem real. Having to go away was real. And her father going away to be a sailor or a soldier. She couldn't imagine her dad harming anyone. All because of the Germans. Why couldn't somebody just stop them?

'I just want to be at home with you and Dad,' she said. 'Not with strangers. And I'll worry about you if I'm not there. I don't care what happens.'

'Well I care.' Nora took Sara's hand. 'You're everything in the world to me, Sara. Just do it for me, so I'll know you're safe. I'm sure they'll find you somewhere nice to stay.'

'Suppose I don't like them, or they don't like me?'

'They will.' She took a pound note out of her handbag. 'Here, take this. Hide it somewhere. Just in case you ever need it.'

Sara held it in her hand. She had never had a whole pound before, just for herself. It seemed unreal, just like everything else that was happening. 'Where shall I put it?'

'Put it in one of your books for the moment. Find a good hiding-place when you get there.'

They arrived at the station. Nora couldn't believe what she was seeing. A constant stream of children was moving over the footbridge to the mainline station. The noise was loud and disturbing – a noise, Nora realized, she had never heard before – the sound of hundreds and hundreds of confused and frightened children. A friendly voice, intended no doubt to be comforting, was repeating over the loud-speakers, 'Hello children. Please go quickly to the train and sit down. Do not play with the doors or the windows.' The platforms were teeming, tiny five-year-olds were looking bewildered, many of the older children were crying, mothers were crying, some of the older boys were misbehaving, running about, jumping and wrestling. There was a pungent smell, the burning coal and oil and steam from the engines, and here and there were little groups of children who, Nora thought, wrinkling her nose, could do with a good wash. The ladies from the WVS, in their dark-green uniforms, were trying to bring order to the apparent chaos.

What a mess, Nora thought. What a heart-breaking mess. The children had their gas-masks slung over their shoulders, carried battered cases or bags for their little possessions, and a teddy bear, a doll. The little ones had labels with their names and home addresses; just, Nora thought, like little abandoned parcels, being posted God knows where. She had never imagined in all her life that she would see scenes like this.

Am I doing the right thing, she thought? She looked around her, really, really frightened. The bombs didn't seem real – not yet – but these dreadful scenes, frightened children, sobbing mothers, these were real and terrible. It's Hell, she thought, Hell come to earth, families torn apart, children leaving. But anything – anything – was better than Sara being hurt.

Sara looked up at her mother's distraught face and knew that she would have to go. She flung her arms around her. 'Oh Mum!'

Nora hugged her, holding her tight. 'Fill in that post card right away and let us know where you are. And write to me. I'll come and see you. I promise.' Sara nodded miserably. 'Help the little ones if you can.' She watched Sara disappear into the maelstrom, her satchel and gas-mask over her shoulder, her little case in her hand. The satchel dragged her shoulder down – books, books. She turned away in despair.

Amy had been at the station since early morning, just waiting in case she was needed. So far she'd treated a couple of grazed knees and a mother who had fainted. She was surprised that more of them hadn't fainted. It was unspeakably stressful. Those little five-year-olds would break your heart, whole classes together with their teachers, most of them looking around for their mothers.

She saw Nora across the heads of the children, and saw her distress. She made her way to her through the throng. 'Mrs Lewis, isn't it?'

Nora was startled. 'Oh, Doctor Fielding.' She paused, and took a deep breath. 'I've just been saying goodbye to my Sara.'

'I'm so sorry,' Amy said. 'It must be terrible for you.'

Nora was crying, blinking, trying to hide it. 'I expect it's worse if you've got really little ones.'

'Sara sounds like a sensible girl,' Amy said. 'She'll be all right, I'm sure.'

'She's mad at me,' Nora said. 'She didn't want to leave her school. She wants to be a doctor – I told you, didn't I?'

'Yes, I remember,' Amy said. 'Did she get the *Gray's Anatomy?*'

Nora nodded. 'She's taken a bit of it with her.'

A train pulled out of the station, steaming and clanking, and the platform began to clear a little. Nora began to shake. Her face drained.

'Come to the tea room with me,' Amy said, 'and have a cup of tea. I could do with one myself.' She spoke to one of the green-clad ladies to tell her where she would be if she were needed.

They walked along the platform to the tea room and Nora sat down shakily at one of the small wooden tables. It was cluttered and messy with used cups and saucers. Amy ordered tea at the counter. She watched as Nora got up to clear the table, carrying the used cups to the counter, then as she borrowed a cloth to wipe the top. She obviously liked things neat and tidy.

'We haven't had a minute to clear,' the woman said behind the counter. 'It's been pandemonium this morning. Those poor kids.'

Amy brought the tea. 'Are you going to stay in London, Mrs Lewis?' she asked.

Nora nodded. 'It's Sara – her school. She might be able to go back to it one day. She wouldn't want me to move.'

'Will your husband be with you? Is he in a reserved occupation?'

'No. He's a carpenter. He wants to volunteer for the Navy.'

'You'll be on your own, then?'

Nora looked down at her cooling tea. 'Yes, I'll be on my own. Too much time to think.' She sipped her tea. 'I'll probably get a job. I'll need the money.'

Amy was thoughtful. 'What did you do before you were married? Did you have a job then?'

'Yes,' Nora said. 'I was in service when I was fourteen. Then when I got older I was a sort of under housekeeper.' She gave her first little smile. 'We had a very good cook. She taught me a lot.'

I wonder, Amy thought. Getting a new housekeeper wasn't going to be easy. She'd think it over, perhaps make some excuse to visit Mrs Lewis's house to see what it was like. She might not want that sort of job. There would be lots of work going. Still it might be an idea worth thinking about.

They finished their tea. 'I'd better get back,' Amy said. 'Will you be all right now?'

Nora nodded. 'Yes, thank you, Doctor.'

Sara left the train with a group of other children, shepherded by a green-clad lady. This station was very small, she thought, only two lines, and a level crossing. She looked around her. Beyond the station were green fields and woods, and sheep and cows. It seemed terribly quiet.

They were led down the village street. The village seemed to be very small, after London. The fields came right down behind the houses and she could hear the sheep calling. But where's the school, she thought? Where am I going to school?

They came to the school, a small, low building with BOYS over one door, and GIRLS over the other. Ancient, she thought. Totally ancient.

There were several women already waiting in one of the classrooms, plump, kindly-looking women. 'Oh, the poor children,' one of them said. Sara looked more critically at the other children. Some of them looked poor indeed, with their ill-fitting clothes and battered plimsolls. The little ones looked tired out and some of them were crying for their mothers.

'These ladies are going to look after you, children,' the WVS lady said. 'Now, ladies, which one do you want?'

The little ones went first, hugged and clucked over. Sara was the oldest and the last. 'It looks as if you're mine,' the woman said. 'My name is Mrs Brooks. What's yours?'

'Sara Lewis.'

'Come along then, Sara.' She led Sara to a house on the edge of the village. It seemed to be bigger than most of the others, and had a big garden. She took Sara up to her room. It was a nice room, Sara thought, flowery paper on the walls and a rug on the wooden floor.

'I think you'll be comfortable here,' Mrs Brooks said. 'I'm glad I've got you. I don't think I could have coped with little children – I've never had any of my own.'

'It's very nice,' Sara said. 'Thank you.'

'Put your things away, and then come down to tea. There's just you and me at the moment. Is there anything you want?'

'I just want to know where I'm going to school,' Sara said. 'I have to go to school.'

Mrs Brooks smiled. 'Of course you do. I expect it'll be the village school, though I don't know how they'll cope with all these new children.'

Mrs Brooks went downstairs. Sara sat on the edge of her bed. Mrs Brooks seemed very nice, but not the village school! What was she going to do? She took the pound note out of her satchel and put it under the mattress.

On 3 September the family gathered round the wireless to hear the Prime Minister's statement at 11.15. They knew what was going to happen. Everyone in the country knew now.

Mrs Parks was crying. 'We know what he's going to say,' she said. Amy took her hand. The words fell, spreading and staining, like drops of blood. 'This country is now at war with Germany.' They played the National Anthem. The family sat for a few moments in silence.

Charlie felt emotion stir, strong enough to bring the start of tears, hurriedly controlled, emotions of patriotism, loyalty, a desire to prove himself. That's it, he thought. I'll probably be called up tomorrow.

'I must ring Granddad,' Amy said. 'He'll be devastated.'

Dan got up. 'We all need a drink,' he said. 'Get the glasses, Tessa. We'll have some champagne. We'll drink to our country, to England, and the rest.' He brought the bottle from the cellar, undid the wire and eased off the cork. He poured the wine. He stood up, holding his glass. 'To us,' he said. 'To our country, to our fighting men, including Charlie, and to victory.'

Before they had time to taste the wine the loud wailing of the local air-raid siren began to howl, up and down, up and down, echoed by others, one after the other, chilling the blood. They gasped, looking at each other, shocked and anxious.

'Good God,' Dan said. 'Already? They don't lose any time, do they? They must have been just waiting for this. Into the cellar everyone.' They trooped down the cellar steps. Dan switched on the light. 'What a mess down here,' he said. 'We'll have to clear it out, Charlie, make it fit to live in. We might be spending a lot of time down here by the sound of it.' They perched on bags and boxes, silent, listening. Amy wondered whether anyone could actually hear her heart beating. Her body was tense, waiting for the next sound, sounds she remembered from the war in France: the drone of aircraft, the crashing roar of anti-aircraft guns, the scream of a falling bomb.

Ten minutes later the siren started again, the long continuous note of the All-Clear. There was a sigh that seemed to come from all of them, from the house itself. They trooped up the steps again.

'False alarm,' Dan said. He handed round the champagne again. 'Can you believe it? I wonder what bloody idiot decided to go for a little pleasure flight today, of all days. Set the whole country off. Lucky if he didn't get himself shot down.'

So it's begun, Amy thought. All over again. Blackout – fortunately they'd got the curtains made – rationing, danger, air raids, crouching in the cellar, and awful, painful goodbyes. Oh Charlie!

Chapter Nine

1939

Amy opened her eyes on to a new world, one that she had hoped she would never see again. Dan was already awake.

'Mrs Parks will be going,' she said. 'I'll have to find someone else, very soon.'

'Tessa's home for a few weeks yet,' Dan said. 'She can help.'

Amy sighed. 'She can help with the housework, but I don't know about cooking. There's a woman – a patient – that I was wondering about. She used to be a housekeeper before she married. I might pop in and see her – see what she's like at home.'

'Good idea,' Dan said.

'Her husband will be called up, so she might be thinking about a job. Her little girl has been evacuated. She's the little girl I told you about – the one who wants to be a doctor.'

'Oh,' Dan said. 'That might be interesting.'

'I don't know,' Amy said. 'All the children. It's unbelievable. God knows what's going to happen now.'

He put his arm around her. 'Don't, darling. You were so strong last time. Don't give up now.'

'I didn't have children last time,' she said.

He held her close. 'We'll get through,' he said. 'We'll all get through. Have faith, Amy.'

Amy drove to the Harrow Road. It was strangely quiet without the children, without the laughter and the shouts and the running about. All the life seemed to have gone out of the world and the streets were silent and empty. The morning surgery was packed. Most of the

116

women wanted contraceptive advice. 'I don't want to get pregnant now,' they said, one after the other. 'I don't know how I'll manage as it is with my husband away, and I don't want to bring another child into all this.'

The mothers were anxious and strained and some of them were openly crying, desperately missing their children, afraid for the future. She found that it needed all her control not to cry herself. Which is worse, she thought, to say goodbye to your little children who need you so much, or to say goodbye to Charlie and all the other boys, knowing the danger they were facing, wondering if she would ever see him again?

After the surgery she did her home visits. There were very few children to see; very few of the mothers had chosen to keep them at home and the false alarm siren on the day war was declared had frightened everyone to death. She saw three of her old ladies, living in the tenements, all anxious and alone. 'What am I going to do, Doctor?' they said, one after the other. 'How am I going to manage?' It was going to be one of her jobs, keeping a regular eye on them. The lady with the pigeons was unperturbed. She looked at the photograph on her chest of drawers. 'Perhaps I'll see my boy again sooner than I thought,' she said. The pigeons looked down on her, silent and broody as ever. Lucky pigeons, Amy thought. They can just fly away, find a nice safe place and forget it all.

She drove to Mrs Lewis's house. She felt guilty, coming to Mrs Lewis's home like this to check up on her housekeeping, but there was really no other way to find out. And anyway, Mrs Lewis might not want the job.

Perhaps, she thought, she would be better advised to go to an agency, but things were in such confusion. She would prefer someone she knew, even slightly, and someone who lived close by and knew the area. Mrs Lewis could even live at home if she wanted to. She seemed so devoted to her daughter, so determined to give her a better life. She was obviously a woman who was thoughtful and caring.

She arrived at the house and parked outside. The knocker was polished, she noticed, the windows shining and the doorstep scrubbed clean.

She knocked at the door. Nora opened it, obviously surprised to see the doctor there. Amy watched her face tighten suddenly in panic. 'What's happened?' she said. 'What is it? Is it Sara?'

Amy was momentarily shocked that she could have upset Mrs Lewis so easily and so much. She should have realized that her immediate response would be to assume that something had happened to her daughter. 'No, no,' she said. 'I'm so sorry if I frightened you, Mrs Lewis. I've just come to see if you are all right. You seemed so upset at the station. I was just passing, so I thought I'd pop in.'

'Oh.' Nora smiled, a relieved, a worried smile, and opened the door wide. 'Come in, Doctor.'

I should have realized that it would upset her, Amy thought. The whole atmosphere, everywhere, was of fear, expecting bad news, expecting the worst. The country had changed at a stroke, peace and safety gone in an instant. Any bizarre, imagined catastrophe could turn out to be true.

Nora led Amy into the kitchen. It was tidy and spotless, the lino shining with shellac polish. 'I'm all right,' Nora said. 'It was just saying goodbye to Sara, and seeing all those children – all those little ones. It's so cruel. It's so wicked.'

'You're right,' Amy said. 'It is cruel and wicked.'

'Sit down, Doctor.' Nora said. 'Would you like a cup of tea?'

'I'd love one,' Amy said, quite truthfully. That morning had been very stressful, very emotional, very cruel. She watched as Nora warmed the teapot, measured in the tea, poured on the boiling water, and got out two fine china teacups and a milk jug and sugar basin. 'Don't go to any trouble, Mrs Lewis,' she said.

'It's no trouble.' Nora poured milk into the jug.

'I don't take sugar,' Amy said.

'Neither do I.' Nora sat down at the table. 'I told you about Sara, didn't I? She didn't want to go. She didn't want to leave her school. But I couldn't risk ...'

'Of course you couldn't,' Amy said. 'You did the right thing, at least until we know what's happening.'

Nora was close to tears. 'You've got children, haven't you, Doctor?'

'Yes,' Amy said. 'My girl is a medical student.' She paused. 'And my boy is joining the Air Force. He's a pilot.' Nora's silence was more expressive than words could ever be. 'What will you do?' Amy said. 'Are you still planning to stay here?'

'Yes,' Nora said. 'My husband's already volunteered for the Navy. I want to be here for Sara – when she comes back.'

'I feel just the same,' Amy said. 'I'm not leaving my home either.'

'I don't know what to do about her now,' Nora said wearily. 'Maybe I should tell her to forget it all – all this being a doctor. My husband's against it. How could we ever manage it? And we don't know how long this war is going to last. He says I'm just fooling myself, and her. But she's so set on it. I don't know what to do. What would you do?'

'Let her try,' Amy said. 'Maybe it won't work out, but at least she should try. We don't know what's going to happen. We'll all have to cling to our hopes for the future. Things might be different after the war.'

'And when will that be?' Nora said. 'It's only just begun.'

Amy drank her tea and got up to go. 'Don't make her give up her dream,' she said. God knows, she thought, it might be all we have. 'I'll look out some more books for her. At least she can feel she's learning something.'

'I don't know what kind of school they'll put her in,' Nora said. 'She'll go mad if it's no good.'

Amy got into her car and drove past the rows of houses. She could see people at the windows, taping up strips of brown sticky paper to stop flying glass, and making sure the blackout curtains met in the middle. A man in a steel helmet with ARP on the front rode past her on a bicycle, his gas-mask over his shoulder. Air Raid Precautions. Gas precautions. Everyone had a gas-mask now. Everyone was obliged to take it everywhere. The streetlights had already been shut off, making this great blacked-out city a strange, fearful place to be at night. She drove home through the silent, childless streets.

She went to visit her father. 'I can't believe it, Amy,' he said. 'Not again.' He looked older, she thought, defeated and lost. 'Come and live here, Amy, away from London.'

'I can't, Father,' she said, 'I'll be needed there.'

His eyes filled with tears. 'It's just the same,' he said, 'all of you in danger. It's the same nightmare, all over again.'

'You can come and stay with us if you like, Father,' she said, 'but you'll be safer here in Kent, away from any bombing We'll keep in touch with you, all the time.'

'It isn't right,' he said. He was trembling. 'Not again. And Charlie in the Air Force. Not again.'

We are walking a tightrope, Amy thought, waiting for them to come and shake us down. Everyone expected the onslaught to start at any moment, but still they didn't come. The Germans didn't come. But they were there – oh yes, they were there. On the 18 September, the aircraft carrier, *Courageous*, was sunk with a loss of 500 lives, and the Glasgow liner *Athena* was sunk with 112 lives lost.

'And we're dropping leaflets on Germany,' Dan said. 'Leaflets! And our esteemed air minister has refused to bomb the Black Forest on the grounds that it's private property!'

It seemed that death would not wait. Dan was horrified at the number of road accidents in the deep blackout. The surgeons were already working long hours, and the wards were filling up.

'This is just road accidents, Amy,' he said. 'Just the beginning. We're moving the theatres down into the basement, the cancer hospitals are burying the radium. They're even killing the poisonous snakes at the zoo. And look at this advertisement in the paper. They're asking people to send in their binoculars. We haven't even got enough binoculars. We're just not ready for this.'

Then, filtering through from the hospital grapevine, he heard a rumour of some dreadful mistake, some hideous mix-up involving the Air Force: British planes shooting at each other, a pilot killed. He didn't know the details, and apparently it was totally hush-hush, but something had gone terribly wrong. He very deliberately kept it from Amy. The details would leak out sooner or later. She didn't need to know now.

Charlie stayed at home, sitting around, or pacing about like a caged tiger. He went for walks, watching them manning anti-aircraft guns in

Hyde Park and Holland Park. He wondered what it would be like flying bombers, flying through this barrage, and over a hostile country.

It all added to his impatience. 'What a waste of time,' he said. 'Why don't they get on with it? I'll have a lot more training to do. I can't fight a war in a Tiger Moth.'

'You can help with the garden while you're waiting,' Amy said. 'Mr Hodge is digging the beds over. We'll be growing vegetables next year. We'll need the all the food we can grow. We're bound to be rationed.'

'OK,' he said. 'It'll be something to do.'

Amy watched him in the garden in his shirtsleeves, young and strong and full of energy. He's nineteen, she thought. Only nineteen. His life has hardly begun. But she could see how he had changed, how manhood had come to him already, thrust upon him too soon. He seemed to have filled out more, perhaps he was even a little taller. She remembered Dan in the last war, how he had changed from the diffident, rather shy young man she had first met, to a tough, hardened soldier. Not a fighting soldier: a surgeon, but a soldier nevertheless. Did it change me, she thought? It must have. But the only change she could feel was one of fearfulness, fear that the horrors she had seen in France could come again. How must the French be feeling now, she thought, with the memory of their ravaged country still clear in their minds? Perhaps I'm tougher than I was, she thought. She sighed. Who could tell? She had never imagined that she would ever be tested again. Whatever happens, she thought, we'll just have to deal with it, like we did before.

Dan found Charlie in the garden. 'I've brought you some lemonade,' he said. 'Come and sit down.' Charlie sat beside him on the garden bench. 'I think we should have a chat,' Dan said, 'before you leave.'

Charlie grinned. 'What about, Dad?'

Dan smiled briefly. 'What do you think?'

'I think I know what goes on, Dad,' Charlie said. He coloured a little. 'Theoretically, as yet.'

'Wars are different, Charlie. The same standards don't apply. Things get looser, less controlled. One tends to live in the moment, whatever that implies.'

'Well, let's not beat about the bush, Dad. You think I'm going to jump into bed with anything that comes along?'

'I don't know, Charlie. You might.'

'Did you?'

'No, of course not,' Dan said. 'But I knew more about the consequences than most. We had to give lectures to the boys about venereal diseases.'

'And you're going to give me one now.'

'Not a lecture, Charlie. Just a warning. At least we have sulphonamides now for gonorrhoea but it doesn't stop reinfection. Be careful, and use a sheath. And don't ever ignore the symptoms – pain passing urine and cloudy pee. And syphilis gives you a rash. And don't ever be too embarrassed to ask me about it.'

'Dad,' Charlie said. 'It's the last thing I'll be thinking about.'

Later, in his room, he realized that it wasn't quite true. He thought about girls a lot. They all did – all the boys. As far as he knew, none of his friends had been to bed with a girl. It was all talk, really, or just a bit of fumbling about in the dark. You were supposed to wait until you got married, which seemed reasonable to him. He was far more frightened of getting a girl pregnant and having to marry her than of getting VD, though he imagined that would be fairly horrible. Not to do it – that was the answer. Wait until you're married.

He lay on his bed, his hands behind his head. Flying. That was the thing. He must get into fighters. He wanted to fly a Spitfire more than anything – more than girls, even. He tried to imagine being in a dogfight, and couldn't. It was going to happen though. It was coming. It rather put girl friends in the shade. He sat up, ran his hand through his hair. Am I going to be frightened? Am I going to be able to do it, again and again? He wanted to go at once, wanted to face it at once, get that first time over with. Then we'd see. It was the waiting that was bad.

The summons came at last. Charlie was confirmed in his rank of pilot officer and ordered to report to St Leonards to an Initial Training Wing for further training. Amy and Tessa went with him to the station. It was alive with young men again, carrying their suitcases and gasmasks, saying goodbye to their families. Everything she did seemed to recall the past. She remembered standing on Victoria station, saying goodbye to her father when she left for France in the Great War. Now she knew how he'd felt. She hugged Charlie close. 'Telephone tonight if you can, darling. Keep in touch, all the time.'

'I'll be all right Mum,' he said. 'I'll only be training.' He kissed her cheek and got into the train. 'I'll see you soon.' The train pulled away, out of the station. The next time I see him, she thought, he'll be in uniform.

She and Tessa drove home and Tessa made some tea. 'I feel so useless, Mum,' she said. 'Girls will be doing all kinds of things and I'll be doing nothing – just going on as if nothing has happened.'

'Life has to go on,' Amy said. 'The war won't last for ever. Your job is to qualify. You'll be of use then.'

'Well, I can help a bit in the vacations,' Tessa said. 'I can be a volunteer firewatcher at a hospital or something. It was in the paper.'

Amy sighed. 'Yes, darling.'

Charlie arrived at St Leonards on Sea to join the Wing. They were to be housed, apparently, in one of the hotels. He got a taxi from the station and joined the group of young men trooping into the hotel: all pilots, he supposed. He wondered how many of them wanted to fly fighters. Competition.

They were given their rooms, and a pep talk and their schedules. There was to be no flying for a few weeks. A groan ran round the room. They were to be introduced into the service as pilot officers, drilling, lectures, and endless PE with a tough-looking gentleman who was a very successful British boxer. No nonsense there then.

He met some of the other pilots in the lounge. 'No flying,' one of them said gloomily. He was tall and fair-haired with eyelids that drooped over an expression of sardonic amusement.

Charlie introduced himself. 'Charlie Fielding,' he said.

'Tim Crighton.' They shook hands. 'Perhaps they'll let us out after dinner, and we can find a pub.'

'A nice thought,' Charlie said, 'but it isn't going to happen – not until the weekend anyway.'

They met again after dinner. 'We can get a beer here,' Tim said. 'What'll you have?'

'Half a pint,' Charlie said. Tim ordered it, and a pint for himself.

'Well, here we are then,' Tim said. 'How did you get into this racket?'

'I learnt to fly at Cambridge – in the air squadron,' Charlie said. 'Then I joined the volunteer reserve.'

'Same here,' Tim said, 'at Oxford.'

'Did you get your degree?' Charlie asked. 'I left early.'

'I'm nineteen,' Tim said. 'So no.'

'What were you reading?'

Tim grinned. 'God knows. I've forgotten. Have another?'

'No thanks,' Charlie said, 'it'll keep me awake.'

'I don't know what all this is for,' Tim said. 'Square bashing and knees bend. Sounds like a waste of time to me. We should be flying.'

'Get us fit, I expect,' Charlie said. 'And what they said – introduce us to service life, discipline, and all that.'

'If you've been to a public school you know all about that,' Tim said. 'Mine was a shocker. I nearly got thrown out. Ill-disciplined behaviour.'

Charlie thought of Arthur. 'A lot of the chaps haven't been to public school,' he said, 'but I don't think they need to be taught anything about self-discipline. They have to have it in buckets to get anywhere.'

'Thank God for that then,' Tim said. 'It isn't going to be that sort of war – me Chief, you Indian. Everybody's going to be in it. The Germans aren't going to care where you went to school when they shoot you down.'

Charlie wasn't sure whether he was joking. He preferred not to think about being shot down. 'What do you want to fly?' he said.

'Fighters,' Tim said. 'I'm too much of a coward to fly bombers.'

Charlie laughed. 'Me too. Spits, I hope.'

Charlie phoned home and Amy answered. He sounded very cheerful, she thought. 'I'm here for four weeks,' he said. 'I'll be square-bashing, doing endless PE, and learning how to behave like a gentleman in the mess. And tomorrow I shall be getting kitted out with uniform and a regulation haircut. You won't recognize me with no hair. No flying. Still, it's not for long. I'll see you soon.'

They did PE every day. 'I feel as I've been beaten up,' Tim said. 'That boxer's a sadist. It's worse than school.'

'Hardly,' Charlie said. 'He's trying to get you as fit as he is.'

Tim sighed. 'He'll never succeed.'

They did endless parades on the promenade, and attended lectures about officers' administrative duties, and one from a short, grim, unsmiling doctor, about venereal disease.

'What a dreary old sod,' Tim said. 'I shouldn't think he's ever had the opportunity.'

Charlie grinned. 'I've already been through all that with my father. He's a doctor.'

'You listen to your daddy then,' Tim said. 'This uniform'll be a girl-magnet, especially when we get our wings. We'll be beating them off.'

Charlie laughed. 'I'd be too exhausted at the moment. And after that I don't suppose we'll have the time. That's if the Germans ever come. They seem to be taking their time.'

'Oh they'll come,' Tim said. 'They'll come.'

They waited for their selection: bombers or fighters, or army support or instructors. 'I wonder how they choose?' Charlie said.

'It's all in the mind.' Tim said. 'They have secret psychological tests that you don't even know you're taking. It's a kind of voodoo.'

Charlie laughed. 'I'll keep my fingers crossed, then.'

On Saturday night they went out to a pub in the town. It seemed to be full of uniforms and girls and the noise was deafening. They managed to get a table in the corner and Tim struggled to the bar and came back with two pints of bitter. 'Just what I said, Charlie, girls everywhere.'

'Go on then,' Charlie said, 'magnetize one.'

Tim gazed round the room, his eyes narrowed. 'She looks nice,' he said. 'That girl over there – the blonde.'

'Go on then,' Charlie said. 'Do your stuff.'

'How do you mean?'

'Go and talk to her,' Charlie said.

'I can't do that.' Tim blushed faintly. 'We haven't been introduced.'

Charlie laughed. 'Tim,' he said, 'you're all talk.'

Tim lit a cigarette. 'Not about everything,' he said. 'We'll see.'

They were even more impatient when they heard that RAF pilots had shot down several German bombers attacking naval vessels at Rosyth. 'And here we are,' Tim said. 'Playing soldiers.'

At the end of the month they were given their assignments. Charlie and Tim had a beer afterwards to celebrate.

'Fighters then,' Tim said. 'Maybe we'll get to the same squadron, so I won't bid you goodbye.' They were sent home again to wait.

Mrs Brooks took Sara to see the headmistress at the village school. The headmistress seemed flurried and distracted. 'I expect you'll be coming here, Sara,' she said, 'until we get ourselves sorted out. I don't know how we're going to cope with all these extra children.'

'I was at a grammar school,' Sara said. 'I have to go to a grammar school. I need to do science and Latin. I was doing them before.'

'I don't know about that,' the headmistress said. 'We certainly don't have those facilities here, or the staff.'

'What about the local grammar school?' Mrs Brooks said. 'Can't she go there?'

'Well, I can speak to them,' the headmistress said, 'but I expect they'll be in the same boat. They'll have a lot of extra children. You'll have to come here for the time being, Sara.'

Sara couldn't believe it. It couldn't be happening. It couldn't all stop, just like that. They couldn't take it all away from her. Her mother said she would come at the weekend to bring her some more clothes. I'm not staying here, she thought. I don't care what happens. She'll have to take me home.

She went to school for the rest of the week, but cried when she came home the first day. Mrs Brooks was concerned. 'What is it, dear?' she said. 'What happened?'

'Nothing,' Sara said. 'But I can't go there, to that school. I've done all that before. It's a waste of time. I want to go home.'

Nora came on Saturday. Mrs Brooks gave her a cup of tea and then left her alone with Sara.

Sara burst into tears. 'I can't stay here, Mum,' she said. 'It's a baby school and there's no room at the grammar. I might as well be dead.'

Nora almost lost her temper, torn between Sara's tears and the prospect of her actually being dead if the Germans bombed London.

She put her arms around Sara, trying to be calm. 'What can I do, Sara?' she said. 'Nearly all the children have left. How would I feel if anything happened to you?'

'I don't care,' Sara sobbed. 'I want to come home. My school's still going.'

Nora sighed. 'I'll speak to your dad,' she said. 'See what he thinks.'

'He'll do what you say,' Sara sobbed. 'He isn't going to be there, is he?'

Three weeks went by. 'Is there a war on or not?' Charlie said. 'What am I supposed to do at home? I'll have forgotten how to fly anything at this rate.' His impatience, he knew, was largely apprehension. He wanted to know how he would react, how he would take it. Staying at home thinking about it wasn't helping.

He went to visit Tessa at Cambridge.

'You look nice in your uniform, Charlie,' she said. 'They've had some RAF pilots staying at Clare, doing training, marching about and trying to make dates with the girls.'

'What are you up to?' Charlie said.

'Thorax and abdo this term,' she said. 'It's an odd feeling, holding someone's heart in your hand, if you think about it.'

'Don't think about it,' Charlie said. He found that he didn't want to talk about anything dead, even to Tessa. Death was something that he preferred not to think about. It was something that happened to other people, something to joke about – 'going for a Burton' they called it. It wasn't going to happen to him. How could it? He was so full of life, there was so much to do, so much going on. 'It's just part of your training – that's all.'

'We're digging up the college gardens to grow vegetables, and we're all doing fire-watching.'

'Surely they won't bomb Cambridge?' Charlie said. 'Surely they're not complete vandals?'

'Who knows?' Tessa said. 'We're fire-watching anyway, and we've got stirrup pumps and long shovels for incendiaries. It's all a bit strange. The place is half-empty. Lots of the boys are going, just like you, Charlie.'

The weeks wore on. The attacks from the air didn't come. Nothing happened. Life seemed to have a strange transparent skin of normality, while underneath wild and horrible things were happening. The British Expeditionary Force left for France, the battle ship, *Royal Oak* was sunk at Scapa Flow, the war at sea was destroying and killing.

In December Mrs Parks gave in her notice. 'I'll be going to my daughter's at Christmas,' she said, 'and I'm afraid I won't be coming back. I'm sorry, Doctor.'

'It's all right, Edith,' Amy said. 'I understand. Keep in touch with us, won't you?'

Charlie got his posting to an advanced training school. Amy drove him to the station.

'Don't come to the platform, Mum,' he said, 'and don't worry. I'll be all right. I'm looking forward to it. I'll be flying again.' She watched him go, knowing that he was going into his own world, where she couldn't follow, that desperate world that she could never forget.

It grew colder and colder; the coldest winter anyone could remember 'Thank God we're not getting raids,' Amy said. 'We'd freeze to death in the cellar.' The Thames froze over for the first time for fifty years. Upstream people were skating on the river, enjoying themselves.

Still there were no air raids, but the war at sea went on, the U-boats attacking shipping, and the German captain of the Graf Spee scuttled his boat and blew his brains out in Montevideo.

It's happening again, Amy thought, the very weather reflecting the anguish that was rising from the world. It was as if the earth was retreating into itself, withdrawing its warmth and beauty, as it had among the cold and the teeming torrential rains of the war in France. She had an extraordinary sense that the earth itself was a living thing, and was turning away its face in horror and shame at what was to come.

Chapter Ten

1940

A lmost the first person Charlie saw was Tim.

Tim grinned at him under his sleepy eyelids. 'Where have you been? I got here yesterday. Come on, I'll help you with your kit. Then we can have a respectable cup of tea.'

Charlie found his room. 'What are we flying?' he asked. 'Do you know?'

Tim put his thumbs up. 'Harvards. We are creeping closer to fighters at a snail's pace. You wouldn't think there was a war on, would you?'

'We've got four squadrons in France,' Charlie said, 'and that seems to be about it. God knows when we'll get a shot at them.'

'Charlie,' Tim said, with exaggerated care, 'young Charlie. Your hour will come soon enough. Don't be impatient.'

'We need to get going,' Charlie said. 'I was in Berlin the summer before last. They're armed to the teeth and trained up to the eyeballs.'

'It doesn't matter,' Tim said. 'It won't do them any good. I'd love to have seen their faces when that half-baked Oxford crew sauntered in and beat their muscle-men in Herr Goering's pet boat race. What a laugh. We all thought it was hilarious.'

Charlie smiled. 'I don't think it's going to be that easy.'

Tim's grin faded. He looked out of the window at the airfield, at the parked machines, at the snow-dusted fields and woods beyond. 'Winning that boat race wasn't easy, Charlie,' he said. 'I knew some of the crew. They just wouldn't be beaten, that's all.'

'We'll be beaten if they don't get on with training,' Charlie said. 'This is just the calm before the storm.'

'The calm of too much snow at the moment,' Tim said. 'We're

starting with lectures. They'll talk us to death. The Germans won't have to bother.'

They started the next morning with lectures on the Harvard, fully aerobatic, retractable undercarriage, Pratt & Whitney engine, speed 156 knots, range 740 miles. 'I'm blinded with science,' Tim said. Lectures continued, on radar and operating with ground control, lectures on formation flying, lectures on aerobatic manoeuvres. And then one day the skies cleared.

Tim was among the first to fly. Charlie watched him take off with his instructor and disappear into the distance. Eventually he reappeared, doing a very reasonable landing.

They met in the mess. 'How was it?' Charlie asked. 'Any tips?'

'Brilliant,' Tim said. 'Spins like a bastard, especially to the right, so watch it. I expect your instructor will drop you into that one.'

Later, Charlie took off on his first flight, eager and intense. They climbed to 4,000 feet.

'Do a spin to the right,' his instructor said.

Spins like a bastard, Charlie thought. It did indeed. Stick forward, he said to himself, full opposite rudder. He came out of the spin with some relief. He was sweating slightly, but his instructor seemed unperturbed. 'Now spin to the left,' he said. Good job I don't get airsick, Charlie thought.

They flew every day, spins, rolls, stall turns, loops. In battle, whenever that might be, they must not fly straight and level for more than a few seconds. Otherwise they would easily be picked off by a hungry 109. All I want now, Charlie thought, is a Hurricane or a Spitfire. A real fighter.

They spent two weeks at a practice camp, air firing at a drogue pulled by a Wellington bomber, learning to allow for the bomber's deflection. Tim seemed to be rather better at it than most. 'It's just like clay-pigeon shooting,' he said. 'You have to allow for the target's speed.'

Charlie sighed. 'I never did any shooting. I expect I'll get the hang of it in the end.'

'It's daft,' Tim said. 'As if the German bombers are just going to trundle along and wait for us to come and shoot them down. And what if they've got fighter escorts? They're not just going to let us wipe them out, are they?'

'Their fighters can't come all the way from Germany and get back,' Charlie said. 'They wouldn't have any time to play with us as well. They'd run out of fuel.'

Tim gave a short laugh. 'Who says they'll be coming from Germany?'

'You're a bit pessimistic, aren't you?'

'Realistic,' Tim said. 'Things aren't going too well in France, are they? We're not exactly forcing them to stay in Germany, and the French aren't doing much.'

Charlie didn't think too much about it. He was happy, throwing his Harvard around the sky and bringing it safely home again. He'd like to get a crack at the Luftwaffe, though. Sometimes he thought about Kurt. Was he doing the same thing? Flying? He hoped not. Better if he was in the army or the navy. It wasn't a pleasant thought, fighting Kurt.

They took, and passed, their Wings Exam. They spent half an hour sewing the wings on to their uniforms, and then went to the pub to celebrate.

'Well, we got there,' Tim said. 'I wonder when we're going to do our stuff?'

'We'll be off to an operational squadron soon,' Charlie said. 'Perhaps we'll get to France.'

Tim shrugged. 'If it's still there.'

'Ever the optimist.' Charlie took a mouthful of beer. 'What makes you think it won't be?'

'We haven't got enough men there,' Tim said, 'and we've got to transport everything by sea and there are a few U-boats about.' He drained his beer. 'I'll get another round.'

Charlie looked about him at the crowded bar, RAF personnel mostly. It was weird, he thought, this waiting. What were they doing in Germany? Planning to invade Britain? Planning to take over the world?

Tim came back with two pints. 'I was in Paris last summer,' he said. 'There was a funny atmosphere. It was as if they didn't even want to talk about what was going on – a kind of paralysis of mind. I expect they were so peed off about what happened to France in the last lot that they just couldn't face even thinking about it. They lost fourteen hundred thousand men – dead. Poor blighters. I'm glad I'm not French. If you ask me we should get all our fighters out of there. We're going to need them here.'

'We can't just abandon them,' Charlie said.

'No?' Tim said. 'Who knows? But they might have to abandon us.'

'Well, let's not worry about it,' Charlie said. 'We've got our wings. We'll be flying fighters soon.'

The next day was fine – a beautiful spring day. Charlie walked out on to the airfield. Good flying weather, he thought, for us and for them. No sign of them, though.

One of the fitters was standing by the hangars. 'Sir,' he said. 'Sir. Look at this.'

Charlie followed his pointing finger. An aircraft was coming in, flying very fast and very low.

'What is it?' Charlie said.

'I think it's one of ours – British – not this squadron, though. I think it's a Hawker Hart.'

Charlie shaded his eyes with his hand. 'What the hell's he doing?'

'Beating up the airfield,' Jenkins said, 'by the look of it.'

'Strictly not allowed,' Charlie said. 'He'll get hell from the station commander. That's if he lands here.'

'He's coming on, sir. He's cutting it a bit fine, isn't he?'

The plane roared towards them. 'Pull up,' Charlie said out loud. 'Pull up man. Climb!'

Half the station personnel seemed to be out now, watching. The plane crossed the perimeter. The pilot seemed to be making an effort to pull up and climb away. The nose rose a little and seemed to shudder, and then the plane stalled. It plunged down. One wing ploughed into the ground, the plane flipped over, and cartwheeled, hurtling over the grass, tearing and screeching. The fire engines and the ambulance roared and streaked across the airfield. It was too late – all too late. The plane exploded, fragments hurled into the air. Charlie and Jenkins both ducked, though the plane was too far away now for them to be hit. Then it burst into flames.

'Oh God,' Charlie said. He watched the fitter, his hands trembling, take a roll-up out of his top pocket and put it in his mouth, without lighting it, his face as white as paper. He felt his stomach clench and churn. He tried to blank out his mind, tried not to think about how the man must have died. His stomach churned again and he felt sweat breaking out on his face. He made it to the latrines before he threw up. He rinsed his face in cold water, leaning over the washbasin. That's the first time, he thought, the very first time he had seen someone die. It wasn't the war, it was an accident. It could have happened at any time, but it was terrible to watch. Whatever had happened, the poor blighter had bought it. But they won't get me, he thought. They won't get me.

That night in the mess they conducted a strange little ceremony. Charlie played the can-can music on the piano and the pilots linked arms and danced, la-la-ing to the music, kicking up their legs. Then they drank a great deal of beer, making a solemn toast to the dead pilot.

'What'll we do this weekend?' Tim said. 'We've got forty-eight hours. We could go up to town and do a show or go to the pictures. Greta Garbo's on in *Ninotchka*, we could go to the Windmill and see the girls. Or we could just get drunk.'

Charlie laughed. 'No thanks. I thought I'd go to Cambridge and see my sister. She's a student there.'

'Oh,' Tim said. 'You didn't tell me she was a bluestocking.'

'She's hardly that,' Charlie said. 'She's a medical student.'

'My God,' Tim said. 'A brain! She sounds terrifying.'

'She's all right,' Charlie said. 'Takes after my mother. She's a doctor too.'

'I'm frightened of her as well then.' Tim put on a pathetic face. 'Can I come too? I don't want to kick my heels here on my own.'

'Yes, of course,' Charlie said, 'but don't you want to go home?'

Tim shook his head. 'My parents are divorced. My father's in Ireland with his new wife and my mother's in Scotland with her new husband. I don't fancy either of them much.'

'OK,' Charlie said, 'I'll look up the trains.'

'No need.' Tim took a car key out of his pocket and dangled it in the air. 'I managed to get some petrol. We'll go in the Morgan. I've never actually been to Cambridge, would you believe? My family all went to the Other Place.'

They set off on Saturday morning. The countryside seemed to be struggling to recover from the bitter winter, the trees still stark in the pale sunshine.

'March already,' Tim said, 'and we haven't had a crack at the bastards yet.'

'Don't say too much to my sister,' Charlie said. 'Don't say anything about the accident. She doesn't need to know about that.' The aircraft flew into his mind – too fast, too low, too late. He was doing his best to forget it. He didn't want his family to know. Tessa was acquainted with death, he thought. She had held someone's dead heart in her hand. But she had not seen what he had seen. Death she had seen, but she had not seen dying.

'All right,' Tim said. 'I wouldn't have, anyway.'

Cambridge, Charlie thought, with a pang of affection, was unchanged, apart from the scattering of uniforms. He had heard that they were taking out the fine old stained-glass windows from King's College chapel, for storage in a safe place – safe from bombs. Surely not. Not here? History stood in bricks and stone, lining the narrow streets. He felt his old feelings of the deep and serene contentment that seemed to reach down through the soles of his feet into the very earth – a feeling of belonging. There was only one other place that gave him this feeling. It came to him when he stood on the perimeter of an airfield in the bright early morning, or when the sun was going down, and watched the aircraft taking off, or coming into land. It was contentment. It was home.

'It's a lovely town,' Tim said. 'The colleges are in front of your face, not mixed up with everything like they are in Oxford. I hope the bloody Germans leave it alone.'

They booked rooms at the Blue Boar, and Charlie went to find Tessa and ask her to lunch.

He brought her back to the Blue Boar. Tim was waiting in the lounge and stood up as they came in. Charlie introduced them. Tim looked his normal inscrutable self, but he was surprised to see that Tessa had produced a very faint blush. Odd, he thought. He had never seen her do that before.

They went in to lunch. 'Rather a restricted menu,' Charlie said. 'They can't get much exotic food in restaurants now, even in London.'

'Well, it's fairer,' Tessa said, 'with the rationing and everything. Otherwise the well-off could just eat in restaurants all the time and wouldn't feel the difference. Hardly democratic.'

'She's a socialist,' Charlie said.

'We all are now, aren't we?' Tim said. 'All for one and one for all.'

Charlie watched them with amusement and surprise. For once Tim seemed to have been struck dumb – or as dumb as he ever got. He seemed to spend his time looking at Tessa, and hurriedly looking away when he caught her eye. And Tessa seemed completely out of character. She was almost flirting.

What's going on here, he thought? It hadn't occurred to him that Tim might be attracted to Tessa, though that wasn't really surprising. She was fairly nice-looking. But he'd never seen Tessa show any interest before. She had always shrugged it off, so set on her career.

After lunch they walked Tessa back to her college – she said she had some work to do – but they arranged to take her to dinner.

Charlie showed Tim around the town, his own college and King's chapel. Then they walked by the river along the Backs in the pale sunshine.

Tim was still unusually quiet. 'Charlie?' he said eventually, 'has Tessa got anyone? I mean a boyfriend?'

'Not that I know of,' Charlie said. 'Fancy yourself?'

Tim smiled. 'I don't know. She's very nice. Would you mind?'

'No,' Charlie said, 'as long as you're decent with her. Not do anything to hurt her, I mean.' He grinned. 'Otherwise I'll shoot you down.'

Tim laughed. 'If I did that, I'd let you. Would you mind if I came back to see her on my own sometime?'

'Not at all,' Charlie said. 'If she doesn't want you to she'll tell you. She's very direct. She doesn't mess about.'

'God, it's cold.' Dan downed his tea and put on his overcoat. 'I've been thinking, Amy, maybe we should put an Anderson shelter in the garden. Mr Hodge and I could dig the pit. They're supposed to resist a lot of blast. If the house was flattened we might be trapped in the basement. That wouldn't be very nice.'

'We'd freeze to death out there,' Amy said. 'We could get paraffin heaters, I suppose.' She smiled. 'Then we'd die of paraffin fumes. Not much of a choice, is there?'

'Well nothing's happened yet,' Dan said. 'Perhaps they won't bomb civilian areas.'

'They did in the last war,' Amy said, 'so I can't see them holding back in this one.'

'Perhaps Lord Haw Haw will tell us,' Dan said, smiling. 'We'd better listen in on Sunday.'

'That traitor,' Amy said. 'He may be amusing but he's British, and he's making broadcasts for the enemy. How can he do that?' She paused. 'I'll see about an Anderson shelter.'

'He'll get his come-uppance,' Dan said. 'I wouldn't like to be in his shoes when the war is over.' He wound a scarf around his neck and put on a trilby and woollen gloves. 'What are you doing today?'

'The free clinic at Hammersmith,' Amy said. 'Then I thought I'd go and see Mrs Lewis and offer her the job. We can't go on like this with no help.'

'Good idea. See you tonight.' Dan kissed her cheek and left, into the dark, icy morning.

The Hammersmith clinic was busy. It seemed that some of the children in the slum areas were still at home. Amy treated coughs and colds, and a little girl with a nasty discharging ear. She cleaned out the ear as best she could, and then packed it with ribbon gauze soaked in antiseptic. The little girl was eleven, scrawny and shabbily dressed. She let Amy deal with her ear without complaining, though it must have been sore.

'You didn't send her to be evacuated, then?' Amy asked.

'No,' her mother said. 'I can't do without her. I've got three more little ones and I have to go out cleaning.'

'Bring her back in two days,' Amy said, 'and I'll do the dressing again.' They left. The mother didn't take the child's hand, Amy noticed. She spoke to her as if she were an adult. This child, Amy thought, was eleven years old and practically bringing up her little brothers and sisters, missing school half the time, no doubt. What future did she have? Things must change. When this war is over, things must change.

She shivered a little in the cold. Was it the cold? What would Britain be like then? Conquered and subject to Germany? Blasted and flattened? No, she thought, no such thoughts. We will win. We will win.

She went to see Mrs Lewis. 'It's just a visit, Mrs Lewis,' she said at once. 'Nothing to do with Sara.'

Nora smiled and took her into the kitchen. 'Cup of tea, Doctor?' she said.

'Yes please.'

Nora put on the kettle and got out the best cups and saucers.

'Has your husband been called up yet?' Amy asked.

Nora nodded. 'He got into the Navy – that was what he wanted.' She bit her lip. 'He would, wouldn't he – go into the one that's doing all the fighting. The Germans are sinking our ships all the time, aren't they?'

'You must be very proud of him,' Amy said. 'We couldn't do without the Navy. It's our lifeline.'

'Yes,' Nora said, 'I am. But he couldn't even say goodbye to Sara.'

'Have you heard from her?' Amy asked. 'Is she all right?'

'No, she isn't,' Nora said. 'She's very upset. She can't get into a proper school. I don't know what to do.'

'It might not be the right time to ask,' Amy said, 'but I wondered if you were thinking of taking a job?'

Nora was surprised. 'I suppose I'll have to sometime,' she said. 'Everybody'll have to do something, won't they?'

'I wondered if you'd like to work for me?' Amy said. 'I need a housekeeper to look after the house and do simple cooking. My husband's a surgeon. We're both out most of the time.'

'Oh!' Nora said, surprised. 'It might be better than working in a factory or on the land. I'd be there for Sara if she comes home. Would I have to live in?'

'Only if you want to,' Amy said. 'Or you could come in each day.'

'Are you sure I could do it?' Nora said. 'I'm not a fancy cook. It would all be a bit plain.'

'We're not fancy eaters,' Amy said. 'Plain food suits us fine. And

PEGGY SAVAGE

there won't be much else when the rationing really gets going. I expect just about everything will be rationed in the end. My daughter will only be home in the university vacations, and my son when he gets leave.'

'Can I think about it?' Nora said.

Amy smiled. 'Of course. I'll come round in a couple of days and see what you think.'

After she'd gone Nora sat down and had another cup of tea. What a surprise that was! It might be a good idea – the job. Sara would come home sometime, she supposed, and she wouldn't mind if her mother was working for a couple of doctors.

Sara went to school every day and came home frustrated and angry. It wasn't the teachers – they were nice, but as every day went by she felt her dream slipping away. They even asked her to teach some of the little ones now and again, they were so short of teachers. She helped the little ones with their reading. The headmistress seemed to think she was very good at it. 'You should be a teacher, Sara,' she said. Her reaction to that had been to feel a bit sick. No, she thought. No. I shouldn't.

Mrs Brooks had invited her mother for Christmas Day and her mother had brought one of her Christmas puddings with the three-penny bits. She had given her a book about zoology – a second-hand one that she had found in the Portobello Road.

'It's lovely, Mum,' she said, 'but I want to come home. Nobody's bombing anybody, are they, and you're all on your own. There haven't been any raids at all.'

'Please, Sara.' Nora was almost in tears. 'We don't know what's going to happen and you're safer here with Mrs Brooks.'

'But I'll miss everything at school.' Sara was crying now. 'I've already missed one term. If I miss any more I'll never get to university.' Her mother didn't seem to know what to do. Nora had been in tears herself before she left, but she hadn't taken her home.

Sara lay in bed at night, restless and unhappy. I'm not doing this, she thought. I'm not just going to let it all be taken away. I'm not staying here. A plan was becoming a certainty. The pound note was still under the mattress, she checked every night. I'm going home, she thought.

138

I'm not a baby, I'm twelve now and my dad was working when he was twelve. Nobody can stop me, and my mum won't send me back. I just won't go.

Mrs Brooks was going out next morning. She said she was trying to get some eggs from one of the farms. If she went home she would have to take her ration book. She knew where it was. Mrs Brooks kept it in a drawer in the kitchen.

She got up quietly, got out the pound note and put it in her satchel. She packed her clothes in her little case and hid it in the wardrobe. Then she tore a page out of her exercise book and wrote a note to Mrs Brooks. 'I have gone home. Thank you for having me. Love, Sara.' Then she went to sleep. Tomorrow she was going home.

She took the train in the morning. It was packed, mainly with soldiers, and she couldn't get a seat. She stood in the corridor, squashed up against a large lady in a damp fur coat that smelt of dog.

'Do you know where I have to change trains to get to London?' Sara asked her.

'Maidenhead,' the woman said. 'Are you on your own? You're a bit young to be going about on your own, especially with all these soldiers about.'

'I'm twelve,' Sara said. 'I'm all right.'

The woman shrugged. 'I don't know what's going on half the time. There's a war on, I suppose. You be careful. I'll tell you when we get there.'

Sara changed trains. The London train was worse, more packed than ever. There were soldiers lining the corridors, all smoking, and the smoke made her cough. They seemed to go so slowly, past the bare fields and woods of the countryside, and the rows of little houses on the edges of the towns. They'd taken all the signs down at the stations to fool the Germans and she'd no idea where she was. Still, the guard or somebody shouted the station names when they stopped.

'Paddington' the guard shouted. 'Paddington station.'

Sara felt a flood of relief and pure joy. She was home. She climbed off the train and went to find the bus.

*

Nora opened the front door. Sara rushed in and threw her arms around her mother's neck.

'I've come home, Mum. Please, please don't send me back.' She burst into tears.

Nora held her close. 'It's all right,' she said. 'It's all right.' She held Sara away from her and looked into her face. 'You tell me the truth, Sara. Did somebody do something to you? Some man?'

'No, Mum,' Sara said. 'Nothing like that. I just wanted to come home.'

Nora took her into the kitchen. 'Sit down there,' she said, 'and I'll make you a cup of tea. Now tell me what happened.' Nora was ready to be outraged – ready to do battle with anyone who had hurt Sara.

'Nothing, Mum,' Sara said. 'Mrs Brooks was very nice, but the school was useless. I was even teaching some of the little kids sometimes. They said I'd make a good teacher. A teacher, Mum!'

'There's nothing wrong with being a teacher,' Nora said. It might be a good idea, she thought, to suggest some other career, just in case.

Sara began to cry again. 'I'm not going back.'

'All right,' Nora said. 'You're not going back.' She put Sara to bed early.

She sat by the kitchen fire. What a world, she thought. Who would have imagined that there would be another war? With Jim away fighting, it didn't seem real. The confusion of the last few months was terrible. But perhaps, in a small way, things were working out a bit for her. If she took the job with Doctor Fielding she wouldn't have to go into a factory or on the land, and she'd be there for Sara. Sara was at home, upstairs in her own bed, and it was lovely. She was growing up – thirteen now. In another year, she thought, she'll be the same age as I was when I went into service. Well, that wasn't going to happen to her.

Someone knocked at the door. It was a young policeman. For a moment she was terrified. Was it Jim? No, they sent a telegram from the Navy if anything had happened, not a policeman. She asked him in. He was checking to see whether Sara had got home safely. Mrs Brooks had contacted the police. She must write to her, Nora thought, and thank her for everything.

She stared into the fire, the flickering flames soothing and calming her. The child was right. Why should we let them spoil everything? No bloody German was going to stop Sara doing what she wanted, war or no war.

Amy did her surgeries in the Harrow Road. There were some children about again, playing in the streets, and coming in with their coughs and colds and runny ears. 'They've come home,' their mothers said. 'They weren't happy there, and there's nothing happening, is there?' It all seemed to have been a panic for nothing. Fears about bombing seemed to be unfounded and the children were trickling home from everywhere. Perhaps the Germans really were going to do the right thing and not bomb civilians.

It began to feel almost normal again, apart from the blackout, and even that had eased a little. Cars had cardboard covers over the lights with little slits in them to let out a modicum of light. Some street lights were lit – blue lamps shaded from above. The road accident rate had gone down a little, according to Dan.

She called on Nora again, praying that she'd take the job. Things were getting difficult at home. The rations were minute, and she didn't have time to stand in queues to get whatever was going. Oranges and bananas and lots of other things had disappeared. Merchant seamen's lives weren't to be put at risk to bring in such luxuries. Our world has contracted, she thought. This little island really is an island now, the horizons drawn in, the walls building.

Nora opened the front door and beamed at her. 'Come in, Doctor.'

Amy followed her into the kitchen. 'You seem very happy today, Mrs Lewis,' she said. 'Have you had some good news?'

Nora nodded. 'Sara's home. She came back. I didn't know how much I missed her till she came back.'

'Is she here?' Amy asked.

'No. She's back at school. She's as happy as could be to be back there. The other school was no good for her – just a little village one. You know what she's like.'

Amy smiled. 'A lot of the children seem to be coming back. I've been seeing them in the clinics.' Some of the older ones, she was well aware, didn't want to come back – back to the poverty and squalor of the slums. Many of them had arrived home clean and nit-free and wearing new clothes, and angry, aware for the first time that other people didn't live like their families did, dirty and hungry, squashed in a couple of squalid rooms, helpless and hopeless. She'd had a letter from Mrs Parks in Marlow. They'd had a little girl from the East End, six years old, billeted on them, she'd written. She was filthy and covered in head lice, half-starved by the look of her, and she didn't know how to use a toilet. 'It's a disgrace,' she wrote, 'children like this, in a so-called civilized country.'

'You've come about the job, I expect,' Nora said. 'I'd like to take it, if that's all right. At least, I could do a month, say, and see how we get on.'

'That's wonderful,' Amy said. 'When can you start?'

'Next week?' Nora said. 'I'll just get Sara settled down. I'd rather live here, if that's all right. When Jim comes home on leave he'll want to be in his own home.'

'We can get our own breakfast,' Amy said, 'so you can get her off to school before you come.'

'Sara would have to come to your house from school,' Nora said, 'but she won't be in the way. She'll only be doing her homework.'

'That's fine,' Amy said. 'You can both have dinner at my house, if you like, and you can leave a meal ready for my husband and me. Have you told her? Is she happy about it?'

Nora gave a broad smile. 'She's thrilled to bits. She'll be living surrounded with doctors.'

Amy laughed. 'So she's still determined?'

'Yes,' Nora said. 'Just the same.'

'Fine,' Amy said. 'Can you come Monday morning, Mrs Lewis, about nine o'clock? I'll take an hour or two off and settle you in.'

'I'll be there,' Nora said, 'and call me Nora.'

Chapter Eleven

1940

At last Charlie and Tim were posted to an operational squadron. 'Spitfires,' Tim said. 'Just look at them.'

The planes were lined up along the airfield. The sleek lines were beautiful, Charlie thought, but the aircraft was intimidating. Its beauty hid a mighty beast, one that he would have to learn to control.

They had more lectures – Tim complaining again – then they actually sat in the cockpit of a Spitfire. They must learn where the controls were: know them with their eyes shut, literally. Charlie chose not to think about smoke-filled cockpits, or worse. They practised taxiing. The Spit had a long nose with no forward vision and they had to swing from side to side to see where they were going.

Then at last on a clear blue-sky day, they went solo. Charlie was strapped in at the edge of the runway. 'Can't give you any dual training, obviously,' his instructor said cheerfully. 'You're on your own. Just get in and get on with it.'

Charlie opened the throttle, not knowing quite what to expect. The Merlin engine roared in front of him. He reached flying speed and the Spitfire rose gracefully into the air. The aircraft was a complete surprise. This great machine responded like a dream – no pushing or pulling on the controls. A gentle touch was all that was needed. Now he knew why they said that playing the piano was good training – flying a Spitfire was gentle, sensitive, like touching the keys. You just had to stroke it, breathe on it, and it obeyed you. It turned on a sixpence and it came out of a spin like a lady. He climbed to 5,000 feet and threw it about the sky a bit. It was far, far better than he'd ever expected. He flew lower and looked below him at the English countryside, at the neat fields and the farms and the woods. Now, in this fabulous machine, he really felt like a dragon-killer. It reminded him of Arthur. He wondered what he was doing now.

They gathered in the mess in the evening. 'What do you think?' Tim said.

Charlie smiled, a daft, dreamy smile. 'Brilliant. I think I'm in love.'

Tim laughed. 'We can play dogfights tomorrow. Chase each other around. Bet I shoot you down.'

'Two pints says you don't.'

They ceremoniously undid the top button of their uniform jackets – the self-awarded privilege of being fighter pilots.

A new pilot had joined the mess, posted back from France. He was the only one they'd met who'd actually been in combat. They gathered round him, eager to hear what he had to say. 'I think I got one,' he said, 'a 109, but you can't be absolutely sure. It's like a madhouse for a bit, and then it all stops – everybody disappears.' He swallowed a mouthful of beer. 'Don't underestimate them – the Germans. They're good. They've been well trained. I think their 109s are a bit faster than the Spits but the Spit will out-turn them every time. Get above them, come in out of the sun and get in close. Two hundred yards is a reasonable range, or even closer if you can. No further out.'

They plied him with beer. He became faintly philosophical. 'Don't be mistaken about them,' he said. 'Don't let anyone tell you that they're good chaps and just like us. They've been shooting up refugees on the roads – women and children. They're bastards. We've got to get them – do what our squadron leader said – get in amongst them and shoot them down.'

Charlie managed to get a word with him on his own. 'What's it really like?' he said.

'Piece of cake,' the pilot said. He grinned. 'Haven't had any brown trousers yet. You're too busy. I suppose you get a bit sweaty afterwards. But it's all right. It doesn't last.' He was smiling, but the smile faded suddenly. Charlie asked no more.

The next day Charlie met his instructor on the field. 'I'm coming up in another aircraft, Charlie,' he said. 'And I'm going to shoot you down.' He grinned. 'Theoretically, of course.'

They took off together. Charlie climbed away at once and did a neat stall turn. He looked around him, circled, flew lower, trying to remember the lectures on combat manoeuvres. There seemed to be no sign of his instructor. Have I lost him, he thought? Already? That didn't seem to be too difficult. He began to feel rather pleased with himself.

The voice came over the radio. 'Takatakatakatak. I'm on your tail, Charlie. You're a dead man.'

'God,' Charlie said aloud. If he hadn't been strapped in he'd have jumped out of his seat.

After a few more abortive attempts on Charlie's part to escape his instructor, they landed and debriefed. 'Not bad, Charlie,' his instructor said, 'but it needs more work. Do not ever hang about wondering who's there or where they've gone. Do your bit and when you run out of ammo get out. And never, never, follow a damaged aircraft down. Let it go, or you'll be a sitting duck and some other crafty sod will get you. Don't do anything predictable, don't fly straight and level for more than a few seconds.'

March wore on; the weather grew warmer. The pilots stripped to the waist and spent their spare time filling sandbags to build up protective walls around the aircraft. There were sporadic reports of encounters in France: some pilots dead, some safely bailed out, some taken prisoner. The loss of pilots was already deeply worrying. Where were their trained replacements to come from? It was all taking too long. The losses in France were too many, for very little tangible return. The Germans weren't retreating.

Charlie flew and flew. He began to feel that his aircraft was part of himself, an extension of his will. He began to feel that he might be ready. More than ready. He wanted to get in there, have that first real experience, prove to himself that he could do it, prove himself in battle. But still their bombers didn't come.

Tessa joined Rita in the dissecting room. 'We'll start on the lung, shall we?' she said. She pointed with her forceps. 'That must be the pulmonary artery.'

Rita seemed distracted, distressed. She opened her book, but closed it again, and began to cry.

'Rita,' Tessa said. 'Whatever's the matter?'

'I can't do this,' Rita said.

'What? Dissection? What's happened? It's never bothered you before.'

'No, it's not that.'

Rita wiped her eyes on her sleeve. 'My fiancé wants us to get married now, right away. He'll be going to France any minute. I can't say no, can I? And I don't want to.'

'Let's pack this up,' Tessa said, 'and go back to college. We can't talk here.'

They sat in Tessa's little room. 'I'm going to marry him,' Rita said. 'He's going into all that danger. I can't make him wait. He might not …' She began to cry again.

'Look,' Tessa said. 'I'm sure you won't have to leave. Surely they'll let you stay, under the circumstances? The war won't go on for ever.'

'He wants to have a child,' Rita said, 'before it's too late. I can't do this and have a baby. I've made up my mind.'

Tessa found that she was, to her surprise, rather shocked. 'Does he really want you to give up all this?'

Rita stared at her, her face drawn. 'He might be giving up his life, Tessa. You don't seem to understand. What can I give, compared with that?'

Tessa was ashamed. 'I'm so sorry.' She took Rita's hand. 'That was a stupid thing I said. I don't know much, do I? I'm sure you won't be the only one leaving. Would you like me to come with you to see the principal?'

Rita got up. 'No,' she said. 'I'll do it myself, but thanks.' She smiled a thin smile. 'I just want to make him happy. I love him, you see. More than anything.'

Tessa sat for a few minutes after she'd gone. Rita was right, she thought, and how could she have been so insensitive? Was she really that hard? She was terrified by the thought that something might happen to Charlie, or her parents or Grandpa. But a man – a lover or a husband? She had no experience, had never loved anyone in that way. She couldn't imagine herself having to make such a choice. Doing medicine was all she had ever wanted. She got up and moved restlessly around the room, straightening the books on her table. The answer was not to get involved with anyone, not with what was going on in the world. It would be difficult enough, without that. And yet she felt a kind of emptiness; a longing, an isolation.

She stared out of the window at the college garden, coming into bloom now, the buds of spring tentatively opening. Despite the war, she felt that lifting of the heart that spring always brought: new hopes, new beginnings. She leant her forehead against the window. Not to get involved, that was the thing, not step over that line. But she was well aware that she'd been thinking about Tim almost continuously since they'd met, half-hoping that he would contact her in some way. More than half-hoping. He seemed nice, that was all: a nice friend. Charlie's friend.

On Saturday there was a knock at her door – one of the college maids. 'There's a gentleman downstairs asking to see you,' she said. 'He's in RAF uniform.'

Tessa felt fear flare up, a new and horrifying fear. What was it? Something to do with Charlie? Had something happened to him? Had they sent someone to tell her? Or had Charlie come to tell her some awful news from home? She hadn't heard of any raids on London. She hurried down the stairs.

Tim was waiting in the entrance hall, smiling. 'Hello, Tessa,' he said. 'I've got a twenty-four-hour pass, so I thought I'd come to see you. Do you mind? I can go away again.'

She was flooded with relief, and with something else: pleasure at seeing him, pleasure at knowing that he wanted to see her. 'No,' she said, smiling back. 'I don't mind.'

'Can you come to lunch?' he said.

'Yes,' she said. 'I think so. Will you wait? I'll get my coat.'

She ran back up the stairs. He's come, she thought. I knew he'd come.

They lunched at the University Arms hotel. Tessa found herself feeling unusually shy, not her normal free-and-easy self. She found it difficult to meet his eye. Every time she did he smiled at her – a warm smile.

'How's Charlie?' she asked.

'He's fine. He's fallen in love with his Spitfire. Utterly besotted.'

Tessa laughed. 'So I understand.'

'He's flying this weekend, so he couldn't come, but he knows I'm here. He sends you his love.'

They chatted, through lunch, of life before the war. 'Charlie said you were up at Oxford,' Tessa said. 'What were you reading?'

'PPE,' he said. 'Philosophy, Politics and Economics. My father seems to have some idea that I might go into politics.'

'Might you?'

'I don't know,' he said. 'Who knows what the world will be like after the war. The old kind of politics might not do.'

'If we win.'

He grinned. 'Oh, we'll win. They'd have to get past Charlie and me.'

She laughed. 'I'll stop worrying, then.' She stirred a small spoonful of sugar into her coffee, surprised that it was still being offered. 'Things will have to be different, though. My mother says some of the slums are terrible. Those children ...'

'We've got a job to do first,' he said. 'That's all I can think about at the moment.'

She pushed her coffee cup away. 'I feel so useless here. There's you and Charlie flying, and girls working in munitions factories and on the land, and I'm just here, as usual, as if nothing had happened.'

'You're not doing nothing, Tessa,' he said quietly, 'you're keeping going – doing what you have to do. You've no idea how important that is, keeping normality, keeping the country as it should be, as we remember it. You've no idea how lovely it is just to be here, in this spectacular old town, with a – a friend.'

She sensed something in his voice, some reticence, some withdrawal. 'What is it?' she said. 'Has something happened?'

He forced away the memory of the accident. 'No,' he said, smiling. 'Flying's wonderful. I'm just as besotted as Charlie.' He glanced away from her, but she caught something in his eyes, a look that struck her as strange – perhaps some kind of bizarre amusement.

They walked along the Backs in the thin sunshine, the river flowing quietly past the great, ancient buildings, King's College Chapel catching the rays of sunlight. She thought of the masons who had built it, generations of them, most of whom never lived to see it completed. They built for the future, for a thousand years. They had never imagined that someone could drop a bomb on it from above, and destroy it in one horrible second. She stopped and looked at it, a lump in her throat.

'I know,' Tim said. 'It isn't going to happen.'

'I hope not.'

They had tea at the Copper Kettle.

'Where do you live, Tim?' she asked.

'I have a little flat in London,' he said. 'My parents are divorced, so there's no real family home – or perhaps I've got two.'

'Oh.' Tessa was surprised, and then annoyed with herself for showing it. 'I'm sorry.'

'It's all right,' he said. 'It's not exactly happy families, is it? I don't mind now. They made sure I was well looked after – the right school and all that.' He smiled. 'I don't think it's done me any harm.'

'I'm sure it hasn't,' she said.

'Not that it matters much now, does it?' He looked away, over the river. 'It doesn't matter much about your background now. All roads lead to war.'

'I expect you're right,' she said.

'I'd better get back,' he said eventually. 'I'll get a taxi to the station.' He walked with her back to college and they stopped outside the door. 'It's been a lovely day, Tessa,' he said. 'May I come to see you again?'

'Yes,' she said. 'I'd like that.'

He touched her hand and walked away down the street, not looking back. What must it be like, she thought, to be like Rita and thousands of other women, to see someone you love walk away like this into God knows what? I don't think I could do it. How would you bear it? She went up to her room, took off her coat and sat down at her table with *Gray's Anatomy*. Then she got up and looked out of the window. He said he would come again.

Nora started work on Monday morning. Amy showed her round the house, and the flat, in case she ever wanted to use it.

Nora looked around her with considerable pleasure, and some

relief. It was a comfortable home, that was all, not some kind of inhab-ited museum like some of the houses she'd seen. She thought she could cope with this.

Her first job seemed to be the shopping, getting the family rations. She took the ration books to their registered shop and waited for the grocer to pat out the little rectangle of butter they were allowed, some cheese, not on ration – yet, and weigh out a few ounces of bacon. She went on to the butcher and, wonder of wonders, managed to get a rabbit, still off ration. If there was one thing she knew how to do it was make a rabbit pie. Jim said her pastry was the best. Then she joined the queues for everything: potatoes, vegetables, bread. When she got settled, she'd make the bread herself. Jim thought that was the best too.

The housework seemed fairly easy – dusting, polishing, making the beds. She'd done it all before. Doctor Fielding might or might not be home for a sandwich at lunchtime. Her husband was Mr Fielding, she'd discovered. Surgeons were called Mister, not Doctor. Funny that, she thought. If you'd taken the trouble to be a doctor, surely you'd like to call yourself one. If Sara ever did it, she'd call her 'Doctor' to every-body. My daughter, the doctor.

She dusted the study, looking at the rows of books on the shelves. There were several rows of medical and science books. She opened one or two. It all sounded like Greek. She wondered again whether she might have understood all this – if she'd ever had the chance. Sara understood it all, the maths and the physics and the chemistry. She sat down with a chemistry book on her lap – elements, compounds, some-thing called the periodic table. Greek again. We could have done all this, she thought, Jim and me, if there was any justice in the world. She looked out at the garden, all dug up now, planted with vegetables. Justice? How could there be another war, so soon? How could Jim be away, in danger of his life in a ship, perhaps killing someone? He was a carpenter, that's all. He made furniture.

She put the books away and went into the kitchen to start preparing dinner. The rabbit had to be skinned and jointed and the pastry made. She had found, to her great surprise, that there was a refrigerator in the kitchen. The only other ones she'd ever seen were in shops selling ice cream and they let out a cloud of steam when they were opened. She wasn't really sure what to do with it.

Perhaps one day, she thought, Sara would have a house like this. She'd have a telephone and a refrigerator and everything. If that happened, she'd die happy.

Sara arrived at half past four. Nora took her into the kitchen and gave her a biscuit and a glass of milk. She settled her at the kitchen table to do her homework. She looked over Sara's shoulder. 'What are you doing now?' she said.

'Algebra.'

Nora looked at the jumble of figures and letters. 'How do you study?' she said. 'What do you do?'

Sara looked up at her mother, wondering how to reply, how to describe something that was second nature to her. 'I have to understand it,' she said, 'and then I have to remember it.' Nora sighed. 'You could do it, Mum,' Sara said. 'I could teach you.'

Nora laughed. 'Not in a million years. What would I want with algebra?' She looked round the kitchen, at the things she'd laid out to do the pastry. This is my life, she thought, cooking and cleaning. And it's fine, as long as Sara is all right and Jim gets home again and gets a job. Maths, physics, chemistry, algebra. Such wonderful things. Bombs, guns, cruelty and killing; what a world. She began to make the pastry.

Amy came home to a delicious smell from the kitchen. Thank goodness, she thought. Thank goodness for Nora. She was tired out. Her patients were worried and upset, wondering what was going to happen. Mothers especially were on edge about the children, thinking that every little cough or cold was some dreadful disease. There were awful rumours that the Germans were somehow dropping diseases on the country. All nonsense, of course.

She followed her nose into the kitchen. Nora was standing at the sink, finishing off the potatoes. 'Hello Doctor,' she said. 'This is my daughter, Sara.'

The little girl stood up. Not so little, Amy thought. Going to be as tall as her mother, and really quite pretty. She looked shy, intelligent though, with direct blue eyes. Amy held out her hand. 'Hello, Sara,' she said. 'I've heard a lot about you.' Sara took her hand briefly. 'Your mother tells me you want to be a doctor.' Sara nodded. 'If you want to borrow any books,' Amy said, 'just take them. I expect your mother knows where they are.'

'Thank you,' Sara said.

Amy turned to Nora. 'That smells wonderful, Nora. What is it?'

'Rabbit pie,' Nora said. 'Off ration.'

'Splendid. It's lovely to have everything done. You can leave it for me to dish up when my husband gets home. You two have your dinner and then get off home. I'll see you in the morning.'

Nora and Sara went home on the bus. 'I don't have to come to their house from school, Mum,' Sara said. 'I could just come home and wait for you.'

'No,' Nora said. 'Suppose there was a raid and you there on your own and I couldn't get to you. I'd go mad.'

'All right,' Sara said. 'I don't mind. Doctor Fielding seems very nice.'

On Saturday morning Amy took a cup of tea out to Dan, who was digging out the pit in the garden for the Anderson shelter. It was going to be a lovely weekend – Charlie was coming home on a forty-eight. Dan parked his spade in the pit. 'Nearly there,' he said. 'We can get the roof on soon.'

Amy looked down into the damp hole, just about big enough for a bunk bed and a couple of chairs. 'Real home from home,' she said.

Dan wiped his brow on his sleeve and sat down on a garden seat. Amy sat beside him. 'Fancy having to do this,' he said. 'Holes in the ground, like animals. What a world.'

'What do you think, darling?' she said. 'What's happening? Do we really have to do this shelter? It looks terrible. I can't imagine sleeping in there.'

'It can't go on like this,' he said. 'It's all too normal. We're just treating ordinary everyday cases in the hospital. All those empty beds everywhere – just waiting.'

Amy had a sudden memory of the hospital she'd helped to prepare in Paris in 1914, of standing in the ward the night before they opened, looking at the rows of empty beds – just waiting. And then of the shock of the wounded men arriving, wounds she had never seen before, bodies torn and injured beyond belief. She closed her eyes briefly. Not again, she thought. Dear God, not again.

Dan drank his tea. 'Sooner or later they'll invade France. Either that, or call the whole thing off, and they won't do that, not unless we agree to their terms, and I don't think that's going to happen.'

Amy looked at his worried face. 'What then?'

He shrugged. 'We'll fight,' he said. 'France isn't very far away, is it? Twenty-odd miles from Dover. Thank God for the Channel.'

'Let's forget the war,' she said, 'just for the weekend. Did I tell you that Charlie is bringing his friend, Tim?'

'Good,' Dan said. 'They can help me get the top on this damn thing. I'll need some muscle.' He got up and picked up his spade.

The phone rang in the house and Nora appeared at the door. 'It's Tessa,' she called.

'Now what?' Dan said.

Amy hurried into the house and came out again, beaming. 'She's coming home too,' she said. 'The college has let her out for the weekend to see Charlie. Won't it be lovely – all being together again.'

He put his arm around her and kissed the top of her head. 'Yes,' he said. 'Sorry I was grumpy. It's all that digging.'

Charlie and Tim arrived just before lunch. Amy settled them into their rooms and then took Charlie into the kitchen to meet Nora. 'Mrs Lewis has saved our lives,' she said. 'I don't know what I'd do without her.' Nora smiled and shook his hand.

They went out into the garden to Dan, and passed Sara in the hall. 'Who's the kid?' Charlie asked.

'That's Sara,' Amy said. 'Mrs Lewis's little girl.'

Dan gave Charlie a hug and shook Tim's hand. 'There's more good news,' Amy said. 'Tessa's coming home. She'll be here after lunch.'

'Jolly good,' Charlie said.

Amy noticed the look of quick pleasure on Tim's face. What's this, she thought? Has something happened here? 'Have you met Tessa, Tim,' she asked.

'Yes,' he said. 'Twice. In Cambridge.'

Tim was being very close, she thought. He said very little but he hadn't been able to hide his pleasure – not from a mother.

Dan dusted off his hands. 'We'll have lunch,' he said. 'Then you can both help me with this thing.'

At lunch Dan tried to ask them about what they were doing. They glanced quickly at each other, and replied with jokes and silly stories. 'Being lectured,' Tim said, 'and filling sandbags.' Charlie nearly made a joke of being shot down, theoretically, by his instructor, but stopped himself in time. His mother would not appreciate that.

They won't talk about it, Amy thought, just as she found it almost impossible to talk about the last war to anyone but Dan. The words wouldn't come. The boys hadn't been in battle yet, but they knew it was coming. They were not going to discuss their feelings, or their preparations of body and mind. They are men now, she thought, in their own world. They are more at home there.

Tessa arrived after lunch, looking, Amy thought, quite blooming. She flung her arms around Amy and Dan and Charlie and shook Tim's hand. Amy watched her. She couldn't detect any change in Tessa when she looked at Tim, but Tim's expression was unmistakable. I wonder, she thought, what went on in Cambridge?

Tessa and the boys went out to have a look at the hole in the garden. Amy watched them out of the window, laughing and chatting.

Dan came up behind her. 'Seems like a nice young man, Tim,' he said. 'I'm glad Charlie's got a friend.'

She took his hand and he put his arm around her. 'He likes Tessa,' she said. 'I can tell.'

'That's not surprising,' he said. 'Everybody likes Tessa.'

'You know what I mean,' she said.' 'I can tell by the way he looks at her.'

'And do you think she likes him?'

'I don't know,' she said. 'It's not a good idea, is it? The way things are.'

'Amy,' he said, 'they're young and full of life. You can't stop nature. You can't stop young people doing what they do.'

She leant against him. 'I know. It's just … all those boys in the last war. Oh Dan.'

'Amy, you can't stop people loving each other – thank God,' he said. 'It gives us a reason for living, doesn't it? War or no war. It didn't stop me falling in love with you.'

She turned and put her arms around him. 'I love you,' she said.

Charlie and Tim changed into civvies and helped Dan to wrestle the corrugated roof over the shelter and cover it with earth. 'It's horrible,' Tessa said. 'I hope we don't ever have to sleep in it. It smells.'

They came in to tea.

'Would you two go and bring it in?' Amy said. 'Mrs Lewis will be busy with dinner.'

'I'll go and wash.' Charlie disappeared upstairs.

Tessa went into the kitchen. 'Hello Sara,' she said. 'Still at it?'

Sara was sitting at the table, a book in front of her. She nodded, 'Yes.'

'Still want to be a doctor?'

Sara smiled broadly. 'Oh yes.'

'You can always ask me,' Tessa said, 'anything you want to know.'

Charlie came in. 'I'm famished,' he said. 'Hello Sara. I'm Charlie.'

'How do you do,' she said.

He leant over her shoulder. 'What are you reading?'

'Biology.'

'Another brain,' he said. 'I'm surrounded by brains. You must be very proud of her, Mrs Lewis.'

'Oh, I am,' Nora said. 'I am.'

They carried in the tea. 'How about going out this evening?' Charlie said. 'A bit of dining and dancing. We could go to the Café de Paris again.'

'Oh yes,' Tessa said. 'We don't get much dancing, do we?'

'Are they having the May Balls at Cambridge this year?' Dan said.

'I think so,' Tessa said. 'That's if there are any men around to take us.' Amy saw her glance briefly at Tim, and saw his quick smile.

In the evening the three of them came into the sitting room. Amy's heart turned over. They look so beautiful, she thought, the boys in their uniforms, and Tessa in an evening dress, so fresh and pretty. 'Have a good time,' she said.

Dan tucked a five-pound note into Charlie's pocket. 'Thanks Dad,' he said. 'We're not exactly overpaid.'

They arrived at the Café de Paris and were given a table and ordered dinner.

'Wartime food,' Charlie said. He took out the five-pound note. 'Still, we can afford champagne.'

Over coffee Charlie looked around the room. 'There's a nice-looking girl over there,' he said. 'The redhead. I think I'll ask her to dance.'

'You don't know her, Charlie,' Tessa said.

'Wartime.' Charlie grinned. 'Anything goes.' He tapped his chest. 'And I've got the wings.' He set off across the room.

'I think you're stuck with me,' Tim said.

They stood up together; Tim slipped his arm around her waist and drew her close. 'That's nice,' he said.

She said nothing. Slowly she leant her head against his shoulder and he rested his cheek against her hair.

'Tessa,' he said. 'Tessa.'

For a moment she leant against him, but then she pulled away and laughed. 'Don't get serious,' she said.

He looked down at her. 'Why not?'

'Because,' she said.

He drew her close again. 'I can't help it,' he said.

This time she didn't pull away.

Nora kissed Sara goodnight. 'Say a prayer for Dad,' she said.

'I always do.' Sara bit her lip. 'I wish he was here.'

'So do I. Maybe he'll come home soon.' Nora brightened. 'They're nice, aren't they, the family? Tessa's nice.'

Sara nodded.

'And that Charlie,' Nora went on. 'I bet he'll be breaking some hearts.'

Chapter Twelve

1940

'It's started,' Dan said. 'We knew this couldn't go on – this false normality. It's the end of this phoney war.'

Amy paled. 'Why Denmark and Norway, for heaven's sake? What do they want with those?'

'They can use the airfields to get at us,' Dan said. 'And it puts them close to the iron mines in Sweden. They're just mopping up the edges – closing in on France – and on us.'

Amy sat down at the kitchen table and held her head in her hand. 'Poor France. All over again. It's unbelievable.'

Tessa telephoned. 'Do you think I should come home, Dad?' she said. 'Don't you think we should all be together now?'

'No, darling,' Dan said. 'The last thing anyone wants is people panicking and running around the country.'

'I'm not panicking,' she said. 'I just want to do something useful.'

'Stay where you are, Tessa,' he said. 'I'll let you know if we think you should come home.'

'I'll want her with us,' Amy said, 'if it looks as if they really are coming.' Her voice trembled, but she wouldn't give words to her fears.

She found it hard to sleep. The Germans wouldn't stop at Norway. Not now. She dreaded hearing the church bells, the signal that the invasion had begun. Church bells, she thought, that most English sound of a quiet, peaceful Sunday morning, now to be the signal for horror and chaos. She hadn't heard from Charlie for several days. No news was good news, wasn't it? She didn't even know whether he'd yet been in action.

She and Dan listened to the Home Service on the wireless. On 10

May, the Germans took the Netherlands and Belgium, and were advancing into France. Chamberlain had resigned and Churchill was now Prime Minister.

'Thank God,' Dan said. 'It was no good Chamberlain patting us on the head and saying Hitler has missed the boat. He patently hasn't.'

They listened constantly to the news. The British and French armies were being forced back, retreating, leaving most of their heavy equipment behind them. The roads were apparently packed with soldiers and thousands of French refugees. The Luftwaffe bombed and strafed them, civilians included, as they struggled on.

'The Germans have reached the Somme,' Dan said. 'They're only sixty miles from Paris.'

Amy was shocked, with a dreadful feeling of déjà vu, with overwhelming memories of her own days in the hospital in Paris in 1914, fearing that the Germans might come any day. She was even more appalled by the realization that the Great War had all been for nothing. Twenty years later exactly the same thing was happening. The next generation, the children of the survivors of that horror, had to go through it all again. Will it never end, she thought? This spiral of destruction and despair?

Every night they sat, tense, beside the wireless. On 26 May the Germans took Calais, cutting off the British forces. Their only remaining escape was through Dunkirk. 'They're trapped, Dan,' Amy agonized. 'All those boys. Have we lost our army? All our boys?'

She came home from an evening surgery, tired out from the emotional strain of trying to help or comfort white-faced women with their sick children; women whose husbands were on those beaches; they didn't know whether they were alive or dead. She found Dan packing a bag.

'Where are you going?' she said. 'What's happened?'

He took her hands. 'I'm going to Dunkirk, darling. They're bringing the men off in anything they can get across the Channel – yachts, barges, pleasure boats, anything. They're ferrying as many as they can to Naval ships lying offshore. I'm joining one of the destroyers to help with the wounded.'

She put her arms around him. 'Oh Dan.'

'We've got to save as many lives as we can,' he said. 'They've been bombed and shelled to hell. I don't have to tell you what's happening.'

'No,' she said. 'We've seen it all before. Is there anything I could do?'

'No,' he said. 'You must stay here. The children. Charlie ... One of us must be here.'

'We'll both be here,' she said, trying to keep the panic out of her voice.

'Of course we will,' he said. 'I'll be coming back.'

She kissed him goodbye at the door where a car was waiting to take him to the coast.

The destroyer arrived off the coast of Dunkirk. Dan looked out, filled with dismay. As far away as he could see, the men stood in lines out in the sea, the water up to their chests. Slowly, one by one, they were picked up by the little boats, shuttling to and fro to the bigger ships. Barges and yachts, pleasure steamers and little motor-launches, their decks crowded with men, set out across the Channel for England and home.

He watched, horrified, as the men, silent and patient, waited their turn. He watched as the Stukas dived and bombed and the beaches screamed and exploded and men died and disappeared beneath the sea. Hell, he thought. It's hell, once again, the horrors of 1914 added to and magnified, but with better weapons, better methods of killing. He went below to help the naval surgeons to care for the wounded until they could reach home and hospital. Once again he was handling the hideous, mutilating wounds of war. He was filled with pure rage. Even in 1914 he had never seen anything like this: men waiting in lines, unable to move, unable to protect themselves, with no cover from the bombers and the machine guns. There was no panic, no pushing or shoving, just patient, selfless bravery. They'll pay, he thought, the Nazis. They'll pay for this.

They took aboard as many men as they could pack in; the decks crowded. Dan moved among the wounded, applying dressings, giving morphine, doing what he could. He heard the crump and roar as another ship was hit; he tried not to think of the men aboard. As the destroyer pulled out into the Channel a squadron of Spitfires roared overhead, making for France. Charlie, he thought. One of them could be Charlie. God go with you.

They were to patrol inland of Dunkirk, to attack any enemy bomber formation approaching the coast.

Charlie took off with the rest of the squadron. Am I afraid, he thought? His mouth was dry and he had an empty feeling in the pit of his stomach. He was, he realized, more frightened of being frightened than anything else – too frightened perhaps to do anything, to do his job. The squadron around him was reassuring.

They crossed the English coast. They could see the fires at Dunkirk already – towering clouds of smoke from the burning buildings and from the burning oil tanks around the town. They gained height over France, looking out for any aircraft bearing the German insignia. The hard, vicious outline of the black crosses filled Charlie with repulsion. They were a reflection, he thought, of their nature. He looked out of the cockpit at the red, white, blue and yellow roundels on the Spitfires. Cheerful colours. Nice to look at. Pleasing to the eye and the spirit. They needed to search out the opposition soon, he thought. The Spits could fly for an hour and a half or so before running out of fuel. Sometimes the squadrons came back without finding anything – fed up at the inaction.

The RT crackled into life, 'Bombers, ten o'clock high.' Charlie looked up. He could see the formation of bombers above them, heading for the coast, for Dunkirk, for the helpless men trapped on the beaches, to bomb them to blazes. They climbed above them, still undetected. Sitting ducks, he thought. They broke into groups of three to attack.

Charlie chose his target. His heart was racing with excitement, elation, the thrill of the chase. He saw one of the bombers hit, the engine on fire, and wondered briefly who had shot it down.

Then, suddenly, the RT again. 'God! Messerschmitts – dozens of them!' The squadron broke off the attack and broke away. In seconds the sky was filled with hurtling aircraft. Charlie, throwing his aircraft around the sky in desperate manoeuvres, could think only of one thing now: taking one of them down. 'Bastards,' he found himself muttering. 'Bastards.' He latched on to one of the Messerschmitts. He saw glowing tracer coming towards him like a row of tiny, glowing lights. It seemed so slow at first – mesmerizing. He felt fear tightening his chest. He threw the plane into a tight turn and the tracer passed him by. He got the Messerschmitt momentarily in his sights and pressed the firing button. His Spit shuddered as tracer shot out from the wings and he watched the enemy dance away, unharmed. He pulled into a steep climb.

He came out of the climb and looked about him. To his amazement he could see no one – no aircraft at all. The sky was empty. He remembered that one of the pilots who had been in combat before had described this strangeness. 'It's weird,' he'd said. 'One minute it's a madhouse and the next there's nobody there and you just go home.'

He turned for home, keeping an eye on his fuel. Strangely, the encounter must only have taken a few minutes. It had felt like most of his life.

Suddenly, below him, he saw the outline of a bomber, a Junkers. He looked around him warily, his heart in his mouth, but the bomber seemed to be alone, returning to France after bombing the ships in the Channel.

He took it by surprise. His Spit shuddered again as he pressed the firing button and he saw his tracer explode along the fuselage and bits fly off the tail. Then, strangely, although it continued to fly straight and level for several seconds, the aircraft seemed to change before his eyes, as if all vitality was draining away, as if it were a living thing and its soul was leaving it. Then slowly, very slowly it seemed, it fell towards the sea. It crashed into the water with a great gout of spray. There were no parachutes.

'Got you,' he shouted, excited and exultant. He could go back and claim a kill. He looked about him again but the sky was clear. He would make it home. He crossed the English coast and blew it a smacking kiss.

How strange that was, he thought, the way that aircraft had died. It reminded him of a film he had once seen of a bull elephant that had been shot by a hunter in Africa. The elephant had been hit – a mortal shot – but it had stood upright for perhaps thirty seconds. Then, its spirit seemed to leave it, slowly and reluctantly, and it fell to its knees, and was dead. The film had thoroughly upset him.

No one had jumped from the bomber. The men inside it had died. He had killed them. He broke out in a light sweat. He must not think of that. They were busily killing his countrymen. He was fighting for his life, for his family, for his country. But the memory of the elephant upset him still.

When he landed the fitters were waiting to help him out and check the aircraft.

'Everybody OK?' he asked.

'Glad to see you back, sir. One missing, sir.'

'Who?' he said. 'Not Tim Crighton?'

'No sir,' they said. 'Mr Crighton got back all right, minus a bit of tailplane.'

Drinks then, in the mess; plenty of beer, raucous songs around the piano.

'You've been blooded then,' Tim said. 'Lucky beggar to find that Junkers. Where did you get to?'

'I don't know what happened,' Charlie said. 'I looked round and everyone had gone.'

Tim downed his pint. 'Tell me, Charlie,' he said. 'Were you frightened?'

Charlie grinned. 'Terrified,' he said.

Before he slept, he thought about the day. Had he been frightened when the tracer bullets floated past him? Not immediately; he had been mesmerized. Perhaps a few seconds later, when he realized how closely death had passed him by. But it was all right. He'd got through, acquitted himself OK.

The destroyer docked in Dover. The men were unloaded on to the quay, into the arms of waiting nurses and WVS ladies with cups of tea and sandwiches, and crowds of people cheering their welcome. Dan found that his eyes were filling with tears of compassion and relief. The men boarded trains to take them away, to camp or home to rest. Hospital trains festooned with red crosses took the wounded away to hospitals further north, away from the overwhelmed hospitals on the coast, and away from the expected raids on England.

Dan went back with the ship.

Two days later he came home, exhausted in body and spirit. Amy met him at the door and hugged him close. She felt his tears on her cheek.

'Darling,' she said. 'Oh darling. I've been listening to it on the wireless.'

'They can't describe it,' he said. 'I can't tell you ...'

She made him take a bath and go to bed. She brought him a cup of tea and lay on the bed beside him.

'I saw Spitfires,' he said, 'going over. Have you heard from Charlie?'

Amy nodded. 'Yes. He's all right.'

'Was he there?'

'Yes,' she said, 'but he's all right.'

He smiled and was instantly asleep.

He came down to dinner in the evening. 'That's it then,' he said. 'We're on our own. Just us and the Germans.'

'Do you know,' Amy said, 'I'm glad. It sounds an odd thing to say, but I'm glad. We know where we are now. We know what we have to do. And we'll do it.'

Dan took her hand. 'That's more like my Amy.'

'It was all those months of not knowing,' she said, 'and half hoping and fearing the worst. Well, the worst has happened, and it's all right. We'll do it.'

He put his arms around her and held her close.

'We're on our own, then,' Nora said.

Amy nodded, eating her sandwich in the kitchen. 'There isn't much to stop them in France now. The French seem to be giving up.'

'What are we going to do, Doctor?'

'Nothing, for the moment.'

'Why have the Italians gone in on their side?'

Amy smiled. 'You know what Churchill's supposed to have said? "That's only fair, we had to have the Italians last time."'

Nora relaxed and laughed. 'No. They're not exactly fighters, are they? They've only been attacking people weaker than they are. Well, they'll find it's a bit different now.'

Amy looked through her post. She picked out a leaflet. 'Look at this,

Nora. The answer to your question. It's what to do if the Germans invade.' She read out from the leaflet. '"Stay put in your homes; don't block the roads and get in the way of our soldiers; don't give anything to the Germans."'

'As if we would,' Nora said.

'Keep watch and report; no careless talk.'

Nora turned to the sink and began to peel the potatoes. Amy could see the tension in her shoulders. 'They won't get here, Nora,' she said. 'The RAF and the Navy won't let them.'

'My husband and your son,' Nora said.

'Quite right,' Amy said. 'How's Sara getting on at school?'

'Very well.' Nora paused. 'If anyone touched her I'd kill them with my bare hands.'

'Me too,' Amy said. 'We'd make a good team.'

Tim and Tessa walked along the Backs beside the river. 'I'm sorry about the May Ball,' he said. 'We were a bit busy.'

'It doesn't matter,' she said. 'I didn't really want to go anyway. We're going down in a couple of days. I'll be glad to get home.'

They walked on. 'What's it like,' she said. 'Is it awful?'

'Not really,' he said. 'You're too busy to think about it at the time, and then it's all over.'

'Everybody all right?' she said.

He laughed. 'If you mean Charlie, he's fine. Shot down a Junkers all on his own. We thought we'd lost one pilot, but he turned up. Got shot down and bailed out. Came down in some posh garden and they gave him a brandy and a cigar and he came back in a chauffeur-driven Rolls.'

She laughed. 'Quite right too.'

He took her hand. There were one or two punts out on the river, but not many people about. 'I want to kiss you,' he said.

She turned to him and put her arms around his neck. 'Yes please.' He kissed her very thoroughly. 'We'd better stop,' she said. 'Someone might see and I'm supposed to be very respectable.'

'You are very respectable, dammit,' he said, 'and so am I, I suppose.'

She laughed. 'No hanky-panky with the WAAFS?'

'No hanky panky with anyone. I'm a one-girl man.'

He kissed her again and they walked on, hand in hand.

After he'd gone she got out her books to study – the anatomy of the brain. Where is it, she thought? Where's the bit that makes you love someone? She'd been so adamant that she didn't want to get involved; her career was all she wanted. And now she wanted Tim too, and the fact that he was in mortal danger every day made it stronger and deeper. There was no time – no time to dance and dream through a couple of May Balls, idle together on the river, think about the future. Since they'd danced together at the Café de Paris they'd managed to see each other now and again, usually in Cambridge, where they couldn't be alone for very long. They hadn't used the word 'love' yet, much less 'for ever', but it was there. They both knew it was there. It seemed too frightening to say the words. Too much like tempting Providence.

Sara marched down to the school cellar. They had an air-raid practice every week. 'Orderly rows,' the teachers said. 'No running or pushing, even if we're being bombed. If the soldiers at Dunkirk can do it, you can.' Some of the girls groaned but Sara didn't care. She was so glad to be back she'd put up with anything.

The girls sat in rows on the benches, whispering and giggling, the prefects trying to look serious. Sara glanced at the teachers. They didn't seem to be concerned.

It wasn't real, was it? It was like fire drill; it wasn't going to happen. All those soldiers had come back from Dunkirk. Everybody seemed to be cheerful, and things weren't much different really, apart from her dad being away and Mum getting a job. The job was nice, and they were all doctors. Tessa was nice; she'd shown her some of her textbooks from Cambridge. Charlie was a pilot and they all worried about him, she could see that. He was nice too. He made her feel a bit shy, though.

'Gas-masks on.'

Sara put the mask over her head. It smelt horrible and was hot and sweaty. How would we get out, she thought, if the school came down above them? She supposed someone would come and dig them out –

her mum, for one. She occupied her mind with a little mental arithmetic. If a falling object accelerates at thirty-two feet per second per second, how long would it take a bomb...?

'Look at these,' Nora said. 'One of my neighbours brought them up from Plymouth. The Germans must have dropped them in the night.' She put a few leaflets on the table.

Tessa picked one up and began to laugh. 'Listen to this, "A last appeal to reason by Adolph Hitler. The Führer sees no reason why the war should continue. He means Britain no harm."' She handed the leaflet to Amy. 'I could give him a few reasons – the Jews, Holland, Belgium, France.'

Nora giggled. 'My neighbour says they're using them for toilet paper down there.'

'It's a dirty trick,' Tessa said, 'trying to get us off guard. Well, I'm still going to do firewatching at the hospital.'

It's extraordinary, Amy thought, how attitudes have changed in the country, now that we are alone. Everyone is much more cheerful. We can see our task more clearly. The British fight best with their backs to the wall. 'One of my little patients told me a joke,' she said. 'What did Hitler say as he fell through the bed?' Nora and Tessa shook their heads. 'At last I'm in Po-land.'

They all laughed. There's laughter again Amy thought. She looked at Tessa's young, glowing face. And love again, perhaps. They had been seeing a good deal of Tim lately. Perhaps love.

The summer wore on, one glorious day after another. There were raids on the coastal towns and on the convoys of shipping in the Channel. The squadron flew every day, in battle nearly every day, taking off, heart in mouth, a few frantic minutes of hurling their Spits around the skies, perhaps an enemy destroyed. Then home again, survival, and an evening in the pub.

Charlie was woken at four o'clock with a cup of tea. After breakfast they climbed into the trucks to be driven to the dispersal hut. They climbed out of the truck and sat about on the collection of rather broken-down old chairs in and around the hut. Charlie and Tim sat outside in the growing light, watching the stars fading. Dawn came, slowly. The scent of the mown grass and the country flowers drifted around them. High in the sky a lark began to sing.

'I had a letter from Tessa,' Tim said. 'She sent you her love.'

'You two seem to be getting along very well,' Charlie said. 'Is there anything in it?'

'I hope so,' Tim said. 'You know how I feel about her.'

Charlie grinned. 'So I won't have to shoot you down.' Tim didn't reply. The NAAFI van arrived with the tea.

'Time you had a girlfriend, Charlie,' Tim said, laughing. 'Give you something else to think about.'

Charlie shrugged. 'Haven't met one I fancied yet.'

They waited. Charlie felt the usual stirring in his bowels. This was the worst bit – the waiting; waiting for the telephone to ring and the shouting voice – scramble, scramble. Then the run to the aircraft and his bowels would settle as he was strapped in.

'I expect it'll be another bloody marvellous day,' Tim said. 'Why can't we have fog and drizzle and spend the day in bed?'

'What day is it?' Charlie asked.

'Tuesday,' Tim said. 'August the thirteenth. Not that it makes any difference, does it?'

They waited. 'I think you might have your wish,' Charlie said. 'It looks a bit murky.'

'Not murky enough. Not enough to stop the bastards.' Tim went off for another cup of tea.

They waited. At half past six the telephone rang. Scramble! Scramble! The squadron took off, and the fear left him. He glanced at the aircraft around him. There was nothing more beautiful, he thought, than a squadron of Spitfires in the early light.

The mass of the Luftwaffe approached from the south-west. 'Good God,' their leader called, 'there's hundreds of them.' Charlie stared ahead of him – Junkers, Dorniers, Me 109s. In the next few shuddering, screaming minutes he threw himself around the sky in a mad mêlée of aircraft, of tracer bullets streaming past, of aircraft falling, parachutes unfolding. Then, suddenly, he found himself alone again, and turned for home.

The airfield was almost unrecognizable; bomb craters, huts burning, people running about. He managed to get down and was set on by the fitters. He was refuelled, rearmed and returned to the skies, to a second wave of enemy bombers.

Every day, every day, they came. Every day, several times a day, they were in battle. 'You must admit they are gentlemen, the Luftwaffe,' Tim said. 'At least they go home nicely in time for us to get to the pub.'

The days became a blur: days of hurtling through the skies, trying not to be killed, and evenings in the King's Head or the mess, beer in hand, playing the fool; toasting, and then forgetting, the pilots who didn't make it.

Charlie began to feel as if nothing was quite real. He fell asleep one night over his dinner, his head on the table. He was given a twenty-four-hour pass, he borrowed Tim's Morgan and went home.

Amy was shocked when she saw him, but she hid it under smiles and hugs. 'Take your things upstairs, darling,' she said, 'and then come down and have some tea.' Ten minutes later she went up to his room. He was lying on his back on his bed, fast asleep. She slipped off his shoes and he didn't wake. She stroked the hair back from his brow and kissed him gently. Asleep, he looked like a boy again. My boy, she thought. My merry little boy. The ache in her heart was almost unbearable.

She went downstairs to Dan. 'He's exhausted,' she said. 'They must all be exhausted. How long can this go on?'

'As long as it takes, my darling. For all of us.'

Amy opened her post over breakfast. Most of it was from the ministry about GP medical care – diphtheria vaccine, orange juice, free milk for the children. One was to remind them about turning off the gas at the mains at night in case of a raid, another was about how to deal with incendiary bombs. The last one was a shock.

'Dan,' she said, 'this one's about Kurt. He's in England, in hospital. He's been badly hurt. He's asking if he can see us.'

'How injured?' Dan said. 'What's happened to him?'

Amy handed over the letter. 'Burns,' she said. 'He's a pilot, apparently. It sounds pretty terrible.'

'I can't go,' Dan said. 'I'm sorry about him, of course, but I can't get away.'

'I don't think I can either,' Amy said. 'Perhaps the children ...'

'It's a bit odd, isn't it?' Dan said. 'Visiting the enemy? And would they let anyone see him?'

'Apparently so. They think he's going to die, Dan.'

'Oh. Ask the children then. I don't know how they'll feel about it.'

Children, Amy thought. We must stop calling them the children: Charlie, a man among men, Tessa, spending nights on a hospital roof, firewatching, looking for killers. Would they want to go? Kurt was an enemy in an enemy country, but he was dying, and dying alone. What if it were Charlie? Would they want Kurt to visit him?

Charlie came home on a forty-eight-hour pass and Tessa found him in the garden. She sat down beside him.

'Vegetables doing well,' he said. 'Nice tomatoes.'

'Charlie,' she said, 'we've had a letter about Kurt. He's in England.'

'Good Lord,' he said. 'A POW then. Where is he? One of the camps? I don't suppose we'd be able to see him.'

'He's in hospital,' she said. 'He's been injured.'

'Badly?'

'Yes.' She hesitated. It wasn't a subject she wanted to bring up. She knew what gave the pilots their worst horrors. 'He's been badly burned,' she said. 'He was flying – fighters. They think he's dying.' She watched him, ready for the wince that crossed his face.

Charlie sat still. He could feel his shoulders tensing and his jaw clenching. This was the nightmare: not death itself, not a bullet in the brain or the heart – not even drowning. The nightmare was burning, trapped and burning. A quick death was far preferable.

'Mum called the hospital,' Tessa said. 'They said we can go to see him if we want, but we'd have to be quick. There isn't much time.'

Charlie said nothing. He didn't know that he could face it: going to see someone who had suffered the worst fate there was. The thought of it terrified them all. They had to block it out of their minds. He didn't want to see it – to look at it. Every part of him shrank away from it. Perhaps that image would never leave him, damage him, haunt him every time he stepped into a cockpit. 'I don't know, Tess,' he said. 'I don't know if I can.'

'He particularly wants to see you,' she said. Charlie had broken out into a light sweat, beading on his forehead. She took his hand. 'It's all right,' she said. 'You don't have to go. I can go on my own.'

'I'll think about it,' he said.

He got his bike out, rode to Kensington Gardens and walked about the pathways. The flower-beds had been dug over and filled with vegetables, cabbages mainly. Several men were weeding the plots; they were Italians, he realized as he passed by and heard them talking. There was a camp for Italian prisoners of war, if any arrived, and internees, somewhere in the park. They didn't seem to be supervised at all. Perhaps the Italians weren't considered to be too much of a threat.

He had brought Kurt here on one of the half terms from school. He had shown him the fairy tree and Peter Pan.

'Oh, you English,' Kurt had said. 'You are so sentimental.'

There had been rumours that boys from the Hitler Youth had been spying while they were holidaying in England before the war. He couldn't believe that Kurt had been up to no good.

The week he had spent in Berlin came back to him vividly – the grim faces under the steel helmets, the brutality of it all. And he remembered Kurt's last words about the oracle at Delphi. If he'd been talking about Britain, he'd got it badly wrong. Or maybe he meant Germany. Weren't they all just the same, all caught up in this dreadful web of killing? Kurt was just another man. He shouldn't die alone.

He went back home. 'I'll come,' he said to Tessa.

They travelled to the hospital on the train and the bus. A staff nurse took them to Kurt. 'He's in a side room,' she said. 'He's very ill.'

'I'm a medical student,' Tessa said. 'Can you tell me what's happening?'

'He's on M and B and saline compresses,' the nurse said, 'but it isn't helping much. He's on morphine every few hours. He's very drowsy. The doctors don't think he'll last the night.'

A faint sickly smell drifted out as the nurse opened the door. 'It's the infection,' Tessa whispered. 'Poor Kurt.'

He was swathed in dressings, his face, chest and arms. His hands, painted with mercurochrome, rested on the cover like the claws of a great bird. They couldn't see his face – only his eyes and his mouth were free.

Tessa bent down to him. 'Kurt,' she said softly. He seemed to be asleep, though his eyes were open. 'Kurt,' she said again.

His eyes turned slowly towards them. 'Tessa,' he whispered, his voice cracked and hoarse.

'Charlie is here,' Tessa said. 'He's come to see you.'

Charlie bent down. 'Hello Kurt,' he said.

Something like a smile flickered in Kurt's eyes. 'You're a flyer, Charlie,' he said. 'Like me.' He winced. 'Do you remember, Charlie, the good days?'

'Yes,' Charlie said. 'I remember.'

The smile flickered again. 'Perhaps it was you who killed me, Charlie,' he said. 'Perhaps it was you who shot me down.'

Tessa began to cry, silently, the tears creeping down her cheeks.

'It's a dreadful mistake, Charlie,' Kurt whispered. 'It's all a dreadful mistake.' He closed his eyes for a moment. 'After the war,' he said, 'will you tell my parents that you were here; that I have been well treated?'

'Yes,' Charlie said. 'If I can.'

Kurt's voice faded and his eyes glazed over.

'I think you'd better go now,' the nurse said. 'It's best if he sleeps.' Tessa gently touched the clawed hand.

They left the hospital. 'There's a Lyons here,' Tessa said. 'I need a cup of tea.'

They went into the teashop and ordered tea. Charlie looked pale, Tessa thought, his jaw working. 'You didn't shoot him down, Charlie,' she said. 'It wasn't you.'

'It might have been,' Charlie said. 'I've shot down a few.'

'You have to,' she said. 'Or they'll get us.'

'I know,' he said. 'Don't go on about it, Tessa.'

She saw the strain breaking through his composure, his eyes, hooded, withdrawn. 'Let's go home,' she said.

At nine o'clock the hospital telephoned to say that Kurt had died. Charlie went up to his room and closed the door.

Chapter Thirteen

Late August 1940

'Mum,' Sara said, 'can I stay the night with Kathy on Saturday? Her mum says it's all right.'

Nora was putting a cheese and potato pie into the oven. 'I thought she was in Kent with her auntie.'

'She's come back home again.' Sara said. 'She says the Germans have been dropping bombs on the airfields and sometimes they just dump them anywhere, so she's safer at home. She's seen our planes having dogfights with the Germans. She says she saw a bomber shot down.'

Nora shut the oven door sharply. What a world, she thought – children watching men kill each other. 'Yes,' she said. 'You go and have a nice time.'

'Will you be all right?'

Nora straightened up and smiled. 'Of course I will.' She put her arms around Sara. 'You don't have to worry about me, love, I'm fine. Just as long as you're all right. That's all that matters to me.'

'And Dad.'

Nora carefully arranged her face into unworried smiles. 'And Dad, of course. He's all right too. We had a letter from him last week, didn't we? And I wrote back and told him what we were doing.' Nora made a point of talking about Jim every day. Just to mention his name kept him in their lives, kept him there for her and Sara. She said her prayers every night in bed, longing for him to be with her to help her through the terrible things that were happening. She tried not to think about what might be happening to him. Imagining and worrying wouldn't help anybody and would upset Sara.

'I'll go first thing Saturday morning, then,' Sara said. 'We're going to play tennis.' She went back to her books.

Thank God for children, Nora thought, playing tennis, doing what children do.

'Dan,' Amy said, 'I want to bring my father here. I'll make him come if I have to. He shouldn't be on his own and he shouldn't be in Kent. So much for us thinking it was safer in the country. They're starting to call it Bomb Alley.'

Dan nodded. 'Of course he should come here. Just make him. You know how stubborn he is.'

'I'll ring him,' Amy said, 'and read him the riot act, and I'll go and get him on Saturday. I'd better tell Nora there'll be one more.'

Nora was in the kitchen, washing up. 'Would you like me to come with you?' she said. 'Sara won't be at home. She's spending the weekend with a schoolfriend.'

'Oh Nora, would you?' Amy took her hand. 'I'd be so grateful. He'll hate leaving and shutting up the house. He'll probably pack everything but the kitchen sink.'

They drove to Kent on Saturday morning.

'Sara's friend was evacuated to Kent,' Nora said, 'but they brought her back. I suppose they're really aiming to bomb the airfields, but they seem to be dropping them anywhere. And machine-gunning. Ordinary people in the streets.'

'I know,' Amy said. 'My father's told me a few tales. One woman hung out her nappies to dry and came out to find them full of bullet holes. And some woman near Biggin Hill watched her own son bale out – safely, thank God.'

'How awful.' Nora looked out at the passing suburbs. 'I've never been to Kent before. I'd like to see the proper countryside – all the orchards. It must be beautiful in the spring.'

Amy smiled. 'The garden of England.' She chuckled. 'Apparently they dropped a bomb near an apple orchard and all the apples fell off the trees. The farmer said he'd never had such an easy harvest.'

They reached Bromley. Amy drove down the familiar road and stopped outside the house. She sat for a few moments, looking at the house, at the familiar front garden, the hydrangeas still in pink bloom, at the old front door under the little porch. She saw herself leaving for France in 1914; coming back again at the end of the war, changed for ever, to the solid, comforting, unchanging home she had left behind.

'I was born here,' she said. 'My mother died when I was little and my father brought me up.' She turned off the ignition. 'He's a dear. He won't want to go. He'll see it as a defeat. Let's hope he's packed and ready.'

They walked up to the house and Amy opened the door. Her father's bags and suitcases were standing in the hall. He came out to them. 'I'm all ready,' he said. 'I've got everything I need.' His eyes filled. 'I'm not just upset,' he said. 'I'm bloody angry. Being forced out of my own home.'

He must be devastated, Amy thought, to use that word in their presence. She put her arms around him. 'It's all right, dear. It'll be here waiting for you after the war.'

He nodded and blinked his tears away. 'I hope so. Perhaps it won't be too long. We'll have a cup of tea before we go.'

'I'll put the suitcases in the car,' Nora said, 'while the kettle's boiling.' After a few minutes she came back into the kitchen. 'There's just a couple of small bags to go. And where's your gas-mask?'

'In one of the bags,' he said. 'Never go anywhere without it and I've got my ration book in my pocket.'

Amy made the tea and they sat down at the kitchen table.

The sound of the siren startled them, the up and down wailing they had learnt to dread. Amy's father put his cup down abruptly. 'They're early today,' he said. 'They don't usually come till later.'

Amy paused, the teapot in her hand, uncertain what to do.

'They go straight for the airfields,' he said, 'but they drop left-over bombs and machine gun anything that moves on the way back. They don't care what they hit.'

'What shall we do?' Nora said. 'Stay or go?'

'We'd better not go till the All Clear,' he said. 'They've been shooting at cars on the roads.'

'Well let's have our tea,' Nora said. 'I'm parched.'

The droning sound of aircraft engines began in the distance, quickly getting louder, an ominous regular thrumming. 'Dorniers,' Amy's father said. 'I know the sound of the engines. We'd better get under the stairs, just in case. Bring your tea.' They squashed into the cupboard under the stairs and sat on the floor. The droning became a roar that seemed to go on and on. 'There must be dozens of them,' he said.

A silence fell, the planes passing away overhead. 'We can get out for a bit,' he said, 'until they start coming back. Have another cup of tea.'

'We'll finish loading,' Nora said, her voice shaking a little. 'Then we can get off as soon as the All Clear goes.' She and Amy carried the last of the bags to the car.

They didn't even hear the solitary aircraft that dropped the bomb. All they heard was the scream of it dropping, and then a huge explosion. For a surreal moment time seemed to move into slow, slow motion and Amy could see everything with unreal clarity. She watched the windows of the house shatter into glittering shards, flying like silver arrowheads, sucked inwards by the blast. Then she was knocked violently off her feet and hit her head against the car. She found herself on her knees, dizzy and disoriented.

Nora seemed to be beside her at once. 'Are you all right?' she said.

'Yes,' Amy said. 'I think so.' She tried to get to her feet, but couldn't seem to get off her knees. 'Are you?'

'Yes,' Nora said. 'I'm OK. I was round the other side.'

'Father,' Amy gasped. 'Where's my father?' They watched, horrified, as smoke began to curl out of one of the gaping windows.

Amy began to struggle towards the house, staggering, half-crawling. 'Father,' she screamed. 'Father.'

Nora ran to the house and disappeared through the empty doorway. Amy got herself to her feet and began to run. 'Nora, Nora,' she shouted. 'Come back. I'll get him.'

Nora appeared at the doorway, half carrying the old man. They were both black with soot. They staggered to the car together. 'I'm all right,' he said. He took a few deep breaths. 'Didn't know what was happening for a minute.'

They bundled him into the car. 'Let's get out of here,' Nora said, almost shouting. 'There's a smell of gas.'

As Amy got into the driver's seat a fire engine roared into the road, bell ringing. She got out of the car and spoke to one of the men. 'There's no one in here now,' she said. 'The house is empty. We're taking my father away. There's a smell of gas.'

'Well get on with it,' he said. 'The gas main's probably gone. Fast as you can.'

Amy drove away, away from the house where she was born, away from the kindly memories of her childhood. She was filled with rage, rage at the destruction, at the shattering of her father's old age, at how close she had come to losing him. The tears ran down her face. 'Nora,' she said. 'You saved my father's life. And you risked your own.'

She felt rather than saw Nora's smile. 'All in a day's work, Doctor,' Nora said.

'No more Doctor,' Amy said. 'Just call me Amy. I was going to say it anyway, you've been such a friend. And now you've saved my father's life. Call me Amy. Just Amy.'

They arrived home to more cups of tea, baths, and a stiff whisky for Amy's father. She insisted that he went to bed.

The two women sat in the kitchen, nibbling at a sandwich.

'I don't know how to thank you,' Amy began, her eyes filling. 'If there's anything I can do…?'

Nora smiled. 'I'm just glad I was there, Doc …' She caught Amy's eye and laughed. 'Amy.'

Amy took her hand and they sat together in silence. Here we are, Amy thought. Nora's husband and her own son were away and in danger, but they had had one little victory. The Germans had tried and had failed to kill her father. Damn their eyes.

Saturday, 7 September. Charlie and Tim and the rest of the squadron sat about at dispersal, ready to go. Charlie glanced around him. Most of the pilots seemed to be asleep. Tim was twitching a little, his eyes rolling under his lids. Charlie closed his eyes. If he could only sleep – real sleep, deep and unconscious. What was sleep now? Nothing but a dream-infested interlude between hours of frantic flying, dodging lines of glowing tracers, the rattle of guns, the frantic effort to stay alive and to destroy. And then the struggle home, to an airfield that had been blasted and bombed in his short absence. He wasn't even sure, sometimes, that he was actually alive, that it wasn't all some hellish, prolonged, exhausting purgatory. The sun touched his face, kindly and warm. It was a lovely day; beautiful bombing weather.

He waited with his friends and comrades for the inevitable telephone call. Scramble, scramble, then the rush to the waiting Spits, the mad, exhausting fight. He didn't question his commitment, the source of his physical and mental endurance. He deeply sensed that the battle was not only for his country, but was a battle between good and evil. One that they had to win. He had sensed the evil in Berlin, the oppression, lack of freedom, the stuck-up pride. It had to go. The NAFFI truck arrived with tea. Most of the pilots woke, squinting into the early sunshine. No one spoke.

An hour drifted by. 'They're late,' Tim said. He closed his eyes again.

Another hour, and another. Charlie began to feel slightly sick. The waiting was the worst thing. Lunch was brought out to them. Cigarette smoke drifted up skywards. Some of the pilots went to sleep again.

'I don't like this,' Tim said. 'The bastards are up to something. They should be here by now.'

'I expect they soon will be,' Charlie said. 'They're not going to just give up, are they?'

The day wore on. Close by a blackbird began to sing, then it suddenly stopped. Perhaps it knows something we don't, Charlie thought. He fell asleep at last. He was woken by the jangle of the telephone. The corporal put his head out of the hut door. 'Scramble, scramble!'

Charlie glanced at his watch as he ran. Quarter past four. Something was definitely up. Something new.

The squadron took off, climbing to gain height before reaching their assigned position to join other squadrons. Charlie looked down and sucked in his breath. He could hardly believe what he was seeing. The sky was black with hundreds of German aircraft, Dorniers, Heinkels and Junkers flying in stacks and hundreds more Me109s flying as escorts. 'Good God,' he said. He felt oddly detached, as if this couldn't be real – as if he were back in another hellish nightmare.

'Tally-ho boys.' His squadron leader's voice broke over the radio. 'Let's surround them.'

In spite of stunned shock and the familiar empty feeling in his stomach, Charlie laughed. Yes, let's do that, he thought. All twelve of us.

They dived out of the sun. In moments they were into the battle. The air was filled with screaming aircraft. The Spitfires attacked the fighters, leaving the waiting Hurricanes to deal with the bombers. Charlie saw two of the bombers go down, streaming smoke. Two bodies swirled through the air within feet of his cockpit, bringing his heart into his mouth. He felt a jolt. His Spit had been hit – somewhere – but it still worked, fuel OK, controls OK. He'd been lucky. He chased an Me109, spurting bullets, missing it. He ran out of ammunition and turned to fly back to base. There must be bullet holes in the fuselage, but they hadn't hit anything important. Especially him.

He expected that the bombers would peel off and change course as usual, making for the airfields. We'll never survive this, he thought, this number. They must have sent every aircraft they've got. The airfields would be bombed to smithereens. There'd be nowhere to go back to. End of Fighter Command. End of everything. But the stacks of bombers didn't turn, or change course. They surged on, a horrifying, stultifying, relentless black swarm. My God, he thought. It's not the airfields this time. They're making for London.

Saturday, 7 September. A beautiful warm sunny day. Londoners were strolling or lying in the parks in the sunshine, or shopping in the West End. In the East End they were at home in the long rows of terraced houses, or working through the next shift on the docks. The women were chatting with neighbours, the children playing in the streets. The rows of houses stood together, close and neighbourly; the river glittered in the sunshine, the great warehouses and yards stood strung along the banks with their stores of wood and paper and tea and sugar and just about everything that the country needed. Just after four o'clock the sirens sounded. Everyone hurried to take cover, but they were not more worried than usual. There had been sporadic raids before, but they always attacked the airfields. They were sleep-disturbing nuisances. In the east the women called their children in. In the west the sleepers and strollers in the parks began to pack up.

Suddenly, over the East End, the sky was black with death.

The guns roared, the bombs screamed and fell. Terrified people ran into their houses and crouched under the stairs, under tables, under anything they could find. Those near the tube stations crowded down the stairs to the safety of the underground stations below. Around them their world exploded and shattered and burst into flames.

In Hyde Park the anti-aircraft guns cracked through the afternoon haze. The people scattered, making for the few shelters, or crowding down the stairs into the underground stations. In the West End, the people surged into the shops and huddled into the basements and cellars of the big department stores.

It was a lovely sunny day, Saturday 7 September, and the family was at home. Amy and Dan and Tessa and Amy's father had tea in the garden. They felt safe enough – safe for today, anyway. The threat of invasion still hung like a pall over every day, no matter how normal it seemed, how sunny and warm. There had been some scattered raids on London, but nothing to disrupt their everyday lives. They did every-thing they should before going to bed at night: turned off the gas, kept torches at the ready, made sure the stirrup-pump was ready in the downstairs cloakroom. The days were as usual: Dan and Amy at work, Nora looking after the house, and Amy's father had taken charge of the garden. Tessa, on vacation from Cambridge, did her fire-watching at the hospital, usually at night, so that the day workers could get their sleep. It seemed very quiet, almost like peacetime. Amy drank her tea and ate her cake, and tried not to think about what Charlie might be doing – must be doing. It was a constant anxiety, underlying every-thing. She did the usual things; went to a concert: Dame Myra Hess was giving piano recitals at the National Gallery. She went to the pictures with Tessa to see *Gone With The Wind*, and *All This and Heaven Too* in Leicester Square. And all the time Charlie was with her. She almost felt that she knew when he was flying.

'What a lovely day;' Dan said. 'You can hardly believe we're at war.'

'I'm glad we did that raid on Berlin,' Tessa said. 'Give them some-thing to think about. They've had things too much their own way.' She went into the house to get some more hot water. As she came out, the siren began to wail. No one moved.

'Why do they have to have that awful noise?' Amy's father said. 'They should have something stirring and British – "The British Grenadiers" or something.'

Tessa laughed. 'What a good idea. And we could have "In The Mood" when they've gone.'

Amy poured the hot water into the teapot. Charlie would be flying again. 'Damn nuisance,' Dan said, 'spoiling the afternoon. I expect the All-Clear will go in a minute.' The minutes passed. There was no All-Clear.

They sat in silence, a slightly nervous silence. Dan stirred his tea, the spoon scraping against the cup. The silence was strange, he thought. It seemed to have a different quality, as if something was happening a long way away, something he could feel rather than hear. He stopped stirring. It's just me, he thought. Letting it get to me. Attack of nerves. Suddenly the crashing sound of the anti-aircraft guns roared around them. The noise seemed to shake the very air. They all jumped, the tea spilling.

'Good God!' Dan said. 'What a hellish noise. Into the shelter, everybody.'

They tumbled down into the Anderson shelter. Dan closed the door and fumbled for the torch he'd stored inside, and for candles and matches. They sat down on the bunks and the two folding chairs. A little trickle of dry earth came down from the roof. After a few minutes the guns stopped, but there was no All-Clear.

'I think I'll get out and have a look round,' Tessa said. 'Is there anything I can get from the house?'

'You're staying here,' Dan said. 'Anything could happen.'

'I'm bored silly,' Tessa said.

Her father frowned at her. 'Better bored than dead.'

Just after six o'clock the All-Clear sounded, and they emerged into the evening sunshine. Nothing was changed. There was no damage that they could see. They went back into the house and Amy put the casserole that Nora had left into the oven. They turned on the wireless. The announcements were horrifying: mass raids on London, on the East End, a monstrous air battle, many enemy aircraft destroyed. They didn't mention losses in the RAF.

Tessa put her arms around her mother. 'Oh Mum,' she said.

Amy held her close. 'They'll be all right,' she said. 'They'll both be all right.' She held Tessa away from her. 'Do you love him, darling?' she said. Tessa nodded, her eyes filled with tears. Amy held her close again.

Dan was upstairs collecting more bedding and a couple of camp beds for the shelter. He felt in his bones that something had changed, that the shelter must be ready for them all to sleep in if necessary. He went into his bedroom. The window faced east, where every summer morning the sunrise lit up the window and shone, bright and golden, into the room. He looked out of the window, puzzled by a strange glow in the sky. 'The sun sets in the west,' he said aloud. 'In the west.' It was a few seconds before he recognized what he was seeing. He felt suddenly cold, frozen. It's fire, he thought. Fire, in the east of London. London is burning, burning badly enough for us to see the light from here. For a few minutes he watched in growing, unbelieving shock. He went downstairs.

The family was listening to the six o'clock news, their faces stricken.

'It's the East End, Dan,' Amy said, her voice shaking. 'The docks and the warehouses and all those poor people. Up to a thousand German aircraft, they say. It's been bombed to blazes.'

Saturday 7 September was a lovely day. Nora and Sara were shopping when the siren went. Among the shops was a cellar that had been made into an air-raid shelter; there was a sign outside. Nora had never been down there. Now she pushed Sara ahead of her and they hurried down. The cellar was gloomy, lit by a single light bulb, and smelt damp and musty.

'Can't we go home?' Sara said 'It's not far. It's horrible down here. The sirens often go and nothing happens.'

'No.' Nora sat down on a bench, under the dim electric light. Today, for some reason, she didn't want to take the risk.

Sara sat beside her. 'I haven't got anything to read.'

Nora just clicked her tongue. Several other people came down into the cellar.

'Nothing much happening up there,' a man said, 'but better safe than sorry, I always say.'

The anti-aircraft guns started in the distance and Sara took her mother's hand.

'Sounds as if something's happening now, though,' the man said. 'If they're bombing London they're getting ready to invade, I shouldn't wonder. Could be this weekend. Then we'll know all about it.'

'Do you mind,' Nora said angrily. 'There's a child here.'

'Sorry,' he said. 'Didn't think.'

They stayed in the cellar until the All Clear went just after six o'clock. They hurried home and Nora made a quick meal. 'I don't know what we should do tonight,' she said, 'if they come back.'

'Stay here,' Sara said. 'I'm not going back to that cellar.'

'Help me get that single mattress down then,' Nora said. 'We'll sleep under the stairs. That's the safest place.'

They humped the mattress down the stairs and brought pillows and blankets.

'There,' Nora said. 'Quite cosy, really.'

Charlie was stood down. He changed and went into the mess. He ordered a pint of bitter and sat down in a shabby leather armchair. He was weary to his bones. He was all right now, till tomorrow. He could sleep. The Spits weren't much use as night fighters. If the bastards came back in the night it would be mainly down to the gunners.

The fact that he was still alive at all seemed crazy. They had lost another pilot from the squadron today. At least, he hadn't shown up, so it didn't look good. The day's battle to get the bombers before they reached London hadn't succeeded too well. The East End was on fire. The numbers had been too great. He had phoned home to tell them he was all right and his mother had cried on the phone with sheer relief. Tim had phoned Tessa, hunched over the phone for ages. He closed his eyes and leant his head back against the chair.

He felt a tap on his shoulder. 'Hello, Charlie.'

He opened his eyes blearily and for a moment thought he must be dreaming. 'Arthur!' he said. 'What on earth are you doing here?' He got to his feet and shook his hand. 'It's good to see you.' He looked down at Arthur's jacket. 'You've got wings!'

Arthur grinned. 'I made the mistake of learning to fly, didn't I? They're running short of pilots. Let's say I was encouraged.'

'Sit down,' Charlie said. 'I'll get you a pint.' He came back with a beer for Arthur and another for himself. 'How's the family? Your mother still making her famous pastry?'

Arthur grinned. 'As far as the rations will allow.' He looked around him. 'And what do you know? They made me an officer. Me – from the wrong side of the track.' He gave a short laugh. 'They must have thought that because I went to Cambridge I must be OK. I've learnt how to use a knife and fork.'

'There's none of that nonsense here,' Charlie said. 'The sergeant pilots are just as good as we are. Some of them are better.' He paused. 'Better pilots, better men.'

Arthur laughed. 'Tell that to the establishment. After the war I expect I'll be back in my place.'

They sat for a few moments in silence. Charlie well knew how Arthur must be feeling now: excitement, apprehension.

'I expect I'll be at it tomorrow, then,' Arthur said. 'They're bound to come back.'

'I expect so,' Charlie said. 'Never a day goes by.' He took a mouthful of beer. 'How many hours have you done on Spits?'

'Not enough,' Arthur said. 'They're turning us out like sausages. It's your turn to teach me now, Charlie.'

Later Charlie lay in bed, listening to the sirens going. *They're back*, he thought, *of course*. The airfield was unusually quiet. The target was London again. The parents, Tessa, Grandpa were there. He said a brief prayer. He thought of Arthur, doing it for the first time tomorrow. Nightmare.

At eight o'clock the sirens went again. At Amy's house everyone but Tessa went back to spend the night in the Anderson shelter. Tessa, carrying her tin hat and her gas-mask, had already gone to do her fire-watching stint at the hospital. Nora and Sara bedded down under the stairs. And that night the real horror began. The roar of the guns, the blood-chilling sound of aircraft overhead, the crash of falling bombs lasted into the early hours of the morning. Nora held Sara close to her, and prayed, 'Our Father, who art in Heaven …' Sara was surprised. She'd never heard her mother praying before. But they'd never been in such danger before. When the All-Clear went they trailed back to bed for a few hours' sleep, Sara sharing her mother's double bed. 'I want you where I can see you,' Nora said. *Oh Jim,* she said silently, *I wish you were here.* She lay in the dark, Sara asleep beside her. *It's really started now,* she thought. *How long? How long is this going to go on?* Could they all take this, night after night? And stay sane?

The next morning Dan went to buy a newspaper. 'It's the East End,' he said. 'It's unbelievably dreadful. Such destruction and so many people dead. And the man in the shop says there were bombs around here too. Warwick Gardens is a mess and a house is down in Pembridge Gardens, and that's not far away, is it? We'll have to make that shelter a bit more habitable.'

'I'd rather stay in my bed,' Amy's father said. 'They've driven me out of my house. I'm damned if they're going to drive me out of my bed.'

'You're coming into the shelter,' Amy said. 'We don't want to have to rescue you again, do we?'

'I shall bring a bottle of whisky then,' he said. 'Drink to the destruction of Hitler and the Nazis.'

On Sunday night the raids came again. They got into their own beds in the early hours of the morning. 'They're going to bomb us at night, then,' Dan said, 'when our fighters can't properly defend us. We're in for a hell of a ride.'

Chapter Fourteen

1940–1941

Nora and Sara crawled out of bed on Monday morning. 'I'm going to school,' Sara said. 'I'm not missing it.'

'We've been up half the night,' Nora said. 'They won't mind if you're a bit late.'

'I'll mind,' Sara said.

'Well, I'm coming with you. You finish your breakfast and I'll just pop down to the phone box and tell Doctor Fielding I'll be late.'

She walked to the phone box on the corner. She was numb with tiredness and fear. She looked around her at the silent houses. They all seemed to be intact, but she was still afraid. The noise of the planes and the bombs and the guns would frighten the dead. She had never believed that anything so dreadful would happen, even after Amy's father's house was hit. That had seemed like an accident, a stray bomb casually dropped. This was deliberate. Deliberate bombing of ordinary people's homes. Hours and hours of dreadful, pounding fear. Sara had trembled beside her and put her fingers in her ears, but she hadn't screamed or even cried.

Nora walked slowly back from the phone box. What would happen to Sara if her mother was killed, and her father far away? Who would look after her? She couldn't bear to think of those children in the East End. Dare she ask? Would Amy say no? Would it just make an awkward atmosphere?

She took Sara to school. The children were to be let out early. 'I'll come back for you,' she said. 'Wait for me in the hall.'

Sara settled down to her lessons. The children trickled in through the morning. Their form mistress didn't approve. 'If our soldiers and sailors and airmen can stay up all night fighting for you,' she said, 'you can come to school on time.'

She's right, Sara thought. She thought of her dad, away at sea, fighting. Everybody had to do their bit, even the children. Anyway, she thought, I'm nearly grown up now. She could leave school next year if she wanted to. She didn't want to, of course. She hadn't told the teachers that she wanted to be a doctor. Not yet. If they could just get through the war, if her dad would come home, if her mum was all right. If, if, if …

Amy had left a note when Nora arrived at the house. 'What a night, Nora. Thank God we all survived. Charlie phoned and he's all right too. See you later.' Nora started on the housework and then went shopping. It was beginning to take an age to get the simplest thing – queues were everywhere, even for common things like potatoes and bread. And more things were being put on ration all the time. What was everybody supposed to eat?

Amy came home for a sandwich lunch. 'Nora,' she said. 'Wasn't it awful? Were you all right? What did you do?'

'Slept under the stairs,' Nora said. 'If you can call it sleeping, with all that dreadful noise and the handle of the gas meter sticking into you. Sara insisted on going to school this morning.'

'Good for her,' Amy said. 'She's a great little girl. Reminds me of Tessa when she was that age. Dead keen.'

'I'm going to pick her up from school this afternoon, but they're coming out early.' Nora hesitated but plucked up her courage. 'I was wondering,' she said. 'If anything happens to me, would you look after her till her dad comes home? I can't bear to think of her in some orphanage or having to go out to work and living God knows where. I've got a bit of money saved up for her keep….'

Amy took her hand. 'Of course we would, but nothing's going to happen to any of us. We have to believe that. We're not going to get gloomy and frightened. That's what the Germans want, isn't it?'

Nora smiled. 'Yes, I suppose you're right.'

'If anything happens to me,' Amy said, 'will you look after my family, keep the house going as a home until it's all over?'

Nora brightened and nodded. 'Of course I will.' They shook hands. 'It's a pact.'

Dan went to work on the tube. According to the wireless, some of the roads were blocked and impassable. As he went into the tube station he met a stream of people coming up the other way, people who had obviously spent the night in the underground station. They looked bleary and dishevelled: children were crying, mothers distraught. When he came out at his destination he could hardly believe what he saw: shattered, collapsing buildings, fires still burning, men digging in the rubble for survivors.

He couldn't believe that it was happening again, that once again he would be treating the brutal wounds of war. But this time it would not be the soldiers, it would be the ordinary people, including the old, women, and children. He remembered his own words to Charlie: 'They'll try to frighten us to death,' he'd said. He looked at the faces around him, grim, exhausted, but extraordinarily calm. Here and there there was even a joke, some laughter. He was filled with a kind of pride, a new respect for his countrymen.

Every night they came; every night the people of London slept in their shelters or under the stairs. Or they crowded down into the tube stations, lying together in cramped rows in blankets and sleeping bags, clutching their children, suckling their babies. Or they streamed out of the cities before night fell, into the countryside villages to sleep in barns and schools and churches as the nights grew colder. Then in the morning they came back, back to their factories and offices and shops, and the children went to school, and Hitler failed in his resolve to break them. The nation waited, nerves strung out, for the invasion, for German troops to swagger around London as they had in Paris. And still the invasion didn't come; the warning church bell didn't ring.

Tessa came home early one morning covered in dust and spotted with blood. 'They got the nurses' home,' she said. She burst into tears on her mother's shoulder, then dragged herself up the stairs to bath and get a few hours' sleep.

'I'll be glad when term starts and she goes back to Cambridge,' Dan said.

'She needs to do it,' Amy said. 'She needs to do something. She says she feels useless compared with Charlie.'

'Her time will come,' Dan said. 'Her job is to qualify. We all have to do what we do and not give in. They are not going to frighten us to death.'

Sunday 15 September, was a warm fine day. The squadron was scrambled early in the morning and ordered to 20,000 feet. Charlie shivered, tired out and feeling the cold, even through his flying jacket and boots. What now, he thought. Rumours had been rocketing round – they were coming, today, tomorrow. Most people seemed to be surprised that the invasion hadn't happened over the weekend. The German boats and landing craft were massed on the French coast, apparently ready to go. Perhaps this was the start of it. He thought of the family waiting at home, waiting for the rumble of German tanks and shouted German orders. Never, he thought. Never.

He looked down at the Dorniers that appeared below them, making steadily westwards for London. Within seconds they were in battle again with Me109s that appeared out of nowhere. He saw the Hurricanes arrive and almost at once three of the bombers went down, trailing smoke, to crash in flames on the Kent countryside. The squadron returned to base to rearm and refuel and took off again into the mêlée.

His eyes and head flicked around constantly in a sky that seemed filled with diving, spiralling aircraft. Then once again, he suddenly found himself alone, high in a clear sky. Out of the corner of his eye he saw a black speck, rapidly getting bigger, a single Dornier, trailing smoke, limping for home. Almost casually he shot it down, and then flew back to the airfield. He flew over the wrecks of bombed houses, and over the wreckage of an enemy bomber, still burning. He flew over villages where the people below turned up their faces and danced and waved.

Once again they refuelled and rearmed and waited for the next onslaught. It didn't come. He changed and showered and went into the mess. Tim was already there with a bunch of pilots, downing a pint. They were laughing, larking about. There was a different atmosphere, a shift, a feeling that something had changed. For the first time it felt as if they had the upper hand. The enemy armies hadn't arrived on the English beaches. Their swarming aircraft had had hell knocked out of them. It felt, Charlie thought, like the day they won an important inter-school cricket match when he was a junior. A victory. Perhaps this was it, what Churchill called the Battle of Britain. It felt as if they had won it. The war wasn't over – not by a long way – but it felt as if they had made a start. They had dented the German confidence.

Tim came over to him, bearing a pint. 'It was a good day,' he said. 'I think we nettled them a bit today.'

'Yes,' Charlie said. 'It was good.'

'There's one thing, I'm afraid,' Tim said. 'It's bad. There's no sign of Arthur.'

'Oh God.'

'He might be all right,' Tim said. 'He might have come down somewhere else and not phoned in yet.' Neither of them really believed it.

Charlie didn't answer. He went to bed early. If Arthur didn't come back he would write to his parents. He thought of Arthur's mother, her kindliness and motherliness, making her pastry. He thought of Arthur's father, so proud of his son, expecting him to change the world. Perhaps he had.

The news was appalling: the East End devastated, and bombing in the West, a hit on Buckingham Palace; Oxford Street devastated, with bombs on DH Evans and Bourne and Hollingsworth, and John Lewis burnt out completely. And then the City of London. Nowhere was safe. Amy went into town to do some shopping. The local shops were running out of elastic, of all things. How to keep one's knickers up? She passed a police station that had been heavily damaged. There was a sign outside. WE ARE STILL HERE, it read. BE GOOD. Despite every-thing, she had to smile.

Dan turned off the radio. 'I don't believe it.'

Amy looked up from her book. 'What?'

'Herr Hitler has apparently kindly consented to stop the bombing over Christmas. A couple of nights off. We'll all celebrate the birth of Christ, peace on earth and good will to men and then he'll start trying to kill us all again.'

Amy frowned. 'Do you think it's real?'

'I wouldn't trust him for a single moment,' Dan said. 'Why would he stop now? After Coventry and Plymouth and all the other cities bombed to blazes?' He sighed. 'It's nearly 1941, Amy. We've been at it for over a year and look at us.'

'Wouldn't it be lovely?' she said, wistfully. 'Charlie could come home. We'd all be together. I asked Nora if she and Sara would like to come but she said she'd rather stay at home. Something to do with thinking about Jim.'

It seemed to be real. The country was to have two nights off. No raids. Charlie managed to get home and brought Tim with him. 'Where shall we go?' he said. 'It's Christmas Eve. I want to go dancing.'

'I still don't trust them,' Dan said.

'We won't go far, then,' Charlie said. 'Let's go to the Hammersmith Palais.'

'Oh yes.' Tessa did a little twirl. 'I've always wanted to go there.'

'It'll be packed,' Amy said.

'Just what I want,' Charlie said. 'A madhouse that hasn't got anything to do with flying. And girls.'

'Can I borrow your silk stockings, Mum?' Tessa asked. 'I've got none left. Otherwise I'll have to paint my legs with gravy browning or something.'

Amy laughed. 'Yes. I've no doubt they'll come back in shreds.'

'Well, we won't be doing old-time dancing, I hope. Maybe we'll get some Glen Miller.'

The dance hall was seething, the band playing 'Chattanooga Choo Choo' when they went in. The crowd seemed to be swirling around the floor in a clockwise direction, 'like a school of fish,' Tim said. He ducked a flying arm. 'I think I'd rather face a bunch of 109s.'

'Come on.' Tessa pulled him into the mêlée. In the middle of the floor two couples were madly jiving, watched by an admiring crowd. The boys were in RAF uniform. 'I wish I could do that,' she said. 'Do they teach you that in the RAF?'

Tim looked at them closely. 'They're Yanks,' he said, 'from Eagle Squadron.'

'They seem very energetic.'

'I believe they are.' Tim said. 'In every way.'

She laughed. 'I think it's jolly good of them to come and help us. It's not their war, after all.'

'Not yet,' Tim said 'We've got pilots from all over the place. You should see the Poles in action. Mad devils. Shoot down more than we do.'

Across the room they could see Charlie dancing with a heavily lipsticked blonde, his arms and legs flying.

Tessa laughed. 'Charlie's off,' she said. 'He said he wanted a madhouse.'

Tim excused himself for a few minutes. 'Nature call,' he said. 'Don't go away.'

The dance ended and the band began to play 'Beat Me Daddy, Eight To The Bar'. Tessa looked around her, smiling. One night, she thought. One night without fear, without crouching in the Anderson shelter or crawling around on some roof, watching for incendiaries. No wonder they were all jumping about like mad things.

'Excuse me, would you like to dance?' The accent was unmistakable. One of the Eagle Squadron.

'I'm sorry,' she said. 'I'm here with someone. He'll be back in a minute.'

He grinned. 'We could give him the slip. He'd never find us in this mob.'

She laughed. 'I'm sorry. I'm rather attached to him.'

'Oh well,' he said. 'OK honey. Happy Christmas.'

She watched him swing away through the crowd. Isn't that odd, she thought? That's the first time I've ever talked to an American.

Tim came back and put his arm around her waist. 'Dance,' he said. 'With me.'

The three of them came home in the early hours. 'It's Christmas,' Charlie said. 'Happy Christmas. He stumbled. 'I think I'm a little bit drunk.'

'What happened to the blonde?' Tim said.

'Not my type,' Charlie said.

'What is?'

'I don't know yet.'

They crept into the house. 'It doesn't matter if they hear us,' Charlie said. 'They'll think it's Father Christmas.'

'They might think we've been invaded,' Tessa said with a grin, 'and give us what for.'

'I hope not,' Tim said. 'I wouldn't like to be a German facing your mother.'

On 27 December the bombers came back, their cynical little holiday over. The raids started again. The year 1941 arrived and wore on in a haze of destruction, with week after week of blistering nights and days of numbing fatigue. The days and the hideous nights went by, and London was given a breathing space from time to time as the other cities suffered. Amy began to spend two nights a week in the Notting Hill Gate underground station, ready to help if she was needed. The WVS was down there too with their endless cups of cheering tea, and a few nurses set up a first-aid station. It began to feel normal, as if life had always been like this. Couples got married, babies were born, people went to the cinemas and dance halls.

'It's strange, Dan,' Amy said. 'Everyone just seems to have settled down to living like this – like moles. Have you noticed? Everyone seems to sing more and laugh more. No one even mentions giving up or surrendering.'

'They thought they'd bomb us into submission.' Dan said. 'So far they've killed more woman and children than fighting men. But they seem to have abandoned invasion plans. I think Mr Churchill has convinced them of what they'd be in for if they did.'

'You look lovely, darling,' Amy said.

'Doesn't she just.' Tim looked down at Tessa, his eyes glowing.

They're in love, Amy thought. Who wouldn't be? It was March now, and spring was coming, and a young man's thoughts … and a young woman's too, by the smile on Tessa's face. Tessa was wearing an evening dress of silver grey, cross-cut and clinging, and Tim was in uniform, of course, the wings bright on his breast. They are so young, Amy thought, so beautiful, so alive.

'Have a good time,' Dan said, 'and if there's a raid get to a shelter. No good dancing on and taking risks.'

'I'll look after her, sir,' Tim said.

Tessa laughed. 'We're going to the Café de Paris, Dad,' she said. 'It's twenty feet underground. We'll be OK there.'

'I don't like it,' Dan said when they'd gone. 'I wish they'd just stay at home. I wish she'd stay in Cambridge. They seem to be very happy about letting the students come home now and again in term-time. It wouldn't have happened in my day. It's the war, I suppose.'

'It doesn't happen very often,' Amy said. 'They need to get out on their own and have some fun. Tim especially, doing what he does. They need to have some normal life or they'll all go mad.'

Dan put his arms around her and kissed her cheek. 'I expect you're right. It was only seeing you in Paris in the last war that kept me sane.'

The Café de Paris was crammed. Tessa and Tim were shown down the long staircase to their table. Tessa looked around her at the men in uniform or evening dress and at the women, carefully made up, glowing in their beautiful dresses and jewels. 'It's amazing, isn't it?' she said. 'All hell let loose and people still like to dress up and dine and dance. Stiff upper lip and all that.'

'I just like to be with you,' Tim said.

They dined and then danced together. Tim held her close, his face against her hair. 'You know I'm in love with you, don't you?' he said.

Tessa pulled away and laughed up at him. 'I sincerely hope so, silly. Otherwise I wouldn't be here throwing myself at you.'

He flushed with pleasure. 'Will you marry me when all this is over?'

She looked up at him for several seconds, pretending to consider his proposal. Then she smiled. 'Yes,' she said. 'Of course I will.'

He held her close. 'Oh darling.'

They went back to their table. 'I've still got a long way to go,' she said. 'I'll be coming to London later this year to start my clinical training. I've got three years of that.'

'I'll wait,' he said, 'my darling girl. Or we can get married whenever you like.'

She hadn't time to reply. Faintly they heard the sound of the sirens above, and then came an announcement that a raid had started. Very few people left. 'We're already underground, aren't we?' Tessa said. 'We'll be all right here.'

The band went on playing, of course. They took a pride in not being intimidated. If the dancers were prepared to go on dancing, then they would go on playing. The dancers danced, the waiters moved about with bottles of champagne, while outside and above the sirens wailed and the crump of bombs and the crashing of the guns shook the air. The band swung into a quickstep: 'Oh Johnny', and the girls laughed and swirled in the khaki and blue and navy arms of their young men.

The first bomb crashed through the roof but didn't explode. The crowd scattered, the girls screaming. There was time only for Tim to pull Tessa to the floor and throw himself on top of her before the second bomb fell and exploded in front of the stage.

For a few moments Tessa was disoriented, conscious only of the devastating noise and the rolling, choking dust, and the weight of Tim's body over hers. Then, as the noise of the explosion died away, and after a few moments of utter silence, she began to hear the sounds of panic and suffering – screams, groans, voices calling – 'Joan, Bill, where are you?' And one voice, quite close, 'My God, I can't see!'

Tim raised himself on his elbows and looked down at her. 'Darling,' he said, 'are you all right?'

'Yes,' she said. 'I think so.'

They struggled to their knees. There was a dim light flickering, one of the table lamps intermittently functioning, and a small, vicious fire, up by the stage. After a few seconds there were occasional small lights from torches, and the limited lights from cigarette lighters. They looked around them. The room was destroyed, covered in rubble and dust; tables were overturned, and bodies lay everywhere, some still and unmoving in death, some staggering to their feet, some moaning in pain.

Tim put his arms around her and looked about him. 'Come on,' he said. 'We've got to get out of here.'

'No,' she said, 'we can't just leave them. We have to help them.'

'That's crazy,' he said. 'We can't do anything. I've got to get you out of here.'

'No,' she said again. 'I have to help.' She began to tear at her underskirt and the bottom of her dress, taking off strips to use as bandages.

'Please darling,' he said. 'For God's sake let's go. You're the only thing I care about.'

'No I'm not,' she said, 'or you wouldn't do what you do. I have to help them.' She looked at him, her mouth twisted. 'It's what I'm for, Tim. Don't you understand?'

He helped her then, until the rescuers came, binding bleeding wounds, putting on tourniquets where limbs had been torn away. The men arrived, the Fire Service and the ARP and then, at last, the ambulances with their stretchers and harassed men, desperately trying to deal with overwhelming casualties.

Tim took off his jacket, put it around Tessa's shoulders and helped her out of the chaos, joining the shambling stream being shepherded out of the wreckage. As he stumbled out he came across a seedy little rat of a man, rummaging through handbags and pocketing the contents. For the first time he actually saw red. His rage exploded, at the whole damn war, at the totally unnecessary destruction and death, at the filth of some men – even his own countrymen.

'You rotten little bastard,' he said. 'I'll kill you.' He threw a punch at the man's head, a glancing blow, and the man ran off, scattering money and jewellery. 'Bastard,' Tim called after him. He felt suddenly sick, empty and lost, and retched over the rubble. God, he thought. God. What's it all for?

They emerged into the shattered street. He stopped an ARP warden. 'Is there a telephone box round here,' he said. 'One that's still working?'

'Try the one down the road, first right,' the man said. 'It's fairly clear down there.'

Tim took Tessa's arm. 'We'll never get anywhere tonight,' he said. 'You ring your family and I'll ring the airfield. We'll have to get back in the morning when the tubes are running. Perhaps we can find a hotel.'

They made their way to the phone box. There was already a queue.

Tessa phoned home. 'I'm all right,' she said, 'don't cry, Mummy. I'll get back as soon as I can. Probably tomorrow.'

To Tim's surprise the taxis were still running and he managed to flag one down. 'Can you get us to a hotel?' he said. 'This lady's been in a bombing.'

'I can see that,' the driver said. 'It'll be a bit tricky tonight.'

Tim took her hand in the taxi. 'I'm very proud of you,' he said. 'You're very brave.'

She squeezed his hand. 'You can talk.' She leant her head on his shoulder. 'Tim,' she whispered, 'don't leave me.'

'Not ever.'

They tried two hotels that were full but the third had one room left. 'We'll take it,' Tim said.

'For two?' the receptionist asked, carefully not looking at them.

'Yes,' Tessa said loudly. 'For two. For my husband and myself.'

The receptionist looked at them then, a look of amused cynicism, but he caught Tim's eye and hurriedly handed over the register.

They were shown to their room. 'Are you sure?' Tim put his arms around her. 'I wouldn't want you to get any kind of a reputation because of me. I could sleep in a tube station or something.'

'No,' she said. 'You're not to leave me.'

'I'll sleep on a chair then,' he said, 'or on the floor. Just give me a kick if I come anywhere near you.'

She leant away from him. 'Look at us,' she said. 'We've both been blown up. We could easily have been killed. Oh Tim.'

He held her close again and kissed her, a kiss full of longing.

'Sleep with me,' she said. 'Make love to me. It might be all we ever have. We could both be dead tomorrow.'

There was a washbasin in the room, and soap and towels. He helped her out of her ruined dress and helped her to wash off as much grime as they could.

'Get into bed, my darling,' he said. 'I'll clean myself up a bit.'

He slipped into bed beside her. 'Are you sure?' he said. 'Are you absolutely sure?'

She flung her arms around him. 'Absolutely, absolutely.'

This time his weight above her was only joy.

He took her home very early the next morning, leaving her at the door, eager to get back to the airfield before he could be regarded as AWOL.

Amy flung her arms around her. 'Oh darling,' she said. 'Was it awful?'

Tessa nodded. 'Pretty bad, but I could help them. I knew how to help. I could do something, at last.'

Amy went up to her room with her while she bathed and changed to go back to Cambridge. 'One nice thing,' Tessa said. 'Tim asked me to marry him and I said yes.' She hugged her mother. 'I'm so happy. Tim's coming to see you as soon as he can.' She laughed. 'To ask Dad's permission. He'd better say yes.'

'Amy,' Dan said, 'have you read this paper? It's about penicillin.'

Amy looked over his shoulder. 'What? What about it?'

'It's very exciting.' he said. 'Sad in this case, but very exciting.'

Amy took the paper. Penicillin had been at the back of the medical profession's mind ever since Alexander Fleming discovered it in 1928, ever since it had killed the bacteria in his petri dish at St Mary's Hospital. It had been arousing sporadic interest ever since. Now, apparently, a man called Florey in Oxford had been trying to purify it for use in humans. She glanced at Dan's eager face.

'Go on,' he said, 'read it.'

She read on. A policeman in Oxford who was dying of septicaemia had been given penicillin by injection as a trial. To everyone's amazement he began to get better. His temperature came down and he began to eat. 'Oh!' she said, reading on. To everyone's great distress they then ran out of penicillin. They extracted it from his urine to use again, but they didn't have enough and sadly, he died.

She put the paper down. For a moment they looked at each other, stunned by the implications. 'That's incredible,' she said, 'and how awful to be so close to saving him.'

'Yes,' he said, 'it was, but it's wonderful too, isn't it? If only they can find a way to make enough.' He took her hand. 'All those boys in the last war who died of infection, Amy. Not of their wounds, but of infection. Do you remember how we agonized, how we'd have given our souls for something like this?'

Tears came into Amy's eyes. She remembered only too well: the horror and the pain, the pus-soaked bandages, the constant fight to keep the wounds clean. She remembered too the constant failure, the deaths of fine young men, not from trauma or blood loss but from the invasion of the tiny, microscopic creatures that killed them in the end. 'How can we possibly make enough,' she said, 'to help us now? The war is now, today.'

'I don't suppose we can,' Dan said. 'If we could build a factory to do it, it might well get bombed and all the research lost. I hear through the grapevine that Florey is taking it to America. They're at peace and they've got the money. We must hope that they can make it there. In time for our boys.'

When Sara came home from school that afternoon Amy gave her the paper to read. She had taken to talking to Sara now and again about medicine, answering her questions, explaining things from the books she borrowed. She looked at Sara's bent head, and shining, fascinated face. It's going to be so different, she thought, for the young ones, for Tessa, and Sara, if and when she makes it. They will have the tools we could only dream of. Medicine had taken a huge leap forward.

The raids carried on, one city after another and then back to London again. Then, in May, after one appalling night, they petered out. Amy had a dreadful sense of déjà vu, the memory of the way the First War had become years of stalemate and suffering and killing. How long, she thought, can we take this? Then, on 22 June, Hitler suddenly, and without warning, attacked Russia. Dan actually laughed, almost unbelieving. 'Now I know he's mad,' he said. 'The fool has signed his death warrant. Has he never heard of Napoleon?'

Chapter Fifteen

1941–42

The raids carried on, one town after another was hit, then the Luftwaffe came back to London again. The House of Commons was destroyed, but St Paul's remained still proudly standing, a symbol of hope.

On 10 May Amy spent the night in the tube station. When she came out in the morning the roads of Notting Hill Gate were covered in broken glass, and shrapnel from the shells lay in the gutter, still hot to the touch. She made her way home, bathed and changed and went to her morning clinic. She visited some of her old ladies. Some of them, to her surprise and delight, had resurrected themselves and were happily helping in the WVS or the food offices or the clothing-exchange shops. Give them something to do, she thought, make them feel needed, and they come alive again. It shouldn't take a war.

'How are we supposed to exist on this?' Amy was looking at the week's rations spread out on the kitchen table. 'Two ounces of butter each, two ounces of cheese, four ounces of bacon, one egg, one pound of meat, eight ounces of sugar. Not much else. What are we supposed to eat?'

'It isn't going to get any better,' Dan said. 'We manage, don't we?'

'Nora does. I don't know how she does it.'

'We haven't had Woolton Pie yet,' Dan said. 'Whatever that may be.'

'It's a vegetable pie. The recipe was on Kitchen Front on the wireless, but I think you just put in anything you've got.'

'Strangely enough,' he said, 'rationing has its advantages. We've had the Ministry figures in. Do you know that heart attacks have decreased, even through the Blitz? It must be because people aren't eating so much fat – more fruit and vegetables.'

'As long as we still get them.' Amy sighed. 'I wonder whether we'll ever see an orange or a lemon or a banana again.'

He put his arm around her and kissed her cheek. 'One day. At least the Blitz has eased off and we can sleep most nights.'

'I don't think Nora sleeps at night,' Amy said. 'Not with Jim at sea. They're still attacking the shipping.'

'We've been very lucky,' he said. 'We'll just have to put up with the shortages of everything.'

'It infuriates me to think of Germany with the whole of Europe to steal from.'

'We'll get there,' he said. 'We've beaten them in the air. We're going to win. Bananas shall rise again.'

She caught his eye and began to laugh. 'You have a very naughty mind.'

At school Sara began to do science in earnest, separate chemistry, physics and biology, getting ready for her School Certificate exam. She had to choose her subjects. Teachers were in such short supply that some subjects had to be dropped. History or chemistry? No contest. Geography or physics? No contest. Latin or needlework? She just laughed. For the first time she told her form mistress what she wanted to do. She was asked to see Miss Jenkins, the headmistress.

'Medicine, Sara?' she said. 'We don't have many girls doing that. What does your father do?'

'He's a carpenter,' Sara said, 'when there isn't a war on. He's in the Navy now.'

'It's a long training,' Miss Jenkins said, 'and it's very difficult for girls to get in at all. There aren't many places for women. And it's very expensive. You'd have to get a scholarship. You'll have to work very hard.'

'I know. I like it.'

'In that case we'll help you all we can.'

'That's if we win the war,' Sara said.

Miss Jenkins smiled. 'Oh, we'll win. You can count on that.' She sighed as Sara left her. It was difficult enough for girls, she thought, without a war to worry about. It was especially difficult for girls from working-class homes. She saw so many – bright, intelligent girls who never made it to university. Such a waste. Perhaps things would change after the war, which, of course, we were going to win. She sighed again. Everything was after the war.

Sara went back to her classroom, feeling elated. The headmistress hadn't told her it was a mad idea, and the raids weren't as bad. It was funny, she thought, how you got used to them. She even managed to sleep through the din most nights. It didn't make any difference, really. Everything went on as usual. She wasn't going to change her mind.

Charlie burst into the mess, the letter in his hand. 'Guess what, chaps,' he shouted. 'Good news. Arthur's alive.'

They gathered around him. 'What? Where?'

'I expect the CO will be informed but I've got a letter from his father. He was shot down over the Channel, picked up by a French fishing boat and hidden by the Resistance. He's been on the run all this time, trying to get back home, but they caught him in the end. He's a prisoner, alive and well.' They raised a cheer and sank a further round of beers.

Charlie sat down and read the letter again. *His mother always said he was alive,* Arthur's father wrote. *She said she'd know if he was dead.* Charlie wondered what he'd been through when they caught him. What had the Gestapo done to him? There were hideous rumours trickling out from Germany. He was lucky not to have been shot as a spy. But he was alive and one day he would come home again. His mother could make her pastry in peace. He wondered what it was like in a German prison camp. Were they civilized and decent? Arthur had done his fighting. How would that feel? Relieved? Would he, Charlie, be relieved? Hell, no. Give me a Spit, he thought, and a chance to get back at the bastards.

The year wore on, privation upon privation, even clothes were rationed. Everything was beginning to look grey and shabby. It was difficult to get anything, Amy thought, to cheer yourself up a bit, even a lipstick or a little bottle of perfume. There was a rush on at Woolworths because there was a rumour they'd got some face powder in. The raids had eased, but ordinary life became more and more difficult.

Tessa started her clinical training in London and found herself on the wards for the first time. She persuaded her parents to let her share a flat near the hospital with two other girls.

'If I live at home, Dad,' she said, 'I'll miss all the fun. It'll be just like being back at school, coming home every night. Anyway, I need to be near the hospital. We'll have work to do at night, and I expect I'll still be fire-watching.'

They gave in in the end. 'I can see her point,' Amy said. 'She's not a child any more – she's twenty-one. And the bombing seems to have petered out.'

Tessa whispered in her ear, 'Thanks Mum.'

Amy smiled at her. Don't think I don't know the other reason, she thought. Much easier to be alone with Tim there. And why not? Why not get as much fun as possible? The war was a long way from over.

She had thought about having a talk with Tessa about the responsibilities and anxieties she was about to face in clinical training, but she almost laughed at herself. Tessa had faced these things already. She had seen suffering and pain. You could hardly live in a British city and not see that. Tim had told them about the Café de Paris, and fire-watching had been no picnic. Neither of them had commented on the night they spent together. So what, she thought. Life was contracted now. You took each day at a time. You took joy where you could.

She wondered when Charlie would get a girl he was really keen on. He seemed to have occasional girlfriends, but nothing serious. In fact he said as much. 'Nothing serious, Mum, not with what's going on. I wouldn't want to have a wife and children and not be there to look after them.' God knows, she could understand that. But one day, she thought, it'll bowl him over. Charlie was like that.

Into December, and on Sunday the seventh they heard the astounding news that the Japanese, without any warning, had attacked the

American fleet at Pearl Harbor. The Americans and the British declared war on Japan and the Germans and Italians declared war on America. 'That's it then,' Dan said. 'It's global now. It's a real world war – everybody everywhere killing each other. What have we all done to deserve this?' He smiled. 'But America is with us now, Amy, with all their riches and their power. The Japs must be out of their minds, crazy, like Hitler attacking Russia.'

But the news was dire. The enemy seemed to be unstoppable. By December the Germans were at the gates of Moscow. Then came the news that two great warships, the Repulse, and the Prince of Wales, had been sunk by the Japanese. Amy had an awful feeling. She didn't know which ship Nora's husband was on; she doubted if even Nora knew, but she had an awful feeling.

She knew what Nora was going to say as she stepped through the door. She was pale as a ghost, white with shock, trembling. Amy brought her into the sitting room and sat beside her on the settee. She took her hand. 'Oh Nora,' she said. Nora burst into tears. Amy put her arms around her and held her against her shoulder and rocked her like a child. She waited until the storm of sobbing had died away and Nora was resting against her, her body shaking. 'Is it Jim?' she asked gently.

Nora sat up, sitting with her head bent, her hands clenched. 'His ship went down,' she whispered. 'They didn't find him among the survivors.'

'Is there any chance he might have been picked up by someone else?'

'The Japanese? No. The War Office says he's dead.'

Amy held on to her hand. 'How dreadful. Does Sara know?'

Nora shook her head. 'No. The telegram came just after she'd gone to school.' She began to cry again. 'I don't know how to tell her.'

'We'd better go and get her,' Amy said. 'I haven't got a surgery this morning. I'll come with you.'

She put Nora into the car and they drove to the school. They asked to see the headmistress urgently.

Miss Jenkins's eyes filled with tears. 'It's the second time this week. Another father has been killed.' She wiped her eyes. 'Keep Sara at home for a day or two if you wish, Mrs Lewis, but not for too long. It's better for her to keep going. She's such a bright, clever girl.' She sent for Sara.

As gently as she could, Nora told her. Sara flung herself into her mother's arms and for a few moments they clung to each other, Sara sobbing on her mother's shoulder.

'I'll take you home,' Amy said. She took them to their house, went in with them and made some tea. 'Do you want to take a few days off, Nora?' she said gently. 'Is there anything I can do?'

Nora shook her head. 'Thank you, but what can anyone do?'

'Would you like me to stay?'

'No.' Nora took Sara's hand. 'We're best on our own for a bit.'

Amy got up. 'If you want anything, anything at all, just telephone, and I'll come.'

Nora nodded. 'I'll see you in the morning.'

She arrived as usual the next day. 'Sara went back to school,' she said. 'It's best. She's very upset but it's best keeping her mind occupied.'

Amy could find no words of comfort. What can I say, she thought, that isn't trite and meaningless. She remembered all too well the pain of losing those she loved in the last war. There was no explanation, no reassurance, no degree of patriotism that could ease that pain. She lived in daily dread of losing Charlie.

Nora began to cry. Amy put her arms around her. 'You must think of Sara now,' she said. 'She's a fine girl. She'll make you proud.'

Nora dried her eyes on her handkerchief. 'That child is going to get what she wants,' she said. 'Her father didn't die for nothing. I'll see to that.'

Charlie came home on a twelve-hour pass. Amy met him at the door. 'Bad news, darling. Nora's lost her husband. He was killed at sea. She's upstairs. Sara's here too.'

'Oh no!' Charlie was brought back again into the world of loss. He'd lost so many friends, and then he'd had the surprise and pleasure of Arthur's unexpected return. Life in the north in the Depression must have been an absolute nightmare. Arthur's return from the dead seemed like a well-deserved miracle. 'Is there no chance?' he said. 'Arthur came back after months of everybody thinking he was dead.'

'He was at sea, Charlie. There's no way of coming back from that.'

He tried to blot out of his mind the pilots who had come down in the Channel, shot up, drowned. He sought out Nora, who was hoovering the bedrooms. 'I'm so sorry,' he said.

'Thank you, Charlie,' she said, 'but I'm not the only one, am I?'

'No.' He paused. 'But it doesn't help much, does it?'

'No. It's Sara I'm worried about. Children losing their fathers.'

He found Sara at the kitchen table, doing her homework. 'I'm very sorry about your father,' he said. He sat down beside her. 'I've lost a lot of friends. I know it's not the same, but I know how you feel.'

She looked as if she were about to say something, but then she began to cry. He put an arm around her, awkwardly. She leant against his shoulder and cried. He could feel her slight body shaking with her sobs. He patted her, trying to comfort her. He felt his own tears rising, tears for the loss of so many men he had known, tears for the strangeness he sometimes felt for his own survival, for the whole hideous, sorry mess.

Amy came into the kitchen. He looked up at her, distressed and helpless and gave a little shrug. She took Sara's hand and led her away to her mother.

He pulled himself together. No use being sentimental. But not for me, he thought. I'm not going to marry and then leave behind a sobbing mother and child.

Amy came back. 'Are you all right?' she said.

He nodded, 'Yes.' He looked out of the window where the lawns and the flower-beds had gone and the winter frost shone on the vegetable plots that were empty now, waiting for the spring. He felt exhausted, physically and mentally. An exhaustion of the spirit. No good feeling like that, he thought. There was still a job to be done. Would it ever end? He turned back to his mother. 'How about a sherry before lunch?'

It was Christmas again and very cold. Charlie and Tessa and Tim came to lunch at home, to laughter and love. And then it was into 1942. The enemy seemed unstoppable; the Germans had been at the gates of Moscow for weeks and at the end of January came the shock of the surrender of Singapore to the Japanese, with 60,000 British soldiers taken prisoner.

In May the RAF sent hundreds of Lancaster bombers to bomb Cologne.

'I'm not sure I agree with this,' Dan said, 'bombing civilians. We don't have to do it, just because they do.'

'Yes we do,' Nora said. 'Serve them right. Give them a taste of their own medicine. They started it. They should suffer it, like we have.'

Dan smiled, a wry smile. 'It's true what they say, Nora. The female of the species is more deadly than the male.'

Then the Germans began to bomb British cities known only for their history and beauty: Canterbury, Exeter, Bath and York. 'Sheer wickedness,' Dan said. 'Those lovely towns have no strategic importance. If they think that's going to make us give up they've another think coming.'

'What did I tell you?' Nora said.

'If I'd known they were going to put clothes on ration last year,' Tessa said, 'I'd have bought a few more things. I'm running out of coupons. My underclothes are falling apart – the lace is coming off everything, and I need a new coat.'

'Lace curtains,' Nora said.

'What?'

'Old lace curtains,' Nora said, 'if your mother's got any. I could take a bit off and use it for lace.'

'Can you?' Tessa said. 'Where did you get that idea?'

'The Ministry of Information booklet, *Make Do and Mend*, featuring Mrs Sew and Sew. All sorts of tips. I've made Sara a dress out of one of mine. She's nearly as tall as me anyway, but she's a lot thinner.'

'Can you sew?' Amy asked.

'Oh yes.' Nora was making dried egg omelettes for lunch. 'You have to be able to do everything where I come from. I've got a nice Singer sewing-machine.' She paused and her voice trembled. 'Jim bought it for me.' She dished up the omelettes. 'Some of those sheets need turning. Charlie put his foot through one of them last time he slept here. We'll never get new ones. We should turn the edges to the middle.'

'Nora,' Amy said, 'you are amazing. Is there anything you can't do?'

Nora grinned. 'Not much. I'll do the sheets for you if you like.'

'Would you?' Amy said. 'If you have time. I'll pay you to do some sewing – only if you have time.'

'I'll have time. I've got the evenings. The sheets won't take long.'

'I don't suppose you can magic a new coat,' Tessa laughed, 'out of old net curtains.'

'No,' Nora said, quite seriously, 'but I could make you one out of that nice grey blanket in the airing cupboard. Nobody seems to use it.'

'Could you really?' Tessa looked amazed. 'That's fantastic.'

'You go and buy a paper pattern,' Nora said, 'and I'll make it.'

'Fantastic,' Tessa said again. 'Thank you so much, Nora.' She got up. 'I'll have to get back to the flat now, Mum. I'm going out tonight.'

'Tim?'

'Of course.'

'Anywhere nice?'

'We'll try to find a nice quiet place to have dinner on our own. It's getting quite difficult. The West End's a madhouse – soldiers from everywhere looking for fun. And hundreds of American GIs.' She laughed. 'The war's certainly cheered everything up. I just wish I could have some new clothes.' She kissed her mother's cheek and bounced out of the house.

Amy sighed. 'Isn't it awful,' she said. 'All this scrimping and saving. In some ways it's harder to bear than the Blitz. Our girls should be able to have a few pretty things. It's part of being young. They can't even get silk stockings. They have to paint their legs with something or other and draw a line down the back.'

'I can remember my first dance dress,' Nora said. 'I made it myself. It was blue with a sweetheart neckline. Times were bad then. I made it out of a bedspread. I thought it was wonderful.'

Amy smiled. 'I expect it was.' She paused. 'It must have been bad, Nora, in the slump.'

'It was. Very bad. In some ways we're better off now. At least everybody's got a job.'

'It shouldn't have to take a war. We'll have to make a better world, afterwards.'

'That's what they said last time, so I won't hold my breath.' Nora picked up a pan. 'We need a new saucepan. This one's got a hole in it.'

'I've no idea where we're going to get one,' Amy said. 'I wish we hadn't given those others to make Spitfires. It seemed the right thing to do at the time. We didn't know how bad it was going to get.'

'I expect it was,' Nora said. 'We wouldn't want Charlie to be flying some old crock, would we?'

Amy laughed. 'Dear me, no.' She looked at Nora, whose head was bent over the saucepan. 'Are you all right, Nora?'

Nora bit her lip. 'Most of the time. I just wish Jim was going to be here to see Sara grow up. It's not right. It's cruel.'

Amy put her arm around her shoulders. 'I know. I know.'

In November the news came that General Montgomery and the Eighth Army had defeated the Germans at El Alamein. They were in full retreat.

'Where's that?' Sara asked. She and Nora looked it up on an atlas at Amy's house.

'North Africa.' Nora said. 'Very close to the Suez Canal. We need the Suez Canal. We get a lot of our supplies through there. Anyway, it's the first time we've given them what for.'

There was a new feeling in the air. 'It feels as if we've turned a corner,' Dan said, 'and the Americans got the Japs at Midway. It's beginning to happen, Amy.'

In December 1942 Dan came home one day from work. He knocked the snow from his shoes at the door. 'I've got one,' he said.' He handed the booklet to Amy. 'The Beveridge Report. I had a struggle to get one, there was a queue.'

She laughed. 'Isn't there always?'

They read it together. 'It's fantastic, Dan.' She put the heavy booklet down. 'A new deal for everybody. I like the way he's described the five social giant evils: Want, Disease, Ignorance, Squalor and Idleness. It's the children who are mainly affected – the state some of those evacuees were in, like that little girl Mrs Parks got, half-starved, filthy, head fill of nits. Some of them didn't know how to use a lavatory. It's a national disgrace.'

'It seems to cover everything,' Dan said, 'and what do you think of the best thing?'

They both smiled. 'A National Health Service,' Amy said, 'free to everyone. When you think of the things we see that people struggle on with because they can't afford the treatment....'

'I know,' Dan said. 'I'll probably spend the rest of my life doing hernias and all the truss companies will go out of business.'

Amy laughed. 'Nothing wrong with that.'

'I don't think it can possibly happen until after the war,' Dan said, 'but what a world to look forward to. It'll put new life into everybody. Now I know we'll win.'

The squadron took off to new battles; now the RAF flew to France to attack and harass the enemy on their own ground. They attacked airfields or trains or barges, anything that looked useful, or tempted the enemy fighters up to waste themselves in useless fights. 'rhubarbs', they called those raids. Or they flew on 'circuses', escorting bombers on raids to French targets. None of the pilots liked these much, having to fly at the slower speeds of the bombers.

As they approached the French coast Charlie felt more apprehensive than usual. If he was shot down over England and baled out he could look forward to a cup of tea or a whisky and a lift back to the airfield. If he was shot down over France it was a prison camp, if he wasn't just shot out of hand. They flew on, expecting trouble. It came, of course. The Me109s appeared above them and once again he found himself in a whirling nightmare of wings and tracer bullets.

He began to feel as if he wasn't in an aircraft at all, as if he were flying free, surviving, watching the fight from the outside. He shook himself. This dreamlike state was the quickest way to dusty death. He watched a bomber go down, the parachutes blossoming. Then he saw a Spitfire, trailing smoke, spinning and spinning. He was struck with shock. He knew the aircraft. 'Get out, Tim,' he shouted, knowing it was useless. 'Get out,' but the Spitfire spun and spun and then came out of the spin and flew into a hillock.

*

'Charlie!' Amy threw her arms around him. 'How lovely. What a surprise.' She led him into the sitting room. For a few moments she didn't notice his silence, the pain in his face. She realized suddenly that he was staring at her, his face twisted and agonized. 'Darling,' she said. 'What is it? What's happened?'

'Where's Tessa?' he said.

Her hand flew to her mouth. 'No,' she said. 'No. He's not dead?' She sat down on the sofa, searching his face. He sat down beside her and took her hand. His eyes filled. 'When?' she said.

'Early this morning. We were attacking targets in France. We were set on by 109s – too many. We lost two pilots. The rest of us were lucky to get away.'

'Are you sure?' Amy said. 'Couldn't he have baled out? Couldn't he be alive, taken prisoner?'

He shook his head. 'I saw him go down. He didn't get out.' Amy began to cry. 'I don't know how to tell her,' he said.

'I'll tell her,' Amy said. 'It's better if I do it. She's shopping. She stayed here last night. She's coming back soon.'

Charlie stood up and stared out of the window. I'm glad I haven't got a girl, he thought. He couldn't imagine how Tessa was going to bear this. He wasn't sure how he was going to bear it. Tim had been his best friend.

He heard the front door open and Tessa's eager voice, 'Hello, anyone about?' His mother left the room. He heard her voice, 'Come here, darling, into the kitchen.' Then silence.

Tessa sat beside her mother at the kitchen table, utterly stricken, her face white as parchment, too horrified to cry. 'I don't want him to be dead,' she said. 'We were going to be married.' She put her head in her hands. 'I might just as well be dead too.'

'Don't, darling,' Amy said. 'Tim wouldn't want you to feel this way. He'd want you to go on with your life. He'd want you to be brave and remember him with joy and love.'

'We were going to be married,' she said again.

'Listen,' Amy said, 'while I tell you something. In the last war I fell in love too, with a pilot in the Flying Corps. He was killed, Tessa, shot down by a German.'

Tessa raised her head and looked at her. 'You never said.'

'I didn't know how to go on,' Amy said, 'but I had a job to do, to help the others as much as I could, to keep going, not to break. That's what they want, darling, to wear us down, to break us.'

'Dad?' Tessa said.

'I fell in love with Dad later, and I love him just as much. He knew about Johnny, my pilot. I'll never forget him, but life goes on, darling. And time heals. I know you don't believe it now, but it does. It does.'

Tessa began to cry. 'I don't know.'

'You're doing your clinical training,' Amy said. 'You're going to meet pain and loss and you're going to have to help your patients through it. Love is never wasted, darling. My father said that to me at the time, and he was right. This pain now will help you to understand.'

'I'll never understand,' Tessa said. 'Why? Why do people do this to each other? What's it all for?'

'I don't know the answer.' Amy took her daughter in her arms, their tears mingling. 'We're all here to love you and look after you. You'll never be alone, darling.'

Chapter Sixteen

1943–45

A my looked across at Dan, reading by the fire. He looked older, she thought. So do I. I feel about a hundred. Life now seemed like walking down a long dreary tunnel. Her patients were tired and stressed, apart from the children who seemed, magically, just to accept everything. She put down her book and sighed. Dan looked at her over his reading-glasses.

'What is it, darling?'

'Oh, everything. Everything is so grey, Dan. Grey and dreary. Everything you look at, everywhere you go, everything you eat. There's no colour. We've been at it for over three years and there's no sign of the end of it.'

He put down his book and came to sit beside her and took her hand. 'I know, darling. It won't go on for ever.'

'It feels as if it might, as if the day will never come. Nora and Tessa are being so brave but Tessa looks like a ghost. And Charlie – on and on. He just sleeps all the time when he manages to get home. And such dreadful things are happening. I can't bear to think of that primary school in Catford, bombed, all those little children dead.'

He put his arm around her. 'Let's think of some good things. The Russians are beating back the Germans, we're doing well in North Africa and the Americans are sorting out the Japanese. And penicillin, Amy. How wonderful is that? Florey is using it to treat the troops in Africa and apparently it's miraculous. And look at the advances in plastic surgery. Archie MacIndoe is doing wonders.'

She leant against him 'I suppose so. Why does it take wars, though? Why do we have to start killing each other before all these things happen?'

'It just seems like that,' he said. 'But we've turned a corner with penicillin. A real tool, Amy, a fantastic, amazing tool. Something we've longed for, for centuries.' He gave her a squeeze. 'It's Wings For Victory week. Why don't we go out in the morning and see the Lancaster bomber they've got in Trafalgar Square. You can go inside.'

They went on the tube. The bomber seemed enormous from the outside, but inside she felt the beginning of claustrophobia. The rear-gunner's station seemed far too small for anyone. Imagine setting off in this, she thought, knowing that you might be blown to bits at any moment. How do they do it, over and over again? How do we all do it, in this grey, grey world?

They stepped back into the square. 'We could go to a matinée and see that film, Mrs Miniver,' she said.

'I don't think I will,' Dan said. 'It's a good film apparently, but it doesn't really describe it, does it?'

He's right, Amy thought. It does all the excitement and the danger and the stiff upper lip but it doesn't show the greyness, the day-to-day grind of keeping going, the loss of everything that enchants, the loss of beauty. Beautiful works of art had to be stored way, beautiful old buildings were being destroyed.

A few days later she put down the morning paper and stared out of the kitchen window. Her father and Mr Hodge were digging over a bed, ready for planting the onion sets. She was filled with a dark emptiness that was slowly giving way to red rage. Who were these people, these Nazis? Were they human at all? The paper reported their latest atrocity. At Katyn, the Russians had discovered a mass grave of 4,000 Polish officers, shot and murdered out of hand. How could they line up 4,000 men and shoot them in cold blood? There were dreadful rumours coming out of Germany. What horror could drive all those Jewish parents to say goodbye to their children, probably for ever, and send them to England? They'll murder anyone, she thought. They've murdered the twentieth century.

In April, when the danger of invasion had definitely gone, one ban was lifted. The church bells, so peaceful and so English a sound, rang out for the first time on Sunday morning. Amy sat up in her bed and cried.

'Are you all right?' Nora said. 'Not nervous or anything?'

'No.' Sara, for once, was going to school without a load of books. She was setting out half an hour early in case there was a long queue at the bus stop. She couldn't risk being late.

'Got your fountain pen?' Nora asked.

'Yes. Don't worry, Mum.'

'What is it today?'

'French this morning and Latin this afternoon. Physics and chemistry tomorrow.'

Nora kissed her cheek. 'Best of luck. Not that you'll need it. You've worked hard enough.'

Sara set off for school as ready as she'd ever be for the exams. School Certificate was the first big step along the way. She knew absolutely that it all depended on whether she did well and got into the sixth form. If not she'd be out, and working in a factory making munitions, or in the Land Army. She thought she'd choose the Land Army if she had to, be out in the open air. She tried not to think about failing; it was making her nervous.

She got on to the bus and climbed up the stairs to the top deck. It was rather smoky; almost everyone had a cigarette on. She looked out of the window. They passed several bombed-out buildings, some of them already scattered with flourishing weeds. In one pile of rubble the weeds had opened bright-pink flowers. For some reason she found that very cheering. It didn't take long for nature to take over, to rescue, to transform. It seemed like a good omen.

Nora went up to Sara's room to tidy it up for her, to save her anything to do while she was busy with exams. Sara came straight home from school now that the raids were easier. She didn't go to Amy's house. She said she could work better at home. Nora picked up a book and something fell out of the back. She picked it up and turned it over. It was a rather crumpled photograph of Charlie, one that Amy had thrown into the waste paper basket because it had got bent and damaged. How long has she had that, Nora wondered? Sara must have fished it out at some time. She looked at it for a few moments. There were lines of strain around his mouth but he still looked like a boy. She smiled to herself. Sara was growing up. She put it back in the book.

The year wore slowly on. It was like one of those dreams, Amy thought, when you desperately wanted to run and your legs wouldn't move.

'We're getting there,' Dan said. 'We've got North Africa and invaded Sicily. Slowly but surely we're getting there.'

Amy smiled. 'Yes. Charlie actually stays awake most of the time when he's home now. I actually see him with his eyes open.'

'Does Tessa say anything?'

'No, but she doesn't look quite so drained. She's working hard. She's got her finals next year.'

'Tessa a doctor,' Dan said. 'Our little girl.'

'And young Sara's done well,' Amy said. 'She got distinctions in everything except French. So she's going into the sixth form next term.'

Dan raised his eyebrows. 'What then?'

'She knows she's got to get a scholarship,' Amy said, 'but we could help a bit. At least she could have Tessa's books and white coats and things. Nora saved my father's life, Dan.'

'I know,' he said. 'We'll do whatever we can.'

In September Italy surrendered and the months of fighting the Germans through Italy began. In the east the Russians continued to advance. Tentatively, as if waking from a long nightmare, people began to think, and even to talk, about the end of the war, about the future.

'They've got to bring in the Beveridge Plan,' Amy said, 'or something much like it. We can't go back to the old ways, charity and handouts. People have a right to a decent life, after all this. Kids like Sara have a right to go to university. That's what her father died for. They're not going to come back from all this and accept being treated as they were after the last one. There'd be a revolution. If we can pay for all this horror we can pay for that.'

'It'll come,' Dan said. 'But we've a long way to go. We've got to get them out of France and the rest of Europe. They're not finished yet.'

Christmas, 1943. 'No turkey,' Amy said. 'It'll be roast beef this year and
we're lucky to get that.' But they're all here, she thought, all the family.
Tessa was beginning to look a little better, not so white, not so withdrawn. She must get over it, she thought. She's young. She can't spend
her whole life grieving. She didn't know what to say, what to do. Just
love her, she thought. Just love her and wait. Charlie was permanently
tired and a bit down. She could understand that. The frantic rush of the
wild battles seemed to be over. Now there seemed to be the daily grind,
flying over France, hit and run. He said it was like knocking at a door
and running away. They were all tired. In a few days it would be 1944.

The winter was bitter. Amy made her home visits, ploughing through
the snow. The children, as always, were enjoying it. Life, Amy
thought. Thank God for the children, for that innocent enjoyment of
the moment, of living in the day, not worrying about the future. Her
old ladies were extraordinarily cheerful, despite their chilblains. After
the war, Amy thought, after the war we'll have to look after them
better than this. The pigeons seemed to have taken up permanent resi-
dence in her patient's room. She smiled. They've got more sense than
we have.

Jenny, one of the final-year girls at the hospital, and a flatmate, met
Tessa in the canteen. 'What are you doing on New Year's Eve?' she
asked.

'Nothing much,' Tessa said. 'Just spend it with my parents probably.'

'One of the American doctors came and asked the girls and the
nurses to a dance at one of the hotels.' Jenny looked excited. 'You've
got to come, Tessa. It'll be fantastic. They're having a buffet supper.
They'll have food like you've never seen. They're sending cars for us.'

'I'll think about it,' Tessa said.

Jenny sat down beside her. 'Don't think about it, Tessa. Just come.
You haven't been anywhere this year. I do know why, but life goes on.
Just come.'

Tessa sat for a few moments over her coffee. I wish Tim was here, she thought. I wish he knew that we're beginning to win. I wish he knew that he'd saved the world, him and Charlie and the rest. Sometimes she felt as if he were still near her, but those times were fading. All that she had now was a memory – a loving memory. Everyone was right. Life went on. She hadn't been out for nearly a year. She'd go to the dance.

She finished her coffee and got ready for her afternoon teaching round. She was on a surgical firm, sometimes helping in theatre, mostly with injured civilians, many of them blackout accidents. There were occasional raids and sometimes she still did firewatching. Up there that night on the roof, with the streetlights blacked out and a clear sky, the stars were overwhelming and magnificent in their brightness and number. They gave her a sense of timelessness and peace. With deep love and thankfulness for what they had had, she said goodbye to Tim.

The dance floor was crowded, an American Army band playing swing and the popular songs: 'We'll meet again', and 'Coming in on a wing and a prayer'. The girls were greeted at once by a group of GIs who swept them on to the dance floor. Several couples were jiving madly, arms and legs flying. It reminded Tessa of the dance at the Hammersmith Palais. I haven't danced for a year, she thought. She began to enjoy herself.

The MC announced that the next dance would be a Paul Jones. There was a lot of giggling among the girls and the dancers formed two circles, the men on the outside, the girls on the inside, facing each other. Tessa joined the ring, ready to dance with whoever was facing her when the music stopped. He stood before her and smiled. He was, she thought, an officer, though she wasn't familiar with the uniforms.

'Hello,' he said.

She looked up at him. 'Hello.' The music started again and they danced. He looked nice, she thought – youngish, not exactly handsome, but a nice face, strong, but open and friendly.

'Are you one of the girls from the hospital?' he asked.

She nodded. 'Yes.'

'One of the nurses?'

'No,' she said. 'I'm a final-year medical student.'

'Oh really?' He looked pleased. 'I'm a doctor – a surgeon. My name's Pete.'

'Tessa,' she said.

'When's your final exams?'

'In the summer.'

'Working hard?'

'Flogging myself to death,' she said. 'I haven't been out for a year.'

'You're working too hard,' he said. 'Look, let's get out of this. Can I get you a drink or something to eat? There's a buffet.'

'That sounds good,' she said.

He took her to the next room, a dining room.

'Good Lord,' she said. 'I've never seen such food. We haven't had anything like this for years.' Her eyes were wide, like a child at a party.

He laughed. 'Help yourself. I guess you guys have been having it rough over here.'

They filled their plates and found a table. He put out his hand. 'Pete Morgan. Hail from Boston, USA.'

She shook his hand. 'Tessa Fielding. Hail from London.'

He's nice, she thought, as they talked and danced. Ordinary and down to earth and nice. It turned midnight, in came the New Year– 1944, but he didn't attempt to kiss her. At the end of the dance he drove her back to the flat. He stopped outside. 'Can I see you again, Tessa? And before you ask, no, I'm not married and don't have a girl friend at home. Been too busy, I guess. What about you?'

'My fiancé was killed,' she said, 'in the RAF.'

There was a silence. 'I'm very sorry,' he said. 'I guess you won't ...'

'Yes,' she said. 'I'd like to see you again.'

He smiled broadly. 'Give me your number. I'll call you.' He drove away.

Jenny was already home. 'Where did you get to?' she said. 'I didn't see you all evening.'

'Oh, I was there,' Tessa said. 'I think I was eating most of the time.'

The sirens went again, startling everyone, and the nightly raids started again, the bombing and the destruction. 'They're all sheltering down the tubes again,' Amy said. 'I don't care any more. I'm not spending freezing nights in that shelter in the garden.'

'We'll get one of those Morrison things,' Dan said, 'and stay in the house.'

The Morrison shelter arrived and was assembled in the dining room, a reinforced metal box. They put in a mattress and slept inside it. 'It's like being in a cage,' Amy said. 'Now I know how the animals feel at the zoo.'

Once again they lay there, night after night in the shattering noise, sleepless and apprehensive. In April the raids died away again.

The weeks went by and tension grew. 'It's got to happen this year,' Dan said, 'invading France. It can't wait much longer.' Then, one day, 'It's beginning,' he said. 'They've closed all the beaches and we're clearing beds again. Soon, Amy. Soon.' Can it really be true, Amy thought? Are we coming to the end? The thought of those empty, waiting hospital beds made her heart contract. All those boys.

Tessa came home for the weekend.

'You look better, darling,' Amy said. 'There's some colour in your cheeks.'

'I've got something to tell you, Mum,' Tessa said. 'I've met someone. He's really nice. I'd like to bring him home to meet you.'

Amy hugged her. 'I'm so glad, darling. I've prayed that you would.' She held Tessa away from her. 'You're still going to take your finals, aren't you?'

'Of course. That's not going to change. He's a doctor. His name's Pete. Charlie likes him – we all met in town.'

'We'd love to meet him,' Amy said. 'Bring him home.'

'There's just one thing,' Tessa said. 'He's American. He's a surgeon in the US army.'

For a moment Amy paused, surprised. Then she shrugged and smiled. 'Good for him. I'm delighted.'

Pete came to dinner. They love each other, Amy thought. You can see that. She's happy again.

Later, lying in bed she said, 'He's nice, isn't he?'

'I like him a lot,' Dan said. 'He seems steady and reliable. He'd make her a good husband.'

'But, America, Dan.'

'She must do what makes her happy;' he said. 'She's had enough pain.'

Charlie came home on a forty-eight hour. 'I believe you've met Pete,' Amy said.

'I think he's great,' he said, 'and she's really happy, Mum.'

'But – America. We'd never see her, Charlie.'

Charlie laughed. 'There's a great big new world out there, Mum. He lives in Boston, on the east coast. It won't be a week on a ship any more, you'll be able to fly there in a few hours. I might even be able to fly you there myself if I get the job I want after the war. You can go every month or two if you want. It'll be no different from her living in, say, Scotland.'

Amy laughed. 'I suppose I'm getting a bit old-fashioned. I'll look forward to it. I'd love to see America.' A new world, she thought. Penicillin, air travel. What else?

The whole of the coast from the Wash to Cornwall was out of bounds to civilians. The numbers of American soldiers increased visibly every day. Tessa came home, quiet and tense. She put her arms around her mother.

'Pete's gone,' she said. 'No one's allowed out of the camps. I don't even know where he is.'

Amy held her close. Oh God, not again, she thought. Don't let anything happen to Pete. Let her go to America. Don't let her go through that again.

They waited, and then Dan came home from the hospital. 'Any day, Amy,' he said, 'any day now. We've been collecting group O blood all day. I gave a pint. It'll be within the week.'

Then on 6 June, at 9.32 a.m., the announcement was broadcast: 'D-Day has come. Early this morning the Allies began an assault on the north-western face of Hitler's Europe.' And then the thrilling messages to occupied Europe: 'We are coming. Be patient. We are coming.'

The joy and relief were short-lived. One week after D-Day a strange black object appeared in the sky over London. It fell on a railway bridge at Bow and killed six people. The first of the flying bombs had arrived. In July Lewisham market was hit with scenes of carnage that Amy had not imagined since the first war, and on the same afternoon twenty bombs fell on Kensington, wrecking and killing.

For the first time Amy began to feel despair. There was something so horrific, so chilling and mindless about these pilotless bombs. There was no mental defence against them. You couldn't even use the defence of hatred. You couldn't hate a machine.

Charlie flew over the battlefields of France. There weren't too many enemy aircraft about now; the Allies seemed to have control of the skies. They flew patrols, searching for enemy bombers, harassing the enemy forces when they could.

The explosion behind him was an unbelievable shock. He hadn't even seen the 109 that caught him. In what felt like a fleeting second he realized firstly, that he was physically unharmed, secondly, that the Spit had lost its controls, and thirdly that he was going to have to jump. His main feeling was one of complete astonishment. The war was in its last stages and he had come through it all. What a time to be shot down! The thought took a second, and he was pulling at his canopy. He wrenched it open and shot out.

It happened so quickly. The parachute blossomed above him before he realized that he had pulled the cord. He looked down at the approaching French countryside. He wasn't at all sure where he was – which side of the line. The Germans weren't likely to be too friendly under the circumstances. They didn't like losing. God, he thought, what an end. After all that.

He hit the ground and rolled over. He balled up his parachute and pushed it into a bush. It was very quiet, there was no one about. He came to a lane at the edge of the field. Which way to go? He walked warily down the lane, hoping to find a farmhouse, French people who would help him.

He saw something in the hedgerow and picked it up. It was an empty cigarette packet. He turned it over. It was an empty packet of Lucky Strike. He gave a great belly-laugh of sheer relief. It's the Yanks, he thought. Thank God for the Yanks. I'm going home again.

Amy took the call a few days later. The messages that he had been shot down and that he was all right and on the way home came together. She put the phone down in the hall and leant against the wall, and wept.

'It won't be over by Christmas,' Dan said. 'The Germans have apparently been told to fight to the death or they'll be shot by their own side. Damned if they do and damned if they don't. In fact thousands of them are doing the sensible thing and surrendering. But a lot of them are fanatical. Young kids, some of them.'

New Year, 1945, and the nation held its breath. Would it be soon, would it be soon? Amy watched Tessa's tense little face, desperate for it to be over and for Pete to come home.

They opened their papers one morning to see the horrifying pictures of the death camps, the piles of corpses, the half-human skeletal figures crawling on their knees, too weak to stand. There were pictures of dead and dying children, and a young British soldier, sobbing, his head in his hands.

'There,' Dan said, his face white. 'That's what it was for. That's what this rotten war was all about.'

They knew when it was over, but they turned on the wireless to listen to Mr Churchill actually say the words. They danced around the room, Amy and Dan and Amy's father hugging and crying. There were crowds in the streets, street parties, lights everywhere, Victory parties and dances. And the boys began to come home.

'Are you going to the dance, Charlie?' Amy asked. 'Tessa wants you to go with her and Pete. It is a celebration, after all.'

'I don't think so,' he said. 'I haven't anyone to go with.'

Dan laughed. 'I find that hard to believe. There are girls everywhere.'

'I'm sort of out of girls at the moment,' Charlie said. 'Everyone I know is spoken for.'

'Why don't you take Sara?' Amy said. 'Nora's daughter.'

Charlie raised his eyebrows in surprise. 'She's a kid.'

'She's nearly nineteen,' Amy said. 'If she passes all her exams, and she will, she'll be starting medical school in September. She's been offered a place at UCH. You haven't seen her for a while. She isn't a kid any more.'

Charlie laughed. 'Another doctor? Is there an ordinary person in the house?'

'Well, she's very clever,' Amy said. 'And she's very pretty.'

'Oh,' Charlie said. 'All right. If she'd come.'

'I'll ask her if you like,' Amy said.

She thought she'd ask Nora first. Nora grinned. 'I'm sure she would. She used to have a bit of a crush on Charlie.'

'Charlie thinks she's still a schoolgirl,' Amy said. 'He'll be surprised. She's really quite pretty, Nora.'

'She would be,' Nora said, 'if she took any interest in it. She's only just out of school uniform. She's only been to a couple of school socials with the boys from their grammar school. She says they're all silly infants.'

They looked at each other and smiled. 'First dance,' Amy said. 'We'll have to get her a dress.'

'I've got enough coupons for some material,' Nora said, 'and there are some lovely Vogue patterns.'

Sara flushed when Nora told her. 'What does he want to take me for?'

'He hasn't got anyone else, apparently.'

Sara laughed. 'That's flattering.'

'It's time you went to a do like this,' Nora said, 'before you start your training. You're going out into the big world and you'll meet a lot of men. Time you went out with a nice boy. You might just as well have been in a convent.'

'He's not a boy,' Sara said. 'He's older than me.'

'Not much. Only a few years. And what does that matter. You're only going to a dance.'

'All right,' Sara said. 'What am I going to wear?'

Nora took Sara to get ready at Amy's house. Tessa had offered to help her with her hair and some simple make-up. She coiled Sara's hair up into a French pleat, showed her how to put on a pink lipstick and lent her a pair of earrings. Sara hardly recognized herself. The dress Nora made was a pale turquoise-blue and fitted her perfectly. She felt a bit nervous. She'd had quite a schoolgirl crush on Charlie and wondered if he'd ever known about it. That would be embarrassing. He probably didn't want to take her at all.

Charlie and Pete arrived and waited in the sitting room. Amy gave them a glass of sherry.

'I expect you'll be going back to the States soon.' Charlie said to Pete. 'You'll be glad to be home again.'

Pete gave a little shrug and smiled. 'That all depends, Charlie,' he said.

Nora came into the room, smiling. Tessa came in, smiling at Pete, and then Sara came in behind her.

Amy found that she was watching Charlie – she didn't quite know why. She saw him get slowly to his feet. She saw his eyes widen and his mouth open a little in surprise, almost shock. He looked at Sara, up and down, and a slow delighted smile spread over his face. 'Wow, Sara,' he said. 'You've changed a bit since I last saw you.'

Amy and Nora exchanged glances. I wonder, Amy thought. I wonder.

Amy sat once more at the kitchen table, sipping her tea, looking out on to the garden. We can grow flowers again, she thought. We can dig up the shelter, that cold cramped little place that had done its job and protected them through so many terrifying nights. Nearly six years, six appalling years, but we've come through. She smiled to herself. Charlie was a man now, the kind of man anyone would look up to and respect. Tessa too, a doctor, soon to be married and to go to America, and Sara, exams behind her, fulfilling her dream, the dream she had cherished through everything that the war had thrown at her. And Nora, tough Nora, who might one day be her in-law, the way things were going. And Dan, strong, unchanging.

A new world, airliners, new surgical techniques, penicillin, a new social order for the whole population. Had it been worth it, the battle?

Yes. She thought of the camps where thousands had died, of Europe bitterly oppressed by an evil regime, of millions murdered for their faith, of freedom, England, her home. Yes.